FRAGILE

A GALLOWS INVESTIGATIONS NOVEL

JUSTIN R. MACUMBER

Gryphonwood

Fragile
Copyright 2016 by Justin R. Macumber
Published by Gryphonwood Press
www.gryphonwoodpress.com
Cover by Scott Macumber

ISBN-10: 1-940095-53-0
ISBN-13: 978-1-940095-53-0

An abomination stalks the streets of Mayfair, snatching children from their homes and leaving in their places dolls, whose shattered porcelain skin and scorched eyes crush the hopes of their grieving families. Maya Gallows, paranormal investigator and psychic, seeks to stop the evil before it can claim another victim. As Maya faces this terrible foe, an even greater darkness stirs within her. Can she save not only the children of Mayfair, but her own fragile soul?

Fragile is the second book in the *Gallows Investigations* horror series, which began with the bestselling *Still Water.*

Praise for Justin R. Macumber

"In FRAGILE, Macumber's spooky follow-up to STILL WATER, the author deftly weaves elements of The Exorcist and all the best witch stories, and slathers a perfect Stephen King sensibility on it, keeping the characters and locations real, and taking time both to delve into the nuances of life and the dripping detail you want in a good horror story. Macumber joins the ranks of Joe Hill, Justin Cronin, Stephen M. Irwin, and Michael Koryta as the new elite caretakers of atmospheric horror." - Kane Gilmour, Bestselling author of THE CRYPT OF DRACULA

"FRAGILE is my most anticipated horror novel of 2016. Macumber spins creepy yarns and keeps me turning pages when I should be sleeping."- Jeremy Robinson, international bestselling author of APOCALYPSE MACHINE.

"Justin Macumber's 'Fragile' is a creepy mix of old school horror and supernatural suspense. Its eerie setting, sinister protagonist, and suspense make for an unsettling but satisfying read." - Paul E Cooley, Author of THE BLACK.

Books by Justin R. Macumber

Horror
Still Water
Fragile

Science Fiction
Haywire
Titans Rise (forthcoming)

Urban Fantasy
A Minor Magic
A Broken Magic

Short Fiction
That Old Hell Magic
Dark Running
The Dame Wore White
Pirates of the Crimson Sand

Dedication

I would like to dedicate this book to my younger brother, Scott. Growing up as Army brats, often was the time when the only friends we had were each other. Older brothers are supposed to be the trailblazer, the one to set the pace, but Scott's sense of adventure was always greater than mine, so more often than not he was the one making new experiences while I sat at home deep into Dungeons & Dragons or writing a new story. Over the years I've come to depend on him more and more, and he's never let me down. I can't adequately express how much he means to me, but I will try.

Scott, I love you, I admire you, and I respect the man you've become. Thank you for always being there for me. You've been my rock so many times in the past, and I trust you'll be there for me in the years to come. Thanks also for helping to create my niece and nephew, whom I adore.

Oh, and thanks for the amazing cover you created for this book. Your work graced the fronts of HAYWIRE and STILL WATER, not to mention many of my short stories, and I couldn't be more proud.

Acknowledgments

I would like to extend my eternal gratitude to Scott "Scotch" Calgaro. Normally my writing doesn't involve sticky legal issues and questions about who can investigate what and when according to the law, but this one did. Scott is not only my friend, but he also has seventeen years of federal law enforcement experience in the Department of Justice and the Department of Homeland Security. For a writer like me, that experience makes him an invaluable resource when it comes to questions of legalities and investigative jurisdiction. So, when I had questions regarding state and federal interactions, he was the first and only person I went to. He had answers and advice aplenty.

Thanks, Scotch, for all your help and support and friendship. It means more than I can say. Any mistakes that were made in this book are purely the fault of me–the writer–and not Mr. Lord Sheriff Agent Special Deputy Calgaro. If you choose to still blame him, I can't stop you.

Chapter One

Raging spirits howled around Estera's head. Their hellish energies churned the air into a roiling storm, but she stood against the black powers she'd summoned with a snarl on her grim, craggy face. No matter how much it hurt her gnarled body, no matter the sins she stained her already damned soul with, she would not be denied–not by man, spirit, or God.

On the black altar before her lay the body of a little girl, her blue eyes bulging in terror, her mouth gaping open in a tortured scream. A green dress covered her quivering form, the same one she'd worn when she was taken the day before, but it was dirtier now. The girl's snowy white skin, though, was as perfect and unblemished as an empty field after a winter storm. Loops of coarse rope held her small feet and hands together. Estera didn't know the girl's name, nor did she care to. The child meant one thing, and one thing *only*, to her –a first step toward immortality. Everything else was meaningless.

"Powers of the ancient realms, I call upon you!" she cried, her ravenous voice nearly ripped from her throat by the spiraling winds. "Polúmētis, rise from beneath your mountain and grant me your magic!"

Light erupted from the stone floor around Estera as intricately painted symbols gained energetic life. What had been swaths of white paint were now shimmering lines of dark light, their ultraviolet glow painful to look at. Her snarl turned upward as the protection glyphs within her casting circle reacted to the sudden rise in supernatural energy.

From a hidden fold in her black robes, Estera drew her athame, the ceremonial iron blade imbedded in a stag horn handle. Symbols lined the ceremonial knife in deep etchings. She then pulled back her left sleeve to reveal a pale, bony arm crisscrossed by scars new and old. With savage determination she held the athame against the mutilated skin of her inner forearm.

"Goddess Hekate, I make this offering in your many names–Chthonia of the Underworld and Kleidouchos, Holder of the Keys. Please accept it and grant me your blessing."

Moving the athame quickly, Estera sliced a deep gouge into the doughy flesh of her inner forearm. Blood immediately welled up from the wound. As it splattered on the stone ground, she turned to her right where a large, copper chalice sat atop a pillar carved from obsidian. She thrust her arm over the vessel, and soon it filled with splattering crimson. Though no fire burned beneath the copper chalice, the blood within it bubbled and steamed. A new strength filtered into her body, a power as ancient as it was terrible.

Before she drained herself completely, she withdrew her arm and waved a wand made of bone over the gash. The wand was carved from the femur of a white wolf slaughtered beneath a new moon, one end wrapped in the dead animal's leathery flesh. As the wand moved, Estera uttered an incantation, the words drifting from her lips in a glimmering red mist. Within seconds the slash on her arm closed until it was just another angry pink wound on her pallid, ruined skin.

Flush with magical energy, she bent forward and grabbed a handful of the young girl's reddish-blonde hair. "Baphomet, Goat of Mendes, bless this child and make her ready, I beseech you." With the invocation complete, Estera brought her athame down in a flash of dull metal, and the hair in her left hand came free. She admired the shine and softness of it, recalled how her own hair had been like that once upon a time, and then she rose and dropped the hair into the bloody chalice. Smoke billowed into the air, adding to the whirling darkness above her. Estera bent again, this time grabbing the girl's dress by the hem. The cotton garment cut as easily as the hair, and the swatch of material went into the roiling chalice as well. More smoke poured forth. Only one component remained for the spell to be complete, but it was by far the most painful.

The greater the spell, she thought with a grimace, *the greater the cost. A primary law of magic.*

"And now I call upon the witches three–Abonde, the goddess; Mayfair, the Beautiful Pilgrim; and Cernunnos, the Horned One. Guide my hand and sustain this body so that I might find new life."

The glyphs flashed again, blinding her for a moment. When her vision cleared, she grabbed the front of her robe and pulled it open. Sagging breasts and doughy flesh turned to gooseflesh as the storm of magical energy crackled against her naked skin. She continued to open her robe until it fell back from her shoulders. The scarves tied around her waist prevented the robe from dropping to the ground.

Now unencumbered, Estera held up her hands, the fingers gnarled into claws and her nails sharp as talons as the dark magic worked within her, corrupting her more than she already was. She then pressed them against her abdomen and felt around until finding what she needed. After a few whispered words, she pushed her deformed fingers into her skin. Razor-sharp nails split flesh, and blood brimmed around her hands. Agonizing pain ripped through her like lightning, but she bit her lips closed to keep from crying out. Like worms digging through loam, her fingers rummaged inside her torso, wiggling through warm, dreadful wetness until they touched bone. She groaned as her right hand curled around her lowest rib, but the pain of that was nothing compared to the torment that racked her body when she pulled at the bone with all her strength. Had she tried to do it on her own she would have died before the bone came free, but the power given to her through her invocations was considerable, and a loud *SNAP!* punctured the air as the rib broke free. Finally the pain was more than even she could take.

"Aarrgghh!" She dropped to her knees as tears dripped down her craggy cheeks.

A hunched figure stirred behind her. "Momma?"

Estera's pained expression transformed into an angry scowl. "Stay back! Enter the circle and you're dead." She didn't need to turn and look to know a lumpy head nodded in response.

Shakily she rose to her feet, her rib bone still clutched in a hand drenched with gore. Again she wove her wand over the wound and spoke whispered incantations, the spell nearly as old as the world itself. Even though the wound closed, the pain stayed with her. It was part of the price she paid to defy the natural order of the universe.

Before her, the girl's eyes were open so wide they would have fallen out of her head if she hadn't been lying on her back, and they were locked on Estera like an antelope staring at a lion bounding toward her with bloody murder on its face. She struggled to get free, twisting her body this way and that, but her eyes never wavered. The girl knew the source of her terror, though the knowledge did her no good. Terrible powers had them both in their grip, their lives bound together in an inextricable knot of ominous, eldritch energy.

Standing as straight as her bent spine allowed, Estera held her rib bone out and dropped it into the copper chalice. Instantly a cloud of noxious fumes curled upward. When it cleared, the bubbling blood was black as tar. With her wand in her right hand and a silver medallion engraved with the stern face of Maalik, the black-winged angel who stood guard at the gates of Hell, dangling from the other, she began the final incantation. Words from a dozen languages seeped from her thin, wrinkled lips, each one committed to memory through years of intense study. It had taken Estera a long time to track down the *Focail de Veles*, one of the oldest grimoires in existence. The fight to make it hers had been brutal—the cathedral in Glendalough, Ireland, had nearly been reduced to rubble—but such was her desire to possess its secrets to life-everlasting. Now she called upon those secrets, written in the blood of demons, to turn her desire into reality.

The girl continued to struggle on the black altar, her panic mirrored by the chaos of the energy churning around the safety of the casting circle, and in the middle of it all the chalice boiled and thundered. Bursts of ichor green light lit the boiling blackness from within and cast shadows like furious ghosts on rough stone walls. This wasn't the first time Estera had attempted the spell; the previous two tries ended in bitter disappointment, but this time she felt more confident than ever.

This is the one, it has to be. This time the gods won't abandon me. Now I'll finally enjoy the fruits that all my toil and blood was sacrificed for.

The obsidian column beneath the chalice trembled as the ground suddenly shook, and the large goblet wobbled from side to side. Thick, black blood crested the rim and splashed to the ground where it sizzled and emitted toxic green smoke. The whirling storm of energy increased its speed, throatless voices cried out, and the air vibrated with horrified anticipation.

With one final burst of verdant light, everything abruptly went silent and still. The chalice belched a thick cloud of fumes before settling back in place.

Now is my time. Estera's eyes gleamed in the sudden stillness, and her mouth curled into a hungry snarl. *Now I live forever.*

Cowering against a far wall, Boden dared a glance at the whirling storm and shivered before ducking his head back down and throwing an arm over his skull. Fear and confusion filled his insides like fire and ice, each emotion battling for dominance, but one thought kept him from fleeing in mortal terror—Boden loved his momma. She'd squeezed him from her womb all by herself not ten feet from where he stood shaking, the stone floor still stained from the juices and chunks of flesh that slid out with him all those decades before. She'd brung him up on her own, a hard task made harder by the lack on his part of a fully functional brain, a flaw he was just smart enough to recognize. As if to make up for it, his body was big and strong, yet the universe still managed to make a joke of him with limbs a bit too long, a back forever hunched, and a face like a Halloween mask. In spite of all that, Momma still took care of him, even if some days her love was as tough as old shoe leather.

Suddenly the storm vanished, and in its absence was a silence nearly as terrifying. Boden lowered his arms from his head and looked to Momma. She stood half naked in the middle of her special circle, a child-shaped lump of ash piled on top of her altar.

"No!" she shouted, her voice filling the basement of their house like an angry animal as she plunged her hand into the ash and felt around as though looking for something, something important. The walls shook from the force of her anger, and his already pained stomach seized up at the thought of her directing it at him next. "Not again! Damn the Gods! Damn all of them!"

Just as he'd feared, Momma turned her scornful gaze toward him as she struggled to contain her rage, wisps of smoke lifting from her reddened skin. Markings on the floor and walls glowed a shade of green that made Boden's head hurt, but the painful light faded with each passing second.

"Or damn me a fool for trusting *you*."

Boden sucked in his lower lip and chewed on it. "Don't say that, Momma."

"I say what I please," she replied, lifting frail arms that seconds ago commanded powers not of this world. "I didn't spend years of my life searching for that spell only to be stopped now. Immortality *will* be mine."

Groaning, Boden gathered all his courage and pushed away from the stone wall pressing against his back. The stink of blood and burnt hair filled his nostrils. Once, long ago, she'd been a loving woman, but that was before the doctors and their big words he didn't understand. Momma cried at first, but then her tears turned to anger. After that she was never the same. The light within her turned dark, changing her into a shadow of who she'd used to be, a shadow that killed and consumed. "I always do what you says for me to, Momma. I swear."

Momma pulled her dark robe over her shoulders, saving her son from seeing her ruined naked flesh any longer. "I'm beginning to wonder if your love is as pure as you claim."

Thin strands of hair swayed on his pale, lumpy skull as Boden frowned and nodded. "Of course it is, Momma."

She glared at him with a squinted eye, once so clear and blue but now riddled with broken crimson veins, then shuffled to the old tree branch she used as a staff, the wood as dark and twisted as her mood. "I hope so. I can befuddle the authorities for only so long. Now clean this place up, and when you're done, gather me some more sage and toad skins. I'm gonna go rest."

"Yes, Momma." Boden glanced up at the hooks dangling from the basement ceiling, dried herbs hanging from some and dead animals sagging from others. Many neighborhood pets had ended up in the basement, their fleeting, fragile lives taken for dark purposes he didn't have the capacity to understand.

She sighed and hobbled slowly up the wooden stairs leading to their home. "Show your love and bring me some supper when you're finished."

He watched her until she opened the door at the top of the stairs and passed through. When she was gone from sight, a heavy weight dropped from his broad, slumped shoulders.

"I *do* love you, Momma."

To prove it he lumbered over to a broom barely clinging to the last of its straw and swept the basement's stone floor. Dust and ash billowed with each awkward motion. It wasn't until he came to the white designs on the floor that he stopped.

He hated the marks. They looked innocent enough, drawings of stars and circles and squiggly lines, but he knew better. When his momma stood amongst them, speaking strange names and words that made his insides turn to mush, they shined with a hideous power. Terrible things happened inside those marks, evil things he'd never thought her capable of back when he was young and she was well and whole. But Momma needed the marks, so he stuffed his hatred for them down deep and went back to sweeping. He didn't let his feet touch the marks, though. Not even barely.

Clink!

Boden jumped and shuffled sideways. When his heart finally dropped from his throat he looked at the ground. A small child stared back at him. *Not again*, he thought as he bent over and picked the tiny figure up.

It *looked* like a child, oh yes it did, but it wasn't. It was a dolly. Porcelain white from head to toe, the dolly looked so much like little Alison Duff, from its light auburn hair to the soft green dress. Sadly, the once-smooth skin was shot through with cracks, and its blue eyes were now black pits. It was as if the doll had burned from the inside out. A pinprick of pain stabbed his heart.

"Hello, Alison. I'm sorry. But don't worry, I'll bring ya home. Just like I did the others. Don't you worry."

Sighing again, Boden gently set the doll on a shelf next to a jar of raven hearts, then went back to sweeping. After that he would bring his mother a bowl of leek and chicken soup and then gather the items she requested. Then–after the sun was down and the streets were clear–he would take Alison home. It wouldn't be his first twilight delivery, and he fretted it wouldn't be the last.

Yes, Boden loved his momma, loved her as only a son could, but he was also afraid of her. She was capable of things he shuddered to think about, and while she hadn't yet turned that dark power on him, nothing said she wouldn't when she had no more need of him, when he was no longer useful. He felt like he was living on borrowed time, and swore to do better. His vow came from love, but with his love came fear, the balance of which shifted each day. He had to help Momma. If not for her, then for the sake of his own skin.

Chapter Two

Maya ran her fingers through Kyle's dirty blond hair, the feel of it brushing her palms stirring primal desires deep within her. His brown eyes stared at her, seeing past the flesh to the true Maya that existed between worlds, half of her with the living and the other half dancing among the dead. Many men–too many–had run from her in the past, scared off by her *otherness*, but Kyle hadn't. He'd embraced it.

"I love you," he said, the words caressing her ears like warm velvet.

Maya's stomach trembled, sending waves of warmth throughout her body. "I love you too."

Reaching out, Kyle took her hips and pulled her against him. The short stubble on his cheeks brushed her skin, the feel of it coarse yet enticing. His hands drifted up to her back, and his arms enfolded her with gentle strength. "I will never let you go, Maya."

"I hope not." His words and embrace made her lightheaded. He was so new to her life, barely more than a stranger, but her heart felt like he'd been within it since the beginning. It was strange and at the same time comforting.

"I will never let you go, Maya," he repeated, his arms tightening.

Her skin flushed as she squeezed him back. "I know."

"I will never let you go, Maya." The embrace tightened even more, turning pleasure into pain.

"Yes, I know," she replied, her voice strained from the pressure. "You can at least loosen up your grip. I'm not going anywhere."

Instead of relaxing his hold, Kyle's arms dug into her ribs and he pressed his head against her face so hard his stubble stabbed her like hundreds of tiny knives. "I will never let you go, Maya."

A chill shivered through her. Confused, she put her palms against his shoulders and pushed, but the harder she struggled, the tighter his hold became. Her confusion was quickly replaced with fear.

"Kyle, let me go!"

"I will never let you go, Maya." He spoke with a slur, as though his mouth was suddenly full. The breath that powered his voice smelled rancid.

"Stop it!" she shouted as she balled up her fists and struck his arms. She wiggled and bucked, kicked at his legs, and fought to be free.

Without warning he released his vice-like hug, grabbed her shoulders, and pushed her to an arm's length distance from him. "I will never let you go, Maya."

Maya screamed. Kyle's face was a nightmare of gray skin, coal black eyes, and gum-splitting fangs. Gone was the man she loved, not even a distant memory of him left in the obscene figure gripping her. Revulsion filled her veins as she lashed out, slapping his arms, kicking his legs and feet. But nothing she did mattered. The monster only smiled, his cold, ashen hands immovable. Dirty nails dug into her arms hard enough to draw blood.

"Let go of me!"

The monster wearing Kyle's face stopped smiling, and mysterious shapes moved within the emptiness of his eyes. She felt molested by his gaze, the murkiness of his aura reaching out for her like the shadow of an eclipse arcing across the Earth. Fear became panic became terror until her heart leapt into her throat and choked her.

"I will never let you go, Maya," he said, smiling one last time before yanking her toward him and plunging his fangs into the soft meat of her neck. Pain and gore exploded across her eyes in a red haze.

Maya screamed again, the shriek ending as she drowned in her own blood.

Maya surged into wakefulness shouting and thrashing, her heart a jackhammer in her chest. She looked around in confusion, unsure of where she was, of what was going on. Things seemed familiar, yet not. She closed her eyes, hoping the darkness would sweep clear her muddled mind, but in the nothingness behind her eyelids she saw Kyle's twisted face, his slavering fangs reaching for her neck.

That wasn't real, she told herself, her inner voice far less confident than she'd have liked. *Kyle isn't a monster; he's…dead.*

The truth was—in its own way—worse than the nightmare. At least she could wake up from a bad dream. The truth clung to her with claws she couldn't shake loose, the pain ever present.

Taking a deep, centering breath, Maya reopened her eyes. Bright blurs filled her vision, but as silent seconds ticked past they changed to soft blurs. When her pupils finished adjusting, she remembered she was in her apartment, sleeping on the couch.

It was nearly three months since the horrific events of Stillwater, West Virginia, and she'd suffered the same nightmare every day since. *No, not the same,* she thought. *It's getting worse. I swear I can feel those teeth at my neck. And that smell…* She sniffed the air, thankful the rotten odor hadn't followed her from the terrible dream.

Sitting in the gloom, she couldn't help but remember water and darkness, silence reigning as she drove a dead man's truck, tears falling every mile of the dreary trip back home to Memphis, Tennessee. Kyle's sister, Taylor, had been with her, as well as Taylor's girlfriend, Morgana. All of them had wept as they took turns behind the wheel. When they finally pulled into Maya's reserved parking spot and labored up the stairs to her apartment, she'd volunteered to sleep on the couch so they could share her bed. It was a small sacrifice given how much the two girls had lost, but now she wondered when she'd get to sleep in her own room again.

"You okay?" The question came from behind her, the words said in a yawn.

Startled, Maya shifted around on the couch and looked over her shoulder. Taylor walked from the open bedroom door to sit next to her. The pale young girl's dark hair shot through with white streaks was disheveled, decorative feathers sticking out like twigs in a nest, and her clothes were a filthy, rumpled mess. Piercings gleamed from her lower lip, nose, eyebrows, and ears.

Typical teenager, Maya mused, recalling her own teen years of fashion experimentation with a shudder that only those in their mid-twenties could understand. "Not really," she replied. She scooted over on the couch and gathered a blanket over her bare legs to make room.

Taylor sat down like a dropped bag of flour and sighed. "Me either. I don't think I'll ever be okay again."

Maya completely understood. Her eyes burned as tears welled up and slipped down her cheeks. "Give it time. Life sucks right now, but... hell, I don't know. As if I have a clue about anything."

More tears seared her face, but Maya was heartened when Taylor took her hand and gave it a squeeze. She looked at the little sister of the man she'd fallen in love with so quickly, and in the girl's eyes was a mirror of her pain. A gray cloud hovered just past her skin, the unsettled aura a clear sign of her sadness. The fact that Maya now saw auras all the time was a signal that she'd been affected in ways she couldn't have foreseen by her brush with the Dark God buried beneath the town.

"At least we can say we literally saved the world. That has to mean something, right?" Maya asked.

Taylor shrugged and leaned against her shoulder. "Save the world, but lose my brother. I don't know if the world was worth it."

"Kyle would probably say it was a fair trade." Maya spread the brown fleece blanket to cover Taylor's pale legs.

"But I don't think so."

"I wish he was here so I could punch him. We didn't ask him to be a big damn hero. We should have just left that shithole town and never looked back when we had the chance."

Maya would have been lying if she said she hadn't thought the same thing repeatedly since Kyle gave his life in the sky over Stillwater. In doing so he'd not only destroyed Ash, the demonic right hand of the ancient evil, but he'd also sanctified the water that rushed in to drown the Dark God and bury it once again in the mountain it had laid dormant in for millennia. Billions of lives now carried on, totally unaware of just how close they'd come to having the world ravaged and their lives consumed by ageless malevolence. In time she would probably see his death as heroic, maybe even divine, but sitting on the sofa next to his orphaned sister she didn't have the perspective. All she wanted was to hold him one more time, kiss him one more time, make love...

"Not that it matters what we want, right?" Taylor asked with a sniffle. "I guess it's like my papaw used to say–'If wishes were fishes we'd all cast nets'."

The absurdity of the image Taylor's words created made Maya laugh, momentarily pulling her from her melancholy. "Ain't that the truth."

Grunting, Taylor patted Maya's covered leg and then stretched her arms over her head. "I'm dying for some cereal. Do we have any left?"

"With the way you two girls eat, I doubt it. If there's any left it'll be in the –"

The metallic sound of a key slipping into a lock suddenly cut through the air. Maya whipped her head toward the apartment's front door and her heart lurched into a gallop. Before she could stand or call out, the door opened in a rush and a large man stomped through the threshold. Taylor grabbed her arm in a fierce grip, but when

Maya saw the man's face she smiled.

"Hey, Alan!" she said as she stood up and walked over to embrace her friend. The fact that she only had panties and a thin shirt on didn't bother her. Alan was gay and in a committed relationship, so whatever she had to offer he wasn't interested in buying. Besides, they'd been friends too long to let some casual immodesty be an issue.

"Good mornin', pumpkin," he replied. Behind him entered a small terrier mix dog, the little guy's coat white with large black splotches.

Alan was more bear than man, if bears could be hipster hippy wannabes. Matted ginger dreadlocks fell past a bearded face with horn-rimmed glasses perched atop a broad nose. A Hawaiian print button-up shirt tried valiantly to cover a broad, hairy chest and tubby stomach, and khaki cargo shorts led down to wooly tree-trunk legs and massive feet clad in Birkenstock sandals. Maya had no idea what her friend weighed, but she figured the six-foot plus frame had to be in the vicinity of three-hundred pounds. She loved every ounce of him.

"And how is Dean doing this morning?" Maya stooped down and gave the dog a serious scratching behind the ears.

Shaking his head, Alan's dreads shifted around, revealing large gauge plugs in his earlobes. "He's never known a hard day in his whole life." After taking off the dog's leash, he hung it on a hook next to the door. The terrier immediately headed for the bedroom, his tail up as he looked for Maya's dog Sam. "Sorry for coming over so early, but with the boss out of town I have to pick up the slack."

"He sure goes out of town a lot," Taylor said from the couch, her face perched on the back cushion as she gazed at them.

Alan rolled his eyes. "Tell me about it. If I don't get a raise for all this extra work, I think I'll kill him. Slowly. And I know where to bury him so no one ever finds his bones."

Death, even in jest, wasn't something Maya found funny

anymore. Judging from the dour look on the girl's face, neither did Taylor.

"It's no problem," Maya said, steering the conversation into safer waters. "Sam loves having Dean over. I don't know if the two of them will let me get any writing done though."

"Speaking of which." Alan dug into his front pocket. After a few seconds he withdrew a much-folded sheet of paper. "You should find this interesting."

Nausea rumbled in Maya's stomach as Alan's aura changed from pale gray to orange. Whatever the article was about, he was excited, and the last time he'd been like that it had ended in death and despair. "Oh, I don't know, Alan. After what I…we…went through, I don't know if I'm ready for another investigation."

"Understood," Alan replied, his aura shrinking so much it became nearly undetectable, "but it *has* been three months, and I think if you read the article you might change your mind. It's got one of your favorite things in it."

Maya looked at him through narrowed eyes. "And what would that be?"

"Dolls." He said the word as though revealing the secret of the universe.

A tremor ran down Maya's back, making her shiver from head to toe. "Dolls? Are you serious?"

Alan nodded slowly, his brown eyes never leaving her face. "Yep. And not *just* dolls, but dolls made to look like missing kids. I was spooked just reading about it. Could be nothing, or it could be just what you need to get that book deal you keep talking about. I can already see the cover—a cracked porcelain doll, maybe blood oozing from the eyes or something. You should at least read the article before you say no."

Maya sighed, but then nodded. Once Alan had a bug up his ass it was either give in or bang your head against a wall until it cracked open and spilled your brains. "All right, let me see it. And Taylor, you should go wake Morgana up. We don't want her to be late on her first day of work."

Everyone laughed but then jumped when a loud noise unexpectedly punched the air. Maya twisted around expecting a monster, but instead she was greeted by the sight of Morgana yawning widely and scratching her sleep-rumpled rear end.

"Did someone say my name?"

Chapter Three

"Ah, here they are."

Maya grunted as she pulled a plastic bin from the top shelf of her bedroom closet. Objects inside it clanked against each other, and her muscles ached as she carried the heavy box to her bed. Once it was set down she took the dusty lid off and looked inside.

"So that's ghost hunter gear, huh?" Taylor sat down next to the bin and stared at the collection of electronics within it.

Nodding, Maya picked up a Nikon camera and pressed the power button. Nothing happened. "Yep. Just need some new batteries."

Taylor dug around in the box, her small, black-lacquered fingers moving slowly to presumably not break anything. "I don't see any traps or proton packs in here. You ever been slimed?"

Maya snorted. "Ah, good ol' Ghostbusters jokes. They never get old. Nope, never."

"Uh huh." The young woman picked up a battered set of night-vision goggles bigger than her head and examined it like it was something from another dimension. "Okay, one more–that's a big Twinkie."

"And expensive," Maya replied as she took the goggles and checked the lenses. They were grimy and had a few scuff marks, but other than that they were in good shape. "I'm glad I kept this old gear when I upgraded to newer equipment. Replacing everything I lost in Stillwater would take every penny I have. This stuff might be old, but it still works."

Morgana, freshly showered and dressed in what Maya thought of as her good Goth clothes of pressed black pants, white blouse, and shiny black combat boots, walked into the bedroom and sat next to Taylor. Their hands intertwined in that immediate-yet-casual way couples who've been together awhile do.

"If you're going on an investigation I assume the new car will be going with you, so how do I get to work?" the pale girl asked.

"You do what I did when I was your age–take the bus." Maya recalled many a hot summer day spent sitting on a bench, the shelter around it providing barely any shade. "There's a stop on the corner, and a bus comes by every forty-five minutes or so. There's a schedule next to the bench. They'll get you anywhere you need to go."

"Speaking of going," Taylor said, her tone hesitant. "What do you think of me going with you?"

Maya's head jerked back as the words entered her brain. She couldn't say the idea was a bad one, but that didn't mean it was a good one either. "I hadn't thought of that. Do you really feel up to it?"

"Honestly, I just want to do something."

Morgana lifted her hand and kissed Taylor's fingers. "Why not get a job, like I did? Or maybe take some college courses? With the new IDs Maya was able to get for us it wouldn't be a problem. Might help you feel productive."

"I know," Taylor replied with a kiss of her own to their clasped hands, "but I feel like…I feel like I left something unfinished, you know what I mean? Back in Stillwater. It's like there's something unresolved, and until I know what it is and resolve it, I won't feel settled or ready to move on."

Maya knew exactly what Taylor meant. She'd wrestled with her own feelings of incompleteness and unfinished business. It worried away in her mind constantly, like a worm digging through churned-up earth. Knowing Taylor felt the same way helped make up her mind.

"If Morgana is okay parting with you for a little while, then I'd be happy to bring you along. Make a Ghostbuster out of you yet."

Taylor immediately burst into applause and bounced on

the bed with excited squeals before turning to her girlfriend. For her part, Morgana didn't look nearly as happy, but at least she tried to hide it. She failed, but she tried.

"If it'll help you, then go," Morgana replied, only one side of her mouth smiling. "It's fine."

"Doesn't sound fine." Taylor bumped her girlfriend's shoulder. "What's wrong?"

Morgana didn't respond for several long seconds, but the emotions that played across her powdered face spoke volumes. "I'm just scared. The last time she went out to investigate something, an entire town died, nearly taking us with it. That sort of luck…we might not be so lucky next time."

"We won't need luck," Taylor said before gesturing toward Maya. "We have her. Her gifts saved the world."

Morgana nodded, but then shook her head. "We also had your brother."

The air left the room as Morgana finished her sentence. In the vacuum left behind, Taylor looked down at her lap and sighed. Seconds later tears dropped onto her pajama bottoms.

"We still have Kyle," Maya said, adding certainty to her words she really didn't feel. "Inside our hearts. We have his courage and his love. Never forget that."

Taylor nodded as she looked back up and rubbed wet mascara across her cheeks. The three women looked at each other, words shared by looks and head tilts, until eventually the matter was settled.

"Are you okay with Morgana staying here on her own?" Taylor asked, her light brown eyes so like her brother's it broke Maya's heart to look at them too long.

Maya laughed. After everything they'd been through, she was glad she still had the ability. "After what we went through, I'm not all that worried about anything anymore. Besides, she handled herself just fine when the shit hit the fan. Fine for a white girl, anyway."

Taylor pursed her lips and glared while Morgana chuckled.

"I'll take the compliment."

Maya winked at the Goth girl before turning her attention to Taylor. "Are you sure you really want to go with me?"

"You might get in trouble out there." Taylor leaned over and took Maya's hand. "Besides, you slept with my brother. That practically makes us family."

Shock smacked Maya across the cheek at the statement, but the innocent boldness with which it was said drove yet another laugh from her. "Excuse me?"

"Taylor!" Morgana's pale face somehow becoming paler.

Taylor, though, wasn't ruffled. "Oh, like it was some big secret or something. Maya, you're all we have. If you're going to investigate something, you should have someone with you watching your back."

Maya opened her mouth, but nothing came out; her brain was too locked up to form words. No, Taylor wasn't family, yet they had shared a great deal over a short period of time, the greatest of which being their love for Kyle, so they *were* bonded in many ways. Taylor was also a very sweet person, intelligent, and resilient. Maya knew she could do worse than have Taylor at her back. But did she have the right to expose the young woman to yet more danger?

"You don't need to worry about me," Taylor said as though reading her mind. "I'm a big girl."

Maya couldn't deny that. "I know you are. I just…after losing your brother and seeing an entire town get destroyed in a flood, I don't want to risk you, too. You deserve a good, safe, long life."

Morgana nodded and squeezed Taylor's hand, but Taylor wasn't having it.

"Before you came along, Maya, I had no idea just how strange the world really was. Now that I have an inkling, I can't bury my head in the sand and pretend I don't. I might not have your gift, but I still want to help. Maybe I'll change my mind later when I meet my first ghost, but for now you're stuck with me."

The young girl's words brought a strange sort of comfort to Maya. Taylor's life was her own, as were the consequences. "You sure?"

Taylor nodded slowly. "Yup, so let's get down to business."

"Speaking of," Morgana said. "If I'm taking the bus, then I better get going if I want to make sure I'm not late."

"Good idea." Maya admired the young woman's work ethic.

Taylor took Morgana's fingers and kissed each one. "Make me proud and bring home that Hot Topic bacon!"

Seeing that everything was settled, Maya finished emptying the bin and gave the collection of old gear a firm nod.

Please let this be an easy one, she said to herself, her body tensing at the thought of tangling with another supernatural terror. *I don't know if I have it in me to save the world a second time. I'm no Buffy.*

"So, remind me why I'm heading out again after nearly being eaten by an Elder God?" Maya asked as she loaded the last of the morning's dishes in the washer.

Alan, who'd come back to visit during his lunch break, tipped back his can of Red Bull and took a long swallow before replying. "Because it's creepy, that's why!"

"So are your pick-up lines," Maya replied. Taylor giggled on the couch.

"Hardy har har." His eye roll was long and accompanied by a sneer. "I'm serious. From what little I was able to gather online, this started a couple of weeks ago. A young girl went missing in the town of Mayfair, South Carolina, and a couple days later a doll was found on her parents' front porch that looked a lot like her, if she was possessed that is. Barely a week or so later–same town, another girl, another doll. Now a third girl has just gone missing, and there's no reason to expect her parents won't get a doll too."

A chill raced up Maya's spine like rats with cold feet. "That's terrible, and yeah, more than a little creepy, but what does it have to do with me? Ghosts don't usually kidnap people. This is a case for the FBI or something."

Alan shook his dreadlock-covered head. "That's one of the really odd things about this one. The local sheriff hasn't requested Federal assistance yet. He's keeping it all in-house, and apparently doing his best to keep things as quiet as possible. Were it not for a story in the local paper getting picked up by *News of the Weird*, I never would have heard about it."

"Okay, it's a *little* odd." Maya felt Alan's excitement creep over her, but she resisted it. Her life was strange enough without falling for every spooky story wafting through the internet.

"There's also this." He leaned over and pulled a folded piece of paper from his back pocket. After unfolding it, he said, "And I quote, 'After extensive testing it has been determined that the Finch doll is made of–wait for it–bone. Method of construction unknown. The bone is of human origin, but the DNA doesn't have a match in the system.'"

"Oh my God," Taylor said, her face screwed up in a horrified expression. "That's disgusting."

Alan winked and took another swig of his energy drink. "Just wait, it gets better. Ahem hem. 'Testing of the doll's hair follicles proved a match with the missing child. How the follicles were anchored in the bone could not be determined, however. X-Ray examination is inconclusive.'" Maya inhaled sharply, but Alan held up a finger to stall her. "'The doll's clothing also appears to be a match with the garments the child was known to be wearing subsequent to her disappearance. End of forensic report.' Boom." Alan tossed the paper onto the table in Maya's direction.

"How did you get hold of a police forensic report?" Maya picked up the paper and examined it.

Alan grinned like a cat with a canary in its mouth. "I have my ways, you know that. But that's not the point. This is some seriously messed up shit. I don't have your gifts, Maya, but I have a hunch about this. Something tells me you need to look into it. Three little girls are already missing, and I don't want to see any more disappear. Those poor parents."

"For a big ol' bear," Taylor said, "you have a gooey candy center."

A blush brightened the skin on Alan's face that wasn't covered by hair. "What can I say? I'm sensitive. Even with breeders."

Maya folded up the paper Alan gave her and put it in her purse. "Whatever you are, you convinced me. This is too weird *not* to check into it."

"I was hoping you'd see it my way," Alan replied with a slap on the table. "Since you've got Veronica Mars here going with you, do you need me to keep watch on your place again?"

A broad smile warmed Maya's face. "Thanks, but no. Morgana's staying here."

"She's barely out of diapers." Alan snorted, finished his drink, and burped loud enough to rattle the furniture. As he stood up he said, "I'll stop by now and then. Make sure the place doesn't burn down. Now, if you'll excuse me, I bid you fine ladies adieu."

Maya stood up as well and gave her friend a long, tight hug. "Thanks for everything," she whispered. "I don't know what I'd do without you."

"You'd probably fall to pieces," he whispered back. "But hey, that's what friends are for. Take care of yourself."

With a final squeeze, Maya released him and dabbed at her lower eyelids. She hated goodbyes, no matter how brief the parting was.

"See you later," Taylor said as she rose from the couch.

Alan waddled over and pulled the girl in for a squeeze. She protested loudly, but a smile lit her face, and she giggled when he let her go. "You're part of the family now, girl, so there'll be none of this handshake stuff. Be good to her, okay? Listen to her. Trust her. If she says run, you run as fast as you can, no questions asked. Got me?"

"I got you, sir!" Taylor saluted sharply.

"Then carry on, and good luck. Let me know when you get to town so I don't have to worry you died on the way there."

Maya nodded and smiled. "We will."

Alan returned her nod, gave both women a wink, and then left. His footsteps clomped down the outer hallway like hammer falls.

"You ready to go?" Maya asked. "We should make it to Mayfair by tomorrow morning if we leave now."

Taylor nodded, her face more eager than Maya cared for.

"Then come on, let's get going. Last one to the parking lot drives first!"

The race out of the apartment was as loud as it was hurried.

Chapter Four

Boden held Alison in his knobby hands as he sat in the threadbare living room, the sun dropping behind black curtains so old they'd turned gray with dust. He did nothing but lightly caress the doll's cracked body and wait. Strange sounds had emanated from his momma's room after he brought her supper as she once again poured over her strange books, and an odd smell fouled the air, but now all was silent save for Momma's snores rolling through the hallways like distant thunder. When the sun finally disappeared, the house plunged into shadows cast by moonlight. He could have turned on a lamp, but the dark didn't bother him; it was an old friend. So he sat in the gloom, his eyes on the doll in his lap.

When the ancient wooden clock his grandpa brought with him from the old country struck three dull notes, Boden lumbered to his feet. With Alison tucked under his left arm he walked to the front door, but before he opened it he reached toward the coat rack standing nearby and grabbed a wide-brimmed hat Momma recently made for him.

"This is a very special hat," she'd said as she handed it to him the first time. "Wear this whenever you go out to do somethin' for me. People won't notice you like they usually do."

And Momma hadn't lied. Whenever he went outside and wore the hat, folks looked everywhere but at him. He wasn't invisible; he cast a shadow same as everyone else. It was more like people didn't want to see him, found something more interesting to look at instead. Deep in his heart he wished she'd given him the hat years ago. The things people said when they saw him lumbering down the sidewalk, the dreadful looks they gave him, the way parents pulled their children close, it hurt his feelings in ways his clumsy mind couldn't express yet still felt.

Taking the girl home wasn't something Momma asked for him to do. In fact, he figured she'd be right darn mad if she ever found out about it. So far as she knew he threw them out or buried them or smashed them and then buried them. Whichever, just so long as she didn't have to look at her failure. But the kidnappings didn't seem right to Boden. He'd taken children from parents–children his momma needed, granted–and it wasn't fair that all he'd left them with was sadness. That's why he took what remained of the girls back home. Now their folks at least had something of their children back. That had to be a comfort. Had to be. So, with Alison secured under his arm, Boden settled the hat on his head, unlocked the front door, and trundled through it, careful to be as silent as his ungainly body allowed.

The world outside was chilly, quiet, and still. A long dirt driveway led away from the house, every foot of it overhung by trees and vines. A full moon shined down, casting shadows like black construction paper cutouts across the ground. As he stepped off the porch, a slight breeze played with his hat and brought gooseflesh up from his skin. The walk to the road was long and dangerous, deep mud holes turning the stretch of earth into an obstacle course. Only a vehicle designed for off-roading would make it all the way from the distant street, which was one of the reasons the house hadn't seen a visitor in many long years.

The walk to Alison's house wouldn't be a long one if he made a straight shot of it, cutting through backyards and play areas, but he couldn't do that *and* stay hidden. Too many dogs and camera lights stood watch that way, and Momma's hat didn't work on them. The last thing he needed was Fluffy or Cujo causing a ruckus and drawing attention, so he kept to the streets, making turn after turn after turn. An occasional bark shot out from the dark as his scent caught some pooch's nose, but that was the only mark of his passing.

After walking for nearly an hour, Boden turned onto Simmons Street, and there at the end of the block was Alison's house. He remembered being there the day before when he'd followed the young girl home from school. The shiny rock his mother had given him to help show which children suited her needs had shined brightly when Alison skipped past him on the sidewalk, not a care in the world, and—because of the hat—totally unaware he was there. When she made it home she decided to swing on a tire hung from a tree in their side yard instead of going inside. That made what he had to do much easier. One moment she was laughing into the sky, and the next she was unconscious from the stinky rag he pressed to her mouth and nose. He carried her to Momma's house in his arms, passing dozens and dozens of people who didn't see him or his sleeping passenger.

In the far back of his dense skull he wished someone would notice and force him to stop. He hated taking the children, hated hearing them cry as Momma prepared them for her magic, but he loved his momma even more, wanted her to live a long, pain-free life. So he did as she asked, taking as many children as she told him to get. Bringing the dolls back home was the only defiance he allowed himself.

Alison's house was completely dark and silent as he left the sidewalk and walked across the front yard. His intention was to set Alison on the front porch, just as he'd done twice before, but when he passed the tire swing he decided to put her on the ground beneath it. She'd been having so much fun on it when he took her that he figured she'd enjoy being near it again. He took Alison from under his arm, smoothed her dress as best he could, and set her down carefully on the ground.

"I hope you like this," he said to her, his whisper sounding like thunder in his ears. "I'm sorry for what happened. Bye now."

As Boden stood back up he noticed a light-colored car

parked on the far side of Straub Avenue. There were lots of cars sitting on the road, all of them like cats hunched down and ready to pounce, but he noticed the pale car because it was the only one with someone sitting in it. He couldn't tell who it was since the car was too far away and sitting beneath a broken street light, not that it mattered. Whoever it was hadn't seen him, thanks to momma.

His task complete, Boden fetched a deep sigh and turned back toward home. If he was lucky he could still get a few hours of sleep before momma woke and got him started on chores. He was already tired, and the more tired he got, the worse it would be.

Deputy Jimmy Fuller was exhausted. After working his regular shift he'd decided to take it on himself to stake out the Duff house in the hope whoever had kidnapped little Alison would stick to their usual modus operandi and bring a doll to the site of the abduction in the wee hours of the morning. If they were so inclined to stupidity, he wanted to be the one who caught them and finally broke the case before anyone else was taken or hurt. Sheriff Bowens hadn't assigned him the task, but if things went his way, Jimmy felt sure the sheriff wouldn't raise a fuss over it.

The wee hours of the morning weren't what Jimmy usually kept, so he drank cup after cup of black coffee from a small collection of thermoses sitting on the passenger seat of his personal car; squad cars weren't exactly low-key stakeout vehicles. The caffeine made sure he stayed awake, but it also ensured he had to pee like a race horse. It was either that, though, or strap on a pair of eye-openers *Clockwork Orange* style, so he chose coffee with little regret.

To distract himself he played music in his head and tapped out the drumbeat on his steering wheel with his thumbs. It also helped relieve the nervous energy created by the constant stream of java down his throat. His eyes were locked on the distant Duff house as he hummed Rush's

"Tom Sawyer," Neil Peart scorching the drums like a master putting on a clinic, when a flash of pain sparked through his nether region, starting at his kidney and ending at what felt like a good foot past his penis.

"Dammit," he whispered to himself as he hissed and readjusted his sitting position. Sometimes that was enough to relieve pee pressure, at least for a little while. This wasn't one of those times though.

Unsure how much longer he could hold out, Jimmy resumed his watch on the Duff house. For a moment he thought he saw something, a tall figure wearing an odd hat hunched over next to the tire swing in the Duff's side yard, but another flash of pain turned his groin into a quivering jumble. He feared he would piss himself there and then, but fortunately his muscles held strong.

Jimmy knew that wouldn't last long, though, so he debated his options. He could leave and find a bathroom, or he could get out of the car and find a tree to piss behind. Neither option was all that great, but leaving the area meant possibly missing his perp, so he decided a tree was his best bet.

As he reached to open his car door he suddenly felt like he wasn't alone, that he was being watched. He turned and scanned the neighborhood, his eyes tracking every shadow like a security camera, and for a brief instant he again thought he saw someone on the Duff's property. But as soon as he tried to focus the image disappeared, his groin gave another painful zap, and all thought of the missing child's abductor fled his brain as he raced to exit the car and pee. He nearly fainted from pleasure when his penis hit the cool night air and unleashed a flood of urine on the roots of an old oak tree.

"Ah yeah," he mumbled, his right arm braced on the tree and him leaning against it. Usually Jimmy was a very by-the-book sort of guy, a deputy who valued the law, but there were times when laws had to be bent, and a burning bladder was one of them. The next time he found Old Man McMullin pissing behind the Misty River Bar & Grill he figured he could look the other way. Then the scales of justice would be balanced once more.

A much lighter deputy returned to the car than had exited it, and he smiled in satisfaction as he resumed his watch. Not only was his groin now pain-free, but the sensation of being watched was gone, too. It wasn't until his eyes settled on the Duff's tire swing that he realized his entire night's mission was busted.

"Shit on a stick," he told himself.

Beneath the swing was a doll. He was too far away to see it clearly, but in his gut he knew what it would look like–cracked porcelain body, eyes like burn marks, and in all other ways the spitting image of Alison Duff. He knew for a fact that the doll hadn't been there when he'd arrived for his stakeout–he'd walked over the property with a fine-toothed comb–and no one had approached since, but here it was now as if by magic. All those hours of sitting and guzzling coffee hadn't gained him one damn thing save for the doll, and since neither of the previous two dolls had given them a single clue as to who had taken the children, he didn't hold out much hope this one would either.

Cursing silently, he opened his evidence kit and withdrew a pair of gloves and a clear evidence baggie. He knew from experience that it would take about an hour to go over the scene and collect the doll, but he figured submitting it could wait until he got some sleep and came in for his normal shift. He'd hoped he would enter the sheriff's building as a hero, the kidnapper in cuffs and Alison safely back with her parents, but those hopes were now a fart in the breeze. Hell, he might even get yelled at by the sheriff for not following proper procedure.

As he opened his door again he sighed and said, "Some days it just doesn't pay to be a good person." He then hoisted up his pants and turned toward the Duff residence.

His guts gurgled as he walked, the coffee letting him know it wasn't quite done with him yet.

Chapter Five

Sheriff Alvin Bowens did not sleep well. Usually he was out like a light as soon as his dark brown head touched the soft whiteness of his pillow, but ever since...what was it...

... Darkness rolled through his head like mist composed of the last breaths of all the damned souls of Hell, and far above him a woman whose face was shrouded in shadow stood glaring down at him...

...something to do with those missing kids, he had been plagued with nightmares. He didn't feel like himself, not one bit. Even his wife, Charlaine, had noticed, and she usually had her face too buried in those shitty tabloids to notice anything. She kept telling him he needed to go see Doctor Kurtz, but he didn't. What if people knew their head lawman thought he was going...

...when her fingers moved he felt his body twitch, a puppet at her command. Sickness filled him as her words slithered into his mind, devouring bits of him while changing others, remaking him to suit her needs. She commanded, and he obeyed...

...crazy.

By the time he made it out of the house and was on his way to work, the sourness in his stomach had only increased. When he finally pulled up to the station and exited his cruiser, the morning sun sat low and fat on the eastern horizon, its rays striking him directly in the eyes, sending flashes of pain into his brain.

Normally he was the picture of good health–certificates for perfect attendance in high school were a point of pride for him, each one framed and mounted in his home office– but lately he'd felt off. His stomach, which normally only gave him trouble if he went overboard on the wing sauce at The Soaring Buffalo, seemed to be in a constant low-level bathroom warning rumble, and his hands had developed a tremble. It was subtle, barely there, but there nonetheless.

The forgetfulness was the worst of it, though. As a lawman, his mind was his greatest asset, yet ever since...since...

I wonder if Charlaine picked up that Imodium like I asked her to, he wondered as his shaky right hand rubbed at his grumbling stomach.

Dammit! There it was, a perfect example. He just couldn't focus anymore. One moment he'd be thinking about work and those strange kidnappings, and the next his mind would slip gears. It was annoying, but he figured that was life now that he was weeks away from the big 50. Next he would need reading glasses and orthopedic shoes.

Bowens muttered as he unlocked the Sheriffs' Station and walked into the low-slung brick building. Once past the threshold, his feet turned toward the break room just as they had every morning for the past five years so he could get the first pot of joe brewing. But at the thought of coffee, his innards twisted into a knot and his butthole puckered, so instead he made for the bathroom. Strangely, by the time his hand touched the Men's Room door he no longer felt like shitting his pants, so he turned away after a second's consideration and went to his office instead.

Squealing like a kicked pig, Bowen's chair let the empty station know he'd snuck in an extra piece of lemon chess pie the night before as he settled onto its cracked vinyl surface. Damn thing had been on a slow roll to the junkyard ever since he'd inherited it from the previous sheriff, a gruff old bastard named Clinton Black who'd died in his cruiser with half a glazed donut stuck in his throat. It was bad enough the son of a bitch had left a massive shit stain on the seat— the scent of which still lingered if the windows were rolled up for too long—but confirming the cop stereotype was what really galled Bowen. He hoped that when he finally checked out he'd do it in his bed surrounded by hysterically sobbing friends and family.

Once his mid-life paunch pressed against his desk, Alvin jabbed the power button on his computer with a brown finger so calloused and dry it was almost gray. The damn thing sounded like a World War II bomber as its internal fans cranked to life. The prehistoric beige monitor turned on with a sharp *snap hiss* as the cathode ray tube sparked to grumpy life. Every morning he expected the relic of a machine to catch fire, and every morning he was disappointed.

Someday, he mused, glaring at the aged machine. *Someday you'll choke on all the dust and dead skin cells I let pile up in this office, and then I'll be able to requisition a new computer and finally move into the twenty-first century with the rest of the world. Might even get on that BookFace or whatever it's called.*

Less than a minute into the computer's boot cycle, Bowens's desk phone rang. His heart kicked against his chest like a spooked mule. He waited a moment to see if it galloped into a full-on attack, but his pulse returned to normal after a few hard beats. He looked at his phone to see who was calling. As soon as the numbers 7-0-4 passed beneath his eyes he sighed and reached for the handset. 704 was the area code of Columbia, South Carolina's capital. It was also where the state's head FBI's field office was located.

"Sheriff Bowens," he said into the mouth piece, his tone as authoritative as he could make it.

"Good morning, Sheriff," a young voice he recognized instantly replied. "I see the state labs have finished going over the second doll. Same results as before. Looks like you have an honest to God psycho out there."

Bowens was pissed. He'd barely started his day, and already he had a Fed up his ass. A Fed who didn't mind sticking his pimply nose where it didn't belong, no less.

"Like I told you last time, Agent Hargrave, we don't require the assistance of the Federal Government at this time." A dull ache tapped the inside of his skull with every word.

"You sure about that? With the disappearance of Alison

Duff you've got three missing little girls, and I'd bet a month's pay you'll find another doll, if you haven't already. You have no leads, clues that ask more questions than they answer, and if memory serves you'll be facing reelection soon. I'd say you need the assistance of the entire bureau, *Sheriff*."

The last world came out in a sneer, as though it was an insult, which was precisely how Bowens took it. "Listen up, *Agent*, I know you're still wet behind the ears and want like all hell to make a name for yourself, but you ain't gonna do it at the expense of my jurisdiction, even if it's within your power to do so. We don't need a goddamn Federal parade going through downtown, scaring everyone and spooking the kidnapper into diving as far into the shadows as they can go. So, until I call you and say otherwise, consider this case handled."

The inside of Bowens's head was a pounding mess, a killer of a migraine in the near distance, and he almost dropped the phone because his hand was shaking so much. The last thing he wanted to think about at the moment was the missing children case.

"I hope you're handling it, because if one more child goes missing and you don't have a compelling lead, I can and **will** bring all the authority I have to bear on you whether you want it or not. You won't have to worry about reelection then, because I'll have you in prison for criminal incompetence. That should make me a name for certain."

Every word was a nail in Bowens's skull, and he knew if he didn't hang up soon his head would implode. "Maybe, but I doubt you'd like it. Now, if you'll excuse me, I have actual police work to do. Goodbye."

Bowens had a hard time getting the phone handset put back on its cradle because of his trembling hand, but after a few shaky attempts he managed it.

"Bad day already, Sheriff?"

For the second time in as many minutes Bowens's heart

lurched in surprise.

"Jesus H Christ, Jimmy," Bowens said as he whipped his head toward the door of his office, beads of sweat popping up across his forehead despite the cool temperature inside the station. "What have I told you about sneaking up on me?"

Sheriff's Deputy Fuller stood in the office doorway looking like a dress-code poster boy. His beige uniform was pressed to within an inch of its life, the pant leg creases were sharp enough to cut steak, and his shoes practically looked like black leather mirrors. Dull brown eyes gazed out from a pale face shaved as smooth as a newborn's ass, his hair cut short and smoothed back with Dapper Dan pomade or some shit. His badge, sidearm, and other accouterments were all perfectly in place and looking brand new. Jimmy was a prissy sombitch, which Bowens hated, but the deputy was also very good at his job, and Bowens liked that just fine. It's why he kept the stiff around.

"To not do it, Sheriff?" Jimmy replied as though commenting on the weather.

"And yet you keep doing it." Bowens reached into his left back pocket and withdrew a white cotton handkerchief, then patted the sweat from his dark brow. "I swear, do it one more time and I'll shoot you. And trust me, it'll be justified. Now, why are you haunting my doorway?"

Jimmy's face brightened, but then he frowned as he reached toward a table sitting just outside the sheriff's office. When his hand came back it held a clear plastic evidence bag. A doll was inside it.

Bowens's stomach sank like an anchor.

"I staked out the Duff place last night," the deputy said, "hoping to catch whoever has been leaving the dolls, but somehow they got past me. I don't know how they did it either. I was loaded with enough caffeine to give a horse a heart attack, and my eyes never left their property. But, here it is nonetheless."

"And who authorized this stakeout?" Bowens's face warmed as anger rose within him. "I don't recall tasking anyone with that."

Jimmy became ghost white, which for him was saying something. "You didn't, Sir, but I thought I'd take the initiative. Anything we can do to save these girls–"

"We'll save them," Bowens said, cutting his deputy off, "but we'll do it my way. This is my goddamn department, and I run it. Not you." Fresh sweat dampened his forehead, and again his bowels twisted into a knot.

"I don't–"

"That's right. You don't. So leave the decision making to me, okay?"

Jimmy's lips tightened and roses blossomed on his cheeks, but after a few silent seconds he nodded. "Yes, Sir. Would you like me to send this to the state forensics office?"

Bowens's pulse pounded harder and harder against his temples as the conversation continued. All he wanted was to finish it and close his door, maybe even lock it too. "Yeah, sure, send it. Results are in on the last one, so look those over too."

After several long seconds, the deputy coughed and asked, "You okay, sir?" Jimmy looked at him like he'd sprouted horns.

Rubbing his forehead, Bowens nodded, but then stopped when the motion made him queasy. "It's just a headache."

"Another one?" Jimmy's tone was concerned despite the dressing down he'd just received. "Ever since Cassidy Finch went missing you've been getting them. If it's stress–"

Bowens sighed heavily and leveled a stern gaze on his deputy. "Jimmy, my mom might be dead, but that doesn't mean I need another one. Just go and tend to your job, all right? Leave me and my headache be."

Jimmy stepped back from the office door, his eyes wide,

but after a moment he nodded and walked away.

Bowens figured he'd have to apologize for that, but it would have to be later in the day, because at that moment he couldn't see well enough to get up and attempt navigating the office. His headache had officially become a migraine.

Great, he mused silently. *Another problem to add to the list. When it rains it pours.*

As the sheriff rummaged through his desk drawers for Ibuprofin, thoughts of the missing girls drifted little by little from his mind. His hand eventually bumped against a plastic bottle, rattling it, and he opened it with what was becoming practiced ease. After dry swallowing five of the white pills, he eased down in his ratty chair and closed his eyes. If he was lucky, he'd be better in time for lunch. Daddy Ray's BBQ had the best brisket in the county, and today it was the lunch special. Nothing made his day better than brisket, a heaping pile of mashed potatoes, and a buttered roll.

Make that two buttered rolls. I damn well deserve it.

Chapter Six

Maya flew, her arms outstretched beside her like wings. Green hills rolled far beneath her like a lumpy shag carpet without end, the occasional road or river breaking up the verdant expanse. The thrill of flight delighted her, made her feel free, unfettered by the constant weight of life. All she had to do was keep her arms held out.

Above her, thin clouds dotted the sun-warmed sky like floating cotton patches, all of them slowly sailing in the same direction. Maya let their movement guide her. As her arms turned, they caught the wind and her speed increased. She laughed out loud, the giddy noise soaring ahead of her. At that moment she realized the truth—she was dreaming, the joy was just too much to be real, but the revelation didn't awaken her. Just the opposite—she grabbed hold of the dream with a greed she'd never felt before and refused to let it go. The real world had problems and pain, danger, reasons to be afraid, but dreams…dreams were carefree, seconds turned into hours of bliss. So long as she was within her own mind, nothing could hurt her.

Is that so, child?

The clouds suddenly turned gray, their cottony undersides mottled and sickly. The words echoed through her head, shaking Maya to her core because they weren't her own. Someone had invaded her dream: someone dark and sickening. Her arms drew close, and she fell halfway to the ground before she caught hold of her dream-self again and rose back into the dimming sky.

"Who's that?" she asked. "This is *my* dream."

The clouds turned ashen and angry and thunder roared, rattling the world. Maya knew the booming sound for what it really was though—laughter.

Look deep within yourself. You know who I am, though you never knew my name. You called me the Dark God, the Ancient One. These are fitting titles, but when I ruled this world, the fearful called me Demael the Defiler, First of the Burning Gods. As for dreams, I know of dreams, child. I was the architect of nightmares, deliverer of the blackest imaginings. After the skies drowned the world millennia ago, I thought my time was done, and then you came, and I woke…

In an instant Maya understood the depth of her danger, and with that dreadful recognition came fear. Her mind pushed away from it as her dream-self drifted backward. "No, I don't want to talk about dreams or nightmares. This is *my* place, *I* say what happens. So go away. You're not real. We destroyed you."

Lightning split the heavens in a blinding explosion. *I am more real than anything you have ever known, as you will soon discover. You fought me, and in the end your feeble ploy succeeded…though at a cost. You didn't truly think you could face power like mine and come away unchanged, did you?*

Every utterance sent chills down Maya's spine, and the question the voice asked hammered an icy spike straight into her heart. "I don't understand," she said, afraid she actually did.

Below her, the rolling grass fields were now a desert of dust and bone.

You think yourself pure and light, Demael said, each word dripping with venom, *but within you lies a dark seed buried so deeply you barely knew it was there. You used the power it granted you, but you never understood the source of it, perhaps—in the darkest hours between night and day—even fearing it. Let me now educate you, my child—you are of ancient blood, descendant of a lineage that goes back to the First, to the Dark Ones. The blood of the Primals—what little is left—flows within you.*

"Liar!" Maya replied, her dream arms wrapping around her chest as she slowly drifted through the darkling sky. "You're just a figment of my imagination."

The air thickened around Maya, pressing against her skin like wool. She could barely catch her breath. Her lungs burned as she drowned in open air. She reached for her neck and tried desperately to remove hands that weren't there.

I am so much more than that, blood of my blood. We held one another, our minds entwined in the silent space between death and life, crossing from dream to waking and back again. That seed within you called to me, but the darkness that **is** *you held me. And now, though I am entombed once more beneath stone and water, I live within you, a part of you, and I will never let you go.*

Maya's heart raced as the whispering voice echoed Kyle's nightmare declaration, and she finally understood what had transpired on that West Virginia mountainside so many weeks before. While she had psychically descended into the sleeping mind of a waking god, so had Demael fallen into her. She and it were joined, closer than lovers. As the realization hit, the dreamscape around her became a hellish mirror of her perfect place, the blue sky now black and the green hills mounds of bones.

"No," she said, part of her refusing to believe it. "This is a dream, it isn't real, so you're not real. I'm making this up. Processing what happened. This isn't real."

Terrible laughter shook the sky and ground, sending tremors through Maya's sleeping mind.

Denying the truth does not unmake it. You and I are one now. Soon you will have no choice but to accept it. Then our journey into darkness will truly begin. You will be the First of my Chosen. Through you I will walk the world once more. Together we will make it tremble.

Terror raced through Maya's body, fearful that the voice was right, horrified that she had brought it on herself. In her panic she soared into the heavens, total blackness in front of her, hoping that if she flew far enough and fast enough eventually she would break through into light. But all she saw was darkness, and all she felt was the cold grip of her oncoming destiny. Into the black she screamed, the noise tearing her throat apart, blood racing into her lungs to drown her.

If only she could reach the light! It would burn the darkness inside her away! It had to!

But the light never came.

"Maya! Wake up!"

Morning light burned into Maya's eyes as she awoke, her hands clutching at her chest. Taylor sat in the driver's seat of the Trailblazer Maya had bought to replace her Honda which currently sat at the bottom of West Virginia's newest lake. The young woman's eyes bored into her as she slowed down and steered onto the road's gravel shoulder.

"Jesus H," Taylor said with a heavy sigh as they rolled to a crunchy stop. "You scared the shit outta me. You okay?"

Rattled, Maya didn't know how to answer that. The horror of her dream, not to mention its implications, had her brain running around inside her skull like a yapping dog chasing its own tail.

"I don't know. I think so, for now anyway."

A crooked smile soured Taylor's face. "What in the hell does *that* mean?"

"I wish I knew." Maya arched her back and stretched her arms out. She never slept comfortably anywhere that wasn't her bed, and her body was a knotted ball of kinks. "Lately I've had nothing but bad dreams. This last one though…" She stopped, unsure how much she believed what had been said, not to mention how much to reveal. After a moment's consideration, she decided there wasn't any point in getting Taylor worked up without a solid reason. Their investigation would likely prove stressful enough. "It just hit harder than usual. Still, it was only a dream, so nothing to worry about."

Taylor continued to scowl. "Uh huh. I don't understand how it is that you do what you do, but I assume with people like you a dream is never *just* a dream. You obviously don't want to talk about it though, so I'll let it go…for now."

"Thanks, *Mom*." Maya was caught in that uncomfortable place between irritation and affection.

Nodding, Taylor let her mouth slip back into its normal

shape. "Speaking of which, do you…uh…sense anything? Mayfair's just a few miles away."

Maya stretched to work out knots in her muscles, then settled into her seat and folded her hands in her lap. "It's not like turning on a light or something, but I'll try."

"That's all we can ask for."

Maya shook her head to clear the dream voice from it, pushed away all thoughts of evil and doubt until her mind felt weightless, and then she gazed at the world around her with closed eyes. At first all she sensed was an empty gray expanse, the spiritual quintessence that exists just beyond the physical realm. Behind her lowered lids, her eyes turned left and right for what seemed like hours, but there wasn't anything to see, just ashen tones everywhere. Eventually, though, vague shadows crept through the blankness. They were barely there, shadows passing through snow, but Maya recognized them as the psychic impressions of people living in the area. Vague echoes were all she usually saw when peering into the aether, so it didn't surprise her that nothing unusual caught her attention.

"Anything?" Taylor asked, her question sending vibrations through the gloom that caused the shadows to vibrate and diminish.

"Sshh," Maya replied with more than a hint of sternness.

Taylor obeyed, and after a few moments the shadows returned. Locking her eyes straight ahead, Maya imagined her mind lifting into the air. The shadows became dots. Once she was high enough she sent psychic tendrils into the aether to search for anything out of the ordinary, anything not of the physical world.

A few minutes later, nothing.

She pushed the tendrils further out, expanding her awareness.

Nothing.

Floating amongst the clouds as she was, Maya still had

enough awareness of her physical body to feel sweat break out on her forehead from the mental exertion. *Come on, girl, don't wimp out now*, she thought. Freshly motivated, she dug deep inside for the fortitude she needed to extend her mind even further, nearly blanketing the—

Searing pain lanced through Maya like a hot poker driven into her forehead. The quintessence abruptly disappeared, and in its place were hazy stone walls. Ancient wooden bookshelves leaned against each other like tired old drunks, their sagging horizontal planks laden with books and jars containing strange things she was glad she couldn't make out. Above her hung the carcasses of small, dead animals, their desiccated flesh stiff and unmoving. Suddenly the vision turned, and strange designs shimmered against wall, floor, and ceiling, each one utterly mysterious and more than a little disturbing. The vision turned again, and this time when it stopped a monstrous figure loomed toward her, its body twisted and terrifying. A high-pitched voice screamed words Maya couldn't understand, but she barely had time to wonder before her mind was repulsed from the bizarre room and slammed back into her body.

"Oww!" she cried out, her eyes jerking open. She grabbed her head with both hands and stomped her feet against the floorboard. "Oh, goddamn! Goddamn!"

Taylor's mouth fell open, her face set in a horrified expression. "What is it, Maya?" she asked, reaching out and touching her shoulders. "What happened?"

Maya kept one hand on her head while grabbing Taylor's arm with the other. Water filled her eyes as tears sprang up from the pain, but then her stomach revolted and sent bile into her throat. "I don't know! I need to—"

Maya flung her door open, stumbled to the grass lying beyond the roadway, dropped to her knees, and puked. She felt like everything she'd ever eaten came out of her—every burger, every salad, every slice of pie—and it only kept coming. By the time the last bit of drool slipped from her lips she was turned inside out. She then pushed backward until she was sitting on the grass away from the steaming puddle.

"Holy shit!" Taylor said as she jumped out of the Trailblazer and hurried over. "I've never seen anything like that! You are a champion up-chucker!"

Maya wiped her mouth with the back of her arm and took a deep breath. "Um, thanks?"

"It's all you, girl." Taylor patted her on the back. "Now what the hell was that about?"

All Maya could think to do was shake her head. "I don't know. I was trying to find anything supernatural in the area, and suddenly I was in a...room of some kind. Maybe a basement, or...or maybe a cave. Hell, I don't even know if it was real or not."

"So...does that mean you found what you were looking for?"

A humorless chuckle fell from Maya's lips. "I don't know. I found *something*, that's for sure, but what exactly...I don't know."

"Huh." Taylor put her hands on her lower back and leaned back in a stretch. "Did anything like that happen when you got close to Stillwater?"

Maya shook her head. "No, that was more subtle, like a sinking feeling in the gut. This was like touching a live wire. Maybe what happened there changed my abilities, enhanced them or something. I don't know. Either way, I'm not going to try that again until I do some real-world investigating."

"I hear ya." Taylor's heavily outlined eyes looked at her like a sympathetic raccoon.

Maya appreciated the girl's understanding. She let herself recover on the grass for a few more seconds, then struggled to her knees and stood up. "Anyway, let's get to Mayfair and find a place to stay. I'm suddenly in desperate need of a nap."

"Hopefully a dreamless one." Taylor wound her arm

against Maya's and walked her back to the Trailblazer.

Maya chuckled, the sound genuine this time. "You're damn right. No more dreams for me."

Chapter Seven

Estera didn't dream. Night after night she lay in bed, her eyes closed, her breathing slow and rhythmic, restorative sleep easing her physical pains, but she did not dream. She hadn't in years. Decades. Dreams were too dangerous. They lowered defenses, made the dreamer vulnerable. The last time she'd slipped into the realm of the Oneiri and dreamed, a rival witch named Agatha Maniae tried to invade her body and steal her power. An attack like that would have been easily defended while awake, but not so in a dream, and Estera–after barely defeating the cunning old bitch–vowed that she would never allow herself to be exposed like that again.

So as the moon ascended into darkness, Estera lay on her bed and drifted into the Hallow, a secret space within her mind where she practiced deadly incantations, monitored the spells she'd cast to protect herself, looked over the invisible glyphs and wards etched onto the walls of her home, and read books she'd transmutated from physical objects to mental. The Hallow was a sacred space, and she valued it greatly, but she also missed the simplicity of dreaming, the illusory freedom it provided. Such was the price of her dark magic.

In that nether space between waking and illusion, Estera stood before a crimson altar. On it rested a large, open book, its calfskin pages perfect reproductions of the material world version. Gaining possession of the *Focail de Veles*–one of the most powerful grimoires ever written, and also the most secret–had cost her terribly. But the promise of long-lost arcane power hidden within its cyphered text was greater still, so night after night she poured over the book of magic, casting various spells in the hope that more of the grimoire's secrets would be revealed. Even those that had, though, weren't always entirely clear, which was why she now stood before the blood altar.

From a pocket of her robe she took out a white candle, its wick dark and short. After taking it in her left hand, she placed her right thumb and middle finger on the wick and whispered, "*Ignis.*" Her fingers tingled for a moment. When she removed them, a bright, solitary flame burned above the candle. She didn't need the light for herself–the Hallow was part of her, so she required no light to see–but it was necessary for the spell. She then held the candle over the *Focail de Veles* and said, "Spirits of truth, speakers of secrets, answer my call! Reveal that which lies hidden before me!"

The flame waivered as she uttered the spell, but when the final word left her lips the candle flared brightly and then went dark. In the gloom she watched smoke from the wick float down until it landed on the grimoire's pages. Wispy tendrils curled around the text, outlining each character and symbol until they glowed with a dark light. The pages began to change.

"Yes!" Estera's eyes widened as she put the candle back in her pocket. "Show yourself to me!"

Suddenly the air trembled, the altar shook, and the *Focail de Veles* tumbled to Estera's feet. She reached for it instinctively, but her fingers barely brushed the leather cover before a gust of wind blasted her, sending the book and altar tumbling into the Hallow's shadowy reaches. That was all she saw before darkness overtook her, too.

Estera turned around in a circle, staring into blackness that should have been as plain to her as the deep lines crinkling the back of her hands, but for the first time since creating the private space she wasn't in control of it.

Nor was she alone.

"Who dares trespass here?"

No reply came back, and the blackness did not lighten. If anything it seemed to become even darker, an inky emptiness coating her skin.

"Show yourself, and I might let you live," she said, her

nostrils flaring and her fingers digging into her palms. "Continue to hide, and I will tear your soul apart."

The black continued undisturbed.

Estera dug into the pocket of her robe. "Very well. You were warned." After withdrawing the white candle she again held the still-warm wick between her fingers. "Ignis!"

Once more the candle ignited, but instead of a strong, steady flame, the wick held aloft a tiny flickering spark that barely pushed back the dark around her. She quickly waved her hand over the candle and cast several illumination spells, but the one pathetic flame was all she got, so she held the candle in front of her, turned in a slow circle, and stared intently into the darkness.

Who's out there? she asked herself, the thought as loud as spoken words in the Hallow. *Who has the power to enter my domain and take control of it? And more importantly, why? Am I being played with? Mocked? If that's the case, then woe unto to them, because I will find them, and then I will destroy them.*

Grinding her teeth, Estera held the candle tightly and flicked it forward. The tiny flame leapt from the candle and flew forward to hover like a firefly just at the edge of her vision. Another flame lit atop the candle, and it too went flying. As she prepared to send a third flame, the two fluttering fireflies blinked out of existence.

In the gloom a shape formed. It was indistinct at first, a dark mass against a darker background. But, second by second it shifted, shrank, until she was able to make out a human shape. Physically it was taller than she was, and by the way it stood it seemed younger, and feminine. Fury exploded in her chest like a bomb, and she called the words of a devastating spell to her lips. A new shape then took form, growing from the mysterious woman like a snake rising from a woven basket. Estera didn't know why, but suddenly she was afraid. She had great power at her command, and few things made her quake, but in front of her rose a power far greater than anything she'd ever known before. It was a power as old as the Earth, and more evil than any demon or devil her magic could summon.

Without warning the shadow woman leapt for her, and the ancient evil being with her laughed. In the darkness Estera screamed and lunged forward, ready to kill with every ounce of savagery she had. It was either that or die, and she'd spilt far too much blood attempting to overcome death already to give up now.

"Arrrgghh!"

Boden went from deep sleep to full wakefulness in less than a second as his momma's scream tore through the walls separating them. He sat up from his bed like his torso was spring-loaded and tossed aside the threadbare blanket covering him, leaped from his dilapidated bed, and stumbled out of his room. Early morning light shone through windows in the hallway beyond his door.

"No!" his momma bellowed. "Get away!"

Fearing she was being attacked, Boden moved as quickly as his still-sleeping muscles allowed. His feet hit like sledgehammers on the stairs leading to her room. At the top he grabbed the knob to his momma's door and twisted it as his shoulder hit the rectangle of wood, sending it flying inward with a bang. His momma's bed, a giant piece of ancient wooden furniture, sat in the middle of a room draped in black cloth. Even the hardwood floor was painted black. Various symbols were sewn into the drapes with silver thread glittering in the light of black candles that always burned yet never dwindled sitting on her dresser and side tables. Normally the candlelight was calm, but not now. Now the flames jittered and flared, sending wild shadows dancing across the walls.

Another scream pierced the air, drawing Boden's eyes back to his momma's bed. The blood red comforter tossed about as though wild animals fought beneath it, so he rushed across the dark floor and grabbed the heavy, crimson material with both gnarled hands. Whoever was attacking his momma was about to learn how big a mistake they'd made.

But no one was attacking her. Momma was alone. Naked from head to toe, her arms flailed and her legs shuffled around, but all they touched was empty air. He reached over to see if her attacker was perhaps invisible–she'd had dealings before with beings beyond his ability to see, and few of them pleasant–but his hands touched nothing, felt nothing. When he looked at her face to see what she was looking at, her eyes were closed. It was then the thought occurred to him she might be dreaming.

"Momma," he said as he leaned over to take her shoulders and shake her awake, "wake up, you're–"

Before he could touch her or finish speaking she shouted, "I said let me go! *Please*!" and threw her hands outward. Suddenly one of the silver symbols on the wall shined as though lit on fire, and the air exploded over the bed, sending Boden flying through the doorway he'd passed through just moments before. He hit the landing at the top of the stairs, tumbled past it, and rolled down the creaky steps. When he finally came to a stop, he was bruised, bleeding, and breathless.

"Aarrgghh!" momma said, this time in a rage.

Boden shook his head to clear it, took a deep breath, and got to his feet. After quickly determining that nothing was broken, he once again climbed the stairs to momma's room. When he got there she was still in bed, but now she was awake and sitting up. Her eyes blazed with anger, and the symbol on the wall still glowed. Her naked chest and neck were flushed with blood, sweat thick on her head and limbs.

"You okay, Momma?"

At first she didn't respond, but after a few seconds she turned to look his way, and he instantly regretted it when her furious eyes landed on him.

"Am I okay? Do I *look* okay? I was just attacked! In my

own home, no less!"

Boden shook his head and rubbed the back of his skull when a dizzy spell threatened to take his legs out from under him. "No, Momma. Wasn't no one in your bed but you."

"Don't be stupid, boy," she replied with a withering glance before looking down at her arms and legs.

"Then how was you–"

Momma balled her hands into fists and pounded the bed. The air in her room suddenly thickened. "I don't know! There was…an otherworldliness to it, powerful and old, but it wasn't magic. Least not a magic I've ever come across before."

Boden hadn't thought that possible. Her entire life was magic. "Do you know who it was?"

Momma shook her head. "I sensed a feminine energy, but that was it. Nothing familiar."

"You sure it was an attack?"

Momma squinted as if she were looking at a bug, then turned to dangle her legs off the side of the bed. "Of course I'm sure! And I tell you this: I won't be taken unawares like that again. Whoever it was, if they want to test my powers a second time, they'll quickly come to regret it." As her feet hit the floor, she hissed and held her side. "Speaking of testing my powers, I need to get down to my casting circle."

"Of course, Momma," Boden replied. "Want me to carry you down?"

"I'm dying," she'd said as she hobbled to a small table against a nearby wall, "but I'm not dead yet." She dipped a small graying towel into a chipped porcelain bowl of water and used it to clean her face, under her armpits and hanging boobs, and then her naughty private area. A dark bruise sat against her right ribcage like a giant black and green birthmark.

He turned his eyes away so he didn't have to look at her wrinkled pink and gray body. "As you say, Momma."

Grunting, she set the damp cloth back on the table and

went to her closet. It was only after she'd pulled a shapeless, dark gray dress over herself that Boden looked at her directly again. Momma had a dozen or so of the same dresses hanging in her closet, some darker than others depending on age. Over that she wore a black, hooded coat.

"Go be useful and make me some breakfast. I'll be famished when I'm done with my circle."

"Yes, Momma."

And so minutes later Boden, being the good boy his momma needed him to be, stood in the kitchen stirring a pot of bubbling oatmeal as he tried to not smell the odors coming from the basement beneath him.

He and Momma were descended from a long line of Romanian gypsies, but unlike most of them, Momma didn't go in for useless decoration. Their house was old, plain, and bare. No white stone animals stood outside their front door, no fancy pictures trimmed in gold hung on the walls. Other gypsy homes had pretty lawns and big cars on perfectly paved driveways, but momma didn't care about any of that. Their lawn was a riot of wild flowers and weeds, and their car—a wood-paneled station wagon older than Boden—sagged like a dying animal on gravel. Their house wasn't a very lively house either. Boden didn't mind, though. It was all he'd ever known, and if was good enough for Momma, then it was good enough for him.

The kitchen, though, was the one room that actually felt loved and lived in. All sorts of cooking equipment sat on wooden countertops, bundles of garlic and spices hung from the walls, a well-worn table was off to the side flanked by chairs whose seats were smooth as glass from years of butts sliding across them, but it was the stove that brought it all together. Sitting like a cast iron engine of food production, its dark metal body was wide and seemingly always hot. Next to it was a bin of wood Boden spent hours a day splitting out back. He stood before it now, sweat beading across his bulging forehead, as he tended the large pot filled with softening oats, water, butter, and sugar.

"Nodens and Sirona, I summon you!" Momma's voice suddenly carried through the floorboards. "Heed my call and heal my wounds!"

When her voice quieted, Boden was thankful. Her magic frightened him, and as she grew older her dependence on it increased. But now, as she'd said earlier, she was dying, and her only hope lay in the very part of her he hated most.

Suddenly the house shook, and a loud sound like a thousand cats being skinned at once burst from the floor. The air around him shifted, turned into a breeze, and howled as it drew downward between the floor planks. He worried the house would come loose as the screaming sound and wind pummeled the walls. Momma let loose a high-pitched cackle, adding to the storm, and screamed, "Yes! Heed me, ye ancient powers! Do my will!"

The storm's power grew. Windows vibrated in their frames so much Boden feared they would shatter. The screaming wind pulled at the loose bits of his skin, fed the fire in the stove's belly, sent dust into his eyes like tiny shards of glass. He thought he was going to be tossed from the room when everything suddenly stopped. No more wind, no more yowling noise, no more words from Momma. It ended as suddenly as it started.

Ignoring his fear as best he could, Boden continued stirring. When the wooden spoon met the proper amount of resistance, he lifted the pot from the stove and moved it to a metal grate to cool atop the counter. Bowls sat in the cabinet above the pot, and utensils were in the drawer below. Boden lowered a ladle into the pot as the basement door opened. A foul gust of wind billowed out.

"Okay now, Momma?" he asked as he opened a canister and spooned a heaping mound of sugar onto the oatmeal in his ladle.

Her hair more distressed than usual, Momma shuffled to the table and set down with a heavy sigh. In her old hands was a clay cup from which wafted a sickly green steam. "When I was a young 'un, a potion like this would've been easy, but now it costs me nearly as much as it gives. If I hadn't invoked the old Celt deities, I might not have succeeded at all. They're pitifully vain Powers though, practically begging to assist the few of us left who remember their names and how to invoke them."

Boden tumped the ladle of sweet oatmeal into a bowl as she slurped down her noxious concoction. His nose twitched at the foul odor filling the air with each glug. After sprinkling some cinnamon on the oatmeal, he carried it to the table and sat the bowl before her, then he settled into the chair opposite. Next to him was a window, which he opened, though the old pane squealed in protest. Within seconds fresh air released his nose from torture.

Despite how much he hated the magic Momma used, not to mention the awful smells and sounds that always seemed to accompany it, he couldn't deny the results. Momma barely had the clay cup emptied before the wrinkles of her face lessened, the tremor in her hands disappeared, and she sat up straighter in her chair. After setting the cup down, she lifted her dress. Boden looked away before he had to see the wild thatch of gray hair between her legs, but when she laughed with delight he risked a glance back and watched in fascination as the bruise on her ribcage faded away. Less than a minute later she looked as healthy as ever.

"That feels so much better." She lowered her dress and sighed. "The old ways are still the best."

Without thinking about it, Boden asked, "If they're the best, why are they old and forgotten?"

He hadn't meant the question to be an insult, but the fire glowing in Momma's eyes made it clear that's how she took it. "Because people are cowardly and stupid, too afraid of true power to take control of it. It's always been the way. Only a rare few have the courage to entreat with the forces of creation, and we always have to do it in the shadows, away from the eyes of the fearful, because if there's one thing they fear more than magic, it's those who choose to wield it. And what do these simpletons do to those they fear, boy?"

Boden gulped. She'd drilled the answer into him his entire life. "They kill 'em."

Momma nodded. "Or at least they try damned hard to. We witches would have taken over the world centuries ago if there'd been more of us. Now we're even more a dying breed."

Boden swallowed and put as big a smile as he could on his face to defuse her anger. "They'll never get you, Momma."

The sound she made was supposed to be a laugh, but it came out too wet and chunky to be funny. "Well, boy, if they don't get me, time's merciless sickle will. Speaking of which…"

Momma moved her clay cup aside and drew the bowl of oatmeal close. After taking a few spoonfuls of it into her mouth, she said, "I'm gonna go with you to pick out the next girl. I thought my finding stone would help you do it for me, but either I miscast the spell or you're just too thick to use it rightly. Like they say–if you want something done right, do it yourself."

In spite of his fear of her magic, Boden was glad. He'd already brought three little ones home to her that hadn't worked out, and he dreaded bringing a fourth. Now it would be on her, and he wouldn't have to feel so terrible.

"All right, Momma. I understand."

"Mmm hmm," she replied around the spoon sticking from her thin lips. "I doubt that. Now get out back and get to splitting more logs. *That*, at least, I know you can handle."

Boden nodded, the motion pushing spit over his lower lip and onto the table. He wiped it up with the cuff of his green plaid shirt, then stood and made for the rear door and the chopping block beyond it.

Chapter Eight

As soon as the Trailblazer came to a stop, Maya opened the passenger door, slid out, and took a long, calming breath. She was so thankful she nearly dropped to her knees and kissed the ground. Her innards had been in turmoil since the strange ethereal encounter, and the bumpy roads leading into town hadn't helped. One more mile and her stomach would have gone into total revolt.

"Verdant Inn." Taylor slung a pink and gray backpack over her shoulder as she exited the Chevy and looked up at a bright green sign with the image of a log cabin in the middle of it. "Free Wi-Fi and HBO. I'm sold."

"No in-room Jacuzzi?" Maya snorted as she looked around. Mayfair looked like any other small town—narrow roads, scattered brick buildings and wooden houses, tall trees older than the Constitution everywhere, railroad crossings, kids playing baseball with sticks for bats, and thin grass growing through cracks in the sidewalks. It was pure Americana, yet something else was present in Mayfair, something sinister at the periphery of her senses, and it cast a shadow that chilled her to her bones. "I guess we'll just have to make do. Stay here while I get us a room, okay? No funny business."

Taylor adjusted her backpack and frowned. "No promises."

Maya tossed the girl a look and shook her head, then headed to the inn's office. Cold air blasted her face as she opened the glass door and passed through. A chime lit the air. Wood paneling with green trim, green accents, and green painted hardware were everywhere. *Apparently the owners of the Verdant Inn are pretty serious about the verdant part*, she thought. A counter sat against the wall to the right, and behind it stood a young woman dressed in a green button-up shirt and skirt. Maya couldn't see the clerk's shoes, but she would have bet every penny she had that they were green too. A small smile pulled at the corners of her lips.

"Welcome to the Verdant Inn," the clerk said in a tone that was peppy without being cloyingly cheerful. "How can I help you today?"

"I need a room for two adults. Two beds, if you have it. Ground floor and around back would be great."

The clerk smiled broadly and tapped away at her keyboard. "Very good. It looks like we can accommodate all that. How many nights will you be staying?"

"That's the real question," Maya replied. "I'm not sure. A couple of days at least."

"You can always extend your stay if you find you need to, so no worries. This is the off season."

Maya nodded and pulled her wallet from her pants' back pocket. She'd never been a purse carrier, preferring backpacks to Burberry, though she kept a small black clutch for occasions when pants weren't in the dress code. Her wallet was made of brown leather, and it was smooth as butter from years of being sat on and oiled by her hands. She took out her Tennessee driver's license and one of her Visa cards and held them out to the clerk.

"Okay, I just need–" the clerk started to say before she saw Maya's hand extended toward her. "Very good. Give me just a moment." Her fingers flew across the keyboard as she entered Maya's information, then she swiped the credit card, clicked her mouse, and bent to retrieve the paper her printer spit out beneath the counter. A moment later she slid the printout to Maya along with a green plastic pen with the inn's name and address engraved on it in white. "If you could sign that please, I'll get your keys ready."

Maya nodded and looked the printout over. It was standard stuff, even the fine print, so a few seconds later she picked up the pen and signed the contract. Even the pen's ink was green. Maya wasn't sure how much more green she could stand. "Here you go," she said as she turned the contract around and pushed it to the clerk.

"Very good, Ms. Gallows. And here are your keys. You're in room 135, which has two beds and is around back, just as you requested. Is there anything else I can help you with?"

"I don't think so." Maya picked up the folded paper pocket the clerk pushed her way. Two plastic keycards sat inside it. One side showed the inn's address and phone number, while on the other was written her room number. She also saw a line labeled Wi-Fi Password. She had to laugh when she saw PASSWORD1 written next to it. *Hackers everywhere, fear the genius of the Verdant Inn IT department.*

"There's always someone at the desk, so if you find you need anything, just pick up the phone in your room and hit 0. We are here to serve you." The clerk's smile turned up several watts.

Maya retuned the smile, said, "I appreciate that, thanks," and walked out of the office. The chime above the door marked her exit. After passing a large hedge, she found her Trailblazer was still where she'd left it. Taylor, though, was nowhere to be seen.

"Shit."

Hoping she left a note, Maya walked over to the Trailblazer and checked the front windshield. No note. She then opened the driver's door and looked around the interior. Nothing but empty drink bottles and snack bags. After closing the door she looked around again, slower this time. As she was about to give up, the sound of someone knocking on glass caught her attention. It took her a moment, but eventually she zeroed in on a large window on the side of a Pancake Paradise restaurant. Taylor sat on the other side of the window, smiling and waving her over. Maya wanted to sigh, but a sudden grumble in her stomach squashed that and compelled her feet toward the restaurant.

Despite it still being breakfast time, Pancake Paradise was barely populated. An older woman with blondish-white hair pulled into a bun and dressed in Pancake Paradise brown stood at a podium just past the entrance door and offered a smile that was pleasant, if a bit forced. On the right side of her chest was a name tag–Noreen.

"Welcome to Pancake Paradise. Will you be dining alone this morning?"

Maya ignored the hostess as she looked for Taylor. When she saw her sitting in a booth next to a window, she shook her head. "No, my friend is waiting for me." She inclined her head toward the Goth girl.

Noreen turned her head to see who she was talking about, then nodded and smiled wider. "That's right, she said someone would be joining her. Please follow me." The older woman grabbed a laminated menu and napkin-wrapped utensils. As they approached, Taylor looked up and smiled. A small glass of orange juice sat before her.

Maya slid into the empty side of the booth. "I'll just take a coffee. Plenty of cream, please."

The menu and utensil roll were placed in front of her, and then Noreen took out her order pad from her apron and a pencil from above her right ear. "Coffee and cream, gotcha. You ladies know what you want to eat?"

"Give us a minute," Taylor replied, picking up her menu.

Noreen nodded and tucked her pencil back into the hair over her ear before blessing them with another smile as she turned and walked away.

"She seems nice," Maya offered.

Taylor studied her menu like she was about to be tested on it. "Of course she is. She isn't living on top of an ancient demon god."

It surprised Maya how well Taylor was doing. The poor girl had not only lost her brother, but also her parents and her home town, all to the very ancient demon god she'd just joked about, yet by all outward appearances she was right as rain. Maya supposed the girl could just have some exceptional coping mechanisms to help her deal with things, but she feared it wasn't something quite that benign. More likely she was floating down the river of denial, pushing the pain into a distant dark corner of her mind so she didn't have to think about it. Maya knew from personal experience that doing that might help for a short time, but eventually her sadness would eat through her defenses and force her to deal with it, and when that happened it would be a lot more painful.

But Maya wasn't Taylor's mother, wasn't her therapist, so she didn't interfere. She had her own loss and sadness to contend with. Not an hour went by that she didn't think about Kyle, didn't recall the touch of his fingers, the softness of his lips, the kindness in his eyes. She'd known him only a little while, but the hole in her heart felt raw and gaping. As much as she'd cried, she knew more tears were on the way when she had a private moment to let them come.

"She's a lot nicer than the waitresses in Stillwater, that's for sure" she said, trying her best to compartmentalize her emotions and thoughts. There was a mystery to be solved, and psychoanalyzing herself or Taylor wouldn't help. "At least no one's called me the 'n' word yet."

"Speaking of which." Taylor set her menu down and locked eyes with Maya. "Are you sensing anything right now? Picking up any spooky vibrations?"

At the mention of her psychic abilities, part of Maya's mind recoiled. Before Stillwater, using her mental powers had required focused effort, and what they revealed to her was usually hazy, uncertain, part third-sight and part guesswork. But now…now her power felt like a bulldog straining at a leash she was finding increasingly hard to hold onto. Once upon a time she would have been thankful for the increased power, but after what happened earlier in the day she wasn't so sure. And then there was the dark presence in her head to contend with, something she didn't even know how to start handling. If the being inside her was who she feared it was, she was well and truly screwed.

But, she had a job to do—a job she'd taken on of her own free will, no less—so she closed her eyes and reached out to probe the area. At first she held herself back, fearful she'd encounter the same painful presence as before, but nothing odd touched her mind. She picked up the townsfolk's general background mental radiation, a mixture of happiness and apprehension, along with several pockets of deep sadness, but that was all. Nothing strange floated through the aether; or, if it did, it was well hidden.

"Nothing," she replied with a head shake.

Taylor frowned. "Nothing? Then how are we supposed to find who or what is up to shenanigans?"

Maya snorted with laughter. "Shenanigans? That's a strange word to use for kidnapping children and replacing them with dolls."

"That's not…" Taylor started to say before frowning again and giving Maya a look filled with daggers. "You know what I meant."

"I do." Maya chuckled, mostly at herself. "Usually when I'm out investigating a supposed supernatural event, I start with the local library. I look up the area's past, see if there's anything weird or out of the norm. I also like to talk to some of the locals, casually at first. You never know what clues and bits of info they'll spill. Luckily, with this one we already have a lead—Todd Collier. He's a reporter for the local newspaper, and he wrote the article that *News of the Weird* picked up. If anyone can get us started, it's him. I'll contact him as soon as we're done here."

Taylor tapped her menu against the tabletop. "Sounds good, but we have a waitress incoming."

Maya picked her menu up again as she saw a brown figure approaching out of the corner of her eye. "You girls know what you want?"

"Yup," Taylor replied. "One hint—I'm gonna empty an

entire bottle of maple syrup on it."

Laughing, Maya figured that while in the Pancake Paradise, do as the Pancake Paradisers do, and looked for the hotcakes section. She didn't have far too look, and the selection left her mouth watering. "Death by Pancakes? Really?"

Chapter Nine

"Is it just me, or does the sheriff look like shit?"

Deputy Jimmy Fuller looked up from his desk so quickly his neck popped, and coffee dribbled from his mouth as he tried to contain a shocked gasp. Luckily most of it landed on the large Rumble Robin truck stop calendar sitting flat on his desktop—turned to the correct month, all the previous days properly marked off with perfectly drawn Xs. A few drops managed to hit his tie, so he quickly reached for a napkin from the neat stack he always kept in his top right drawer and dabbed at the coffee before it could stain his uniform. Then he dabbed at the calendar for good measure. Even so, nothing could erase the small, wet, brown blemishes from the paper, each one a blight he would have to look at every day for the rest of the month.

"You really should see someone about your OCD, Jimmy. Seriously."

Jimmy rolled his eyes as he carefully balled up the soiled napkins in his hands and deposited them in the trash bin next to his desk. With everything back in order, he glared at the figure sitting at the desk across from him.

Deputy Harold Dunn leaned back in his chair past the point of safety, a Funyun ring held between yellow-powdered fingers resting on his round beer belly. The twinkle in his gray-blue eyes showed his delight at causing Jimmy distress. This didn't surprise him in the least. Harold, while being a more than competent officer of the law, was just as prone to mischief as many of the people they arrested. The fact that he was nearly fifty years old and should know better didn't seem to matter at all to the older deputy.

"A desire for cleanliness isn't a disorder," Jimmy said before turning his attention back to his desk and the strange figurine sitting atop it.

Harold chuckled as he ate his Funyun in loud, crunchy bites. "It is when it's taken as far as you do. But I'm not worried about that nearly as much as I am about the sheriff. Come on, tell me you haven't noticed."

Jimmy's lips twisted as he considered Harold's words. Of course he'd noticed. How could he not? While Sheriff Bowens had never been the most gregarious man, his demeanor over the past couple of weeks had turned particularly sour. Looking back on it, Jimmy supposed it had started with–

"These damn kidnappings," Dunn said, pulling the words straight from Jimmy's mind. "That's what it is. It's like he's taken them personally or something. That's the only reason I can see him declining federal assistance." As he finished speaking, he fished another Funyun out and tossed it into his gaping maw.

Talk of the missing children drew Jimmy's attention back to his desk and the bagged doll sitting atop it. Even through the plastic he could see its blackened eyes glaring out at him, the words EVIDENCE floating above it in bold red letters. Without thinking about it, he reached out and touched the bag, felt the tiny child-like arm through the plastic, its little fingers barely able to fit one of his in its grip. Even though he knew it was impossible, he swore he felt warmth coming from the doll, the heat of flowing blood and life.

"And don't even get me started on those creepy fucking things," Dunn said with audible disgust, his pale eyes glaring at the object in Jimmy's hands.

"I don't know." Jimmy shifted the bag so light fell on the doll's soft auburn hair. "I think they're rather beautiful in a…gothic sort of way."

Dunn spat out a harsh laugh. "They're twisted is what they are, psycho gifts from a psycho kidnapper who wants those poor parents to never stop suffering. When we find the sick bastard responsible for this, I'm gonna feed him those dolls, one broken piece at a time until he fucking chokes on them."

The idea of shattering the dolls made Jimmy flinch, though he didn't know why, and he set the fractured-looking doll down in front of the IN and OUT boxes on his desk so Dunn couldn't see it, then made a note to get the evidence sent off to the state capital as soon as possible. As he completed the note and put his pen back in its usual resting spot to the right of his keyboard, Dunn suddenly sucked in air.

"Uh oh, we've got problems."

Jimmy looked up and followed Dunn's eye line. The glass front door to the Sheriff's Station banged off the walls, and between them stormed Doug Finch, scuff marks on his face and one eye bloodshot and surrounded by a bruise. His feet took him directly toward Sheriff Bowens's office. Jimmy slipped the doll into a desk drawer as casually as he could. No use upsetting the man any further than he already looked.

Betty, the receptionist, jumped up in a flurry of white hair and flower prints. "Mr. Finch, what can I do for you?"

Doug Finch gave her a single baleful look as he went past her.

"Sir! Doug! Stop! I must insist!" Betty waved a pencil at Doug's back like it was a wand she could cast a spell on him with, but whatever magic the receptionist thought she had did nothing to stop or stall him as he continued toward the sheriff's office.

Jimmy shifted his eyes from Doug to Bowens's office door, expecting to see the sheriff coming out, alerted by the commotion, but the open doorway was empty and stayed that way. Betty rounded her desk and attempted to head Doug off, but she was far too slow, getting as far as the obligatory framed picture of the President before the real yelling started.

"Where the hell is my daughter?" Doug yelled, the deep

base tones shaking the walls. "You said you'd find her, you son of a bitch! And now another girl's done been taken?"

Dunn and Jimmy stood up and scrambled for the sheriff's office. Betty neared the door as they approached, but she hesitated inserting herself into what seemed likely to become a knockdown, drag-out fight.

"Mr. Finch," Bowens replied from within his office, his words sounding weary rather than angry at being ambushed, "I told you, these investigations take time to–"

"You ain't got time! I watch TV, I know how these things go! My Cassidy's been gone near two weeks! She could be…could be dead right now and you're no closer to finding her than you were the night she was taken. That monster is still out there, still taking little girls! So tell me what you're gonna do about it before I get my boys together and take care of it ourselves?"

Jimmy came up behind Doug, one hand on his taser and the other reaching for Doug's arm. Over the angry father's shoulder he saw Sheriff Bowens sitting at his desk, his eyes sunken and the dark skin around them tinted a feverish red. Jimmy knew from their encounter earlier in the day that the sheriff wasn't well, but *not well* had rapidly turned into looking like ten miles of bad country road.

"What are you talking about?" Bowens asked with a sigh.

Doug grabbed the doorframe so tightly his entire body twitched. Jimmy noticed the father's plaid blue work shirt sleeves were torn in several places, and the skin beneath it was scratched. "The gypsies dammit!"

Sensing the rise in anger, Jimmy grabbed Doug's left arm at the elbow. "Let's calm down now, Mr. Finch."

Doug jerked his head around and glared at Jimmy before yanking his arm free. "Don't you fucking touch me!"

"If you calm down I won't have to." Jimmy felt his face redden at being addressed like he was some punk on the street.

"Oh for the love of Christ," Bowens said as he rose behind his desk. "Jimmy, go sit down."

Jimmy's anger increased. "Sir, I think—"

"I don't care what you think, son. Just do as you're told and go sit down. If I need you to save me, I'll let you know."

"If…" Jimmy slowly removed his hold on his taser and stepped back. "If you say so, sir."

Bowens nodded and hitched his thumbs over his belt. "I believe I just did."

Shifting his gaze from the sheriff to Doug and back again, Jimmy echoed the nod and took a step back. "Yes, sir." He then turned and walked back toward his desk, but instead of going all the way he stopped just out of sight of the sheriff at the reception area. Just because the sheriff didn't think Doug was a threat didn't mean he had to think the same thing.

"Sheriff, I'm telling you right now," Doug said, this time keeping his arms at his sides, "those gypsies are nothing but trouble, and have been ever since they caravanned in here. I've waited on you to do something to save my daughter, but I'm through. I never should have waited at all."

"So then what did you do?" The sheriff's voice rolled out of his office with all the strength and sourness of a sick animal. "Did you decide to take your accusations to them yourself? Looks like they didn't much care for it. When I go ask them about what happened—which I'm gonna have to do since you barged in here looking like a punching bag—are they gonna tell me you started it?"

Doug dragged a hand through his mussed hair and sighed heavily. "Who gives a shit? I'm not here about me! I'm here about my daughter! That shiftless bunch of trailer trash took her, and if you're not man enough to do something about it, I know people who are. This," he said, gesturing at his torn shirt and scuffed face, "is nothing compared to what will happen next."

Now it was Bowens's turn to sigh. "Not that I have to

explain myself to you or run my investigation by your orders, but I've already talked to them. Me and my boys did a thorough sweep through their area, interviewed everyone, and we didn't find anything worse than a couple pot plants. So please, go home, stay out of trouble, and let us do our jobs."

Doug raised his right hand and hit the wall next to the door. Jimmy edged forward, but stopped when the crazed father lowered his arm.

"Sheriff, all I *want* is for you to do your damn job! Stop sitting here on your ass and get out there! Call in the National Guard if you have to! The CIA and the FBI too! Just find our daughters!"

The sound of wood scraping against linoleum rushed out of the sheriff's office, and Doug gasped. That was all the warning Jimmy had before the sheriff barreled through the doorway and slammed Doug against the wall to the left of the door.

"You don't order me around, you got that?" Spit flew from Bowers's mouth with each word and flecked Doug's face, and his eyes were those of a crazed animal. "I don't care how stressed you are or what you think. You come into my office and start trying to tell me how to handle my business, and I'll stomp a mud hole in your ass!"

"I think he gets it, sir," Jimmy said as he ran over and grabbed the sheriff's shoulders. "Let's all cool off now."

It took several tugs, but eventually the sheriff let go of Doug's tattered shirt and backed away. For his part, Doug's face was so red it bordered on purple, and his hands were curled into sledgehammer fists, but he didn't retaliate.

"Yeah, like Barney Fife here said, I got it." Doug's fists opened and his shoulders relaxed. "But you should know I'm not the only angry parent in Mayfair. Billy Clayton's daughter Fiona is still missing, too, and he's ready to drop a bomb in that gypsy commune you say had nothing to do with it. Jeff Duff called me this morning, crying and swearing he'll get the bastard who took his girl. And don't think parents who still have their little ones aren't angry too, 'cause they are. Unless you want some very bad things to happen soon, you'll do what you promised and find our girls."

Bowens's paunch trembled as he flexed his hands, but after a few seconds of silence he dropped his head and turned back toward his office. "You tell everyone I'm doing all I can. If someone decides they want to play Lone Ranger, I'll lock 'em up and forget where I put the key. Now get out of this office and spread the word, Mr. Finch. I have work to do."

As soon as the sheriff crossed the threshold of his office he slammed the door behind him. Doug stared at the closed length of wood and glass, shook his head, and looked up at Jimmy. "What the hell is wrong with him?"

"I have no idea," Jimmy replied, wishing he had more to offer.

Doug sighed. "I do too, because shit is rolling downhill fast, and if someone doesn't stop it, Mayfair could turn into a warzone." Shaking his head, he shambled toward the exit. As he opened it, he stopped and leveled a red-rimmed gaze on the three people standing at the reception desk, tears brimming above his abraded cheeks. "All I want is my baby back. Is that too much to ask for?" The door closed a second later, stopping Jimmy from replying, not that he had an answer to give.

"Whew, that was close!" Duff said behind him. "Good job reacting as fast as you did, Jimmy."

Betty nodded in quick agreement.

Unsure what more he could do, the deputy walked past his fellow officer to his desk. "That's what the citizens pay me for."

Duff cast a skeptical glance at the sheriff's door. "You think I should talk to him? Maybe try and find out what's going on?"

Jimmy shook his head. "I wouldn't. Not right now, anyway. Give him a few minutes to calm down. Meanwhile I'm going to get this doll sent off ASAP. Maybe we'll get lucky and it'll have more to give us than the previous two."

Duff nodded as he reclaimed his desk chair and took a seat. "I doubt it, but yeah, maybe we'll get lucky."

Jimmy shared his fellow officer's lack of enthusiasm, but he still had a job to do, so he picked up the bagged doll and headed for the mail room with feet heavier than they'd been earlier in the day.

Chapter Ten

The bullpen of the *Mayfair Daily Gazette* wasn't hopping with activity, but that didn't surprise Maya. She'd been in enough small towns and visited enough local newspapers to know they didn't remotely resemble the newsrooms found in most movies and television shows. Phones didn't ring off the hook, fax machines didn't spit out reams of toner-covered paper, and reporters didn't shout at each other confirming sources and details. The *Mayfair Daily Gazette* was just a simple brick building with a cluster of cubicles in the center and a few offices along the walls around them. A receptionist's desk sat several feet in from the door, but no one occupied the black plastic chair behind it.

"So what do we do now?" Taylor picked up the receptionist's nameplate from the desktop–Dora Reed. "Just yell for our guy?"

Why not? Maya thought. She lifted her chin and called out, "Mr. Todd Collier? Are you here?"

In the near silence of the bullpen it was easy to hear a chair squeak as someone swiveled around and stood up. A blond-haired head popped up over a cubicle wall like a prairie dog. "That's me. You Ms. Gallows?"

Maya nodded. "Yes, but please call me Maya."

Collier stepped out of his cube and walked over, his hands smoothing the front of his white button-up shirt before extending his right hand. A smile spread across his young, pale, goateed face. He didn't have much of an aura–most people didn't–but what little ethereal glow he had was benign white mixed with gray. "It's a pleasure to meet you, Maya. Can't say I've ever had a private investigator come see me over one of my articles before." He then looked at Taylor, confusion crinkling the skin around his eyes. "Are you her…assistant?"

"I'm her manservant." Taylor clicked her heels together

and pushed her shoulders back.

Laughing in a way that said he wasn't sure if he should, Collier walked them back to his cube and sat down on a chair that looked older than the person occupying it. Another chair similar to it sat against the fabric wall next to him. He gestured toward it. "You can have a seat right here. Your manservant can get a spare chair from the cubical over there." He pointed across the hall and looked at Taylor with a wink. "The young lady is welcome to join us, if you like."

"Young?" Taylor laughed as she grabbed a chair and dragged it over. "You look barely older than me, dude."

Collier snorted. "I have a baby face. It's my curse."

Once everyone was seated, the reporter straightened his green paisley tie and locked eyes with Maya. "Okay, how can I assist you? In your message you mentioned my article on the kidnappings and dolls."

Maya nodded, removed a voice recorder from her purse and set it on the desk beside her, then took out a pad and pen. "I read your article on the first kidnapping and doll, but I'd like to hear it all from you personally. And, going from that, what has happened since that article was written?"

Collier leaned back in his chair with a loud creak of old metal and unlubricated springs. "The first girl to go missing was Cassidy Finch. Cute little thing. All brownish-blonde curls, strawberry cheeks, and long lashes. When her mother called 911 to report her missing, everyone thought she'd simply gotten lost. It happens on occasion. Kidnapping, though, doesn't. Mayfair's never had a reported kidnapping. Ever. Not in the two-hundred plus years of its existence."

"What changed the thinking from missing to kidnapping?" Maya asked, her pen scribbling across her notepad.

"The doll," he replied with a shiver. His aura rippled as well, dimming to darker gray as his mind moved into murky territory. "It arrived two days after Cassidy went missing. Her parents found it sitting on their front porch right next to the door. I was able to get a look at it after it was handed over to the sheriff, and I have to tell you, it's the creepiest thing I've ever seen."

Maya, who'd seen more than her fair share of creepy, sympathized. "Because of its resemblance to the child?"

"Resemblance?" The reporter looked at her like she'd just said the sun was a bit toasty. "It was almost an exact copy. Pint-sized, of course, but still. It was the eyes that really freaked me out, though."

"How so?" Taylor asked. She glanced at Maya and mouthed the word "Sorry," but Maya shook her head and waved the apology away. She was about to ask the same thing.

The reporter's lips twisted into a crooked frown, and he looked up for a moment as if he was considering something difficult. "I really shouldn't, but…" After a couple of silent moments, he reached into his front pocket and pulled out his mobile phone. His thumb slid across the glass surface as he opened an app, then swiped back and forth before finally handing it to Maya. "A picture's worth a thousand words, right?"

When Maya touched the phone a sudden jolt of pain raced up her arm and the room tilted for a moment as every instinct inside her urged her to push away and avoid the phone at all costs. If she'd been alone she probably would have done just that, but Taylor's presence next to her gave her courage just enough of a boost to continue forward. Swallowing hard, she took the phone and turned its screen toward her. When she saw what was on it, her stomach dropped, leaving her feeling empty and cold. The room tilted again.

"What the fuck?" Taylor said, her voice carrying through the bullpen like a wrecking ball. "Seriously, what the holy fuck?"

As the reporter had said, the doll was of a young girl, dark blonde hair, china white skin, and a green dress. But there the cuteness ended. Two black pits sat where eyes should have been, soulless and empty, with dark streaks radiating outward as if the eyes had burned from the inside out, and the doll's body was cracked from head to foot, the gray fissures like a map of Hell. But there was something else about the picture of the doll that made Maya want to throw the phone as far as she could hurl it, something deeper that she felt but couldn't voice. It was evil, that much was obvious, but it also felt...alive.

No, not alive, she said to herself. *It's just the opposite—a mockery of life, a cruel imitation created by someone more demon than human. It's an abomination against everything good and pure and natural. It needs to be destroyed, as does the person responsible for it.*

Maya shivered as she handed the phone back. "You should delete that picture."

"I know." Collier slipped the phone back into his pocket. "I can't even bear to look at it. I don't want to imagine how that poor girl's parents felt when they found it." He paused to take a deep breath. "After it was discovered, the thinking quickly changed to kidnapping. When the second girl, Fiona, went missing and then a doll showed up the following day, there wasn't anything else *to* think."

Maya made a quick note. "Has the Sheriff's Department come forward with any leads or information?"

Collier shook his head slowly and rolled his eyes. "Not a single word. I've tried to get more details, through channels both official and...not, but I keep hitting a brick wall. All I've heard is that Sheriff Bowens is seemingly handling the investigation entirely on his own."

A long black ink line marred Maya's notes when her pen slipped. "On his own? What about his deputies?"

"Not a one of them."

"And he's still refusing FBI help?"

The reporter's glasses winked in the light as he nodded. "Last I heard."

Maya coughed and made swirl marks on her pad as her mind reeled. "That's insane. Two girls have gone missing and been replaced with dolls made to look just like them, but the federal government hasn't done anything?"

The gray aura surrounding Collier's body darkened until it was nearly black. "Make that three girls. Alison Duff went missing yesterday, and today a doll was found right where you'd expect."

"No way," Taylor said, her voice hitting the air like a thunderclap.

Maya's hands fell to her sides in sad astonishment and she opened her mouth to echo Taylor's feelings, but her attention was suddenly caught by a shadow in the corner of her right eye. It appeared to be one bit of darkness amidst others, but something about it felt wrong to her. She turned to look directly at it, and when she did the shadow moved, sliding across the wall into an empty cubicle. Her skin tingled and her jaw clenched as something hard pressed into her temples.

"Umm…Maya?" Collier said.

She heard him clearly, but her focus was locked on the distant darkness. Slowly the black shape rose above the cube wall, a shadow free of constraint.

You are not prepared for this, child, a familiar voice said, the words sliding into her skull like daggers of ice. *Turn away now.*

Maya's jaw clenched hard enough to make her facial muscles jump. "No."

"Excuse me?" Collier said, drawing her attention away from the shadow. "No what?"

A flush crossed Maya's face as she realized what she'd said. "I'm sorry, I–"

The shadow slid over the cube wall toward them like a giant snake made of smoke, then reared its head once again. *I have plans for you, foolish girl. Defy me at not only your peril, but the peril of all those you love, everyone you touch.*

Chills ran up Maya's arms like thousands of pins

stabbing her over and over again. The Dark God's shadow pulsed with evil, its dark form black beyond black: a hole in the fabric of reality. She even smelled it, the stench of decaying meat and burnt flesh filling the air in foul, noxious waves. Her gorge rose as the shadow slipped over another cube wall, then another, until it was hidden by the wall behind the reporter's computer.

"Are you okay, Maya?" Taylor asked. The young woman touched her shoulder. "You picking up on something?"

Maya didn't know how to answer. Again the darkness reached out to her, reminding her of its presence inside her like an ominous passenger. With each visitation its presence became more solid, more real, its ravenous roots burrowing into her very soul, bringing them closer and closer together.

The reporter coughed. "What do you mean, 'picking up on something'?"

"No," Maya replied, the word leaving her mouth like a dying animal. "This is something–"

Demael's shadow rose above Collier's cubical wall, the black figure so close she could almost make out its horrific features. *I am beyond the limitations of your pitiful mind, as unknowable as the darkness between the stars. But with time, my love, you will understand me all too well. You will know the sweet flavor of blood and the tender caress of raging fire. Together, as one, Death itself will bend to our will.*

Dread coiled in Maya's chest as she heard his words and realized part of her yearned for the truth of them, longed for their union, and the vast power that would come with it, but the rest of her withdrew in horror. *I want nothing to do with you!* she screamed in her mind, wishing it was true but shamed in knowing it wasn't.

Slowly the shadow arched over the cubical wall like a snake, a wolf, a bird of prey with razor wings spread out toward the reporter. *You deny your hunger, but I am within you, I taste your desire. Watch as I offer but a small demonstration of the power you will soon wield.*

Maya looked on in revulsion, locked in place, as the shadow descended on the reporter and curled dark claws around his throat. Instantly Collier jerked in his chair and gasped. Blotches appeared on his neck where the shadow choked him, his skin bruising around the spectral fingers. His eyes bulged behind his glasses.

"Stop it!" Maya shouted, her mouth the only part of her she could move.

Taylor leapt to her feet. "What's going on?"

Collier reach for his neck, but his fingers passed through the shadowy grip that squeezed harder and harder. He opened his mouth, a scream in his throat, but he didn't have the wind to let it out, so he choked on his own terror.

Do you feel that? the Dark God asked. *Do you feel the power of his life entering you?*

She didn't…until she did, and then it was all she could feel. Suddenly she was overwhelmed by sensation, her chills warmed away by the heat of stolen life. It was exhilarating, and she watched Collier grow pale as he struggled weakly in his chair. The closer to death he came, the more power crackled through her veins. She was nearly drunk from it, and she laughed. When the sound of her joy hit her ears she cringed in disgust at what was happening to her, what she was allowing, and in desperation she fought back. Little by little she reclaimed her mind and body, reclaimed who she truly was, and as she came back to herself she lunged forward and struck at the shadow lingering over the reporter. The darkness dissipated like smoke as soon as her skin passed through it.

"Oh my God!" Collier said as he slumped into his chair, color returning to his face in a crimson blush. He looked over his shoulder, then turned to face Maya. "What the hell?"

Maya staggered backward and sat down before the rush of conflicting emotions hobbled her. Waves of hot and cold broke against her, and air struggled to work its way into her lungs. It was only when Taylor hugged her from behind, her thin white arms wrapping tightly around her shoulders, that she felt a semblance of normalcy return.

"What just happened?" the young woman asked as she leaned in close.

Maya didn't know where to begin explaining, so she simply said, "I'm sorry. I wish I had the words."

"I have a few." Collier rubbed his bruised throat. "Get the fuck away from me. I don't know who you really are, or what you're doing here, or what the fuck is going on, but I want you gone. You're lucky I'm not calling the police."

"Please," Maya said, her stomach a swirling pit of nerves. "I wish I could explain, but–"

Collier frowned and stood up, his chest puffed out despite the pained expression on his face. "But nothing. I said go, so go. Whatever it is you two are part of, I want nothing to do with it. Leave. Now!"

Maya debated between explaining what she could and just giving up. After a couple seconds she decided discretion was indeed the better part of valor, so she nodded and rose as well. "I'm sorry, Mr. Collier. None of this went as I'd hoped, but I appreciate the information you offered. We'll be on our way now."

The reporter didn't move when she exited his cube, nor did he follow as they headed to the exit. Maya dared a final look over her shoulder, and Collier's head was just visible from his cube. There wasn't a sign of the Dark God's shadow now, but the reporter's aura was a very murky gray shot through with black veins. When Taylor opened the *Gazette's* front door and they passed back into South Carolina daylight, she hoped the shadow's harm to him was done, and that the color of the reporter's aura was caused by his mood, and not something more sinister. If another person was harmed because of her, she didn't think she could bear it.

Chapter Eleven

A loud gurgle filled the patrol car, accompanied by a sour churning sensation in his stomach as Sheriff Bowens turned off Matheson Road. He knew he'd never been the picture of perfect health, but the bouts of sickness he'd suffered over the past several weeks was worse than anything he'd ever felt before. It was enough to make him consider going to the doctor, something he only did in the direst of circumstances.

They can't give you bad news if you don't let them poke at you, he thought for the millionth time in his life.

The patrol car rolled over a short wooden bridge spanning a dried-up creek bed. Bowens then followed the asphalt road around a right turn. As the trees pulled back, a tight cluster of RVs appeared like a lost caravan of carnival workers. Some of the vehicles were old, boldly wearing their 60s and 70s designs like hipsters who thought defying the times was the essence of style, while others were new enough to still have their showroom shine. Scattered around them were a smattering of single and doublewide mobile homes.

The gypsy invasion—or, as they preferred to be called, Romanichal—of Mayfair started about ten years ago. Old Estera had lived on the outskirts of town for as long as anyone could remember, but she'd arrived alone and pregnant with her dimwitted son decades ago. Over the years they'd kept to themselves, which the townsfolk were just fine with. But when a local farm went belly-up, the acreage was bought and parceled out to a group - Bowens thought of them more like a plague - of gypsy families. The earliest arrivals came in recreational vehicles, but eventually those were replaced with mobile homes, a clear sign they were settling in, something the people of Mayfair weren't happy about in the least.

Bowens remembered the angry talk that sprang up in

barber shops and watering holes. "Goddamn gypsies," was usually the opening refrain, quickly followed by irate remarks and questions. Fortunately they tended to stay close to their own area, and whenever a group of them wanted to go get loaded they usually did it in nearby Granville since it had a larger selection of bars. Occasionally a scuffle would break out between a gypsy and a townie, but the fault usually rested on both participants and not just the reclusive Romanichal. Maybe if they'd made more of an attempt to integrate with the rest of Mayfair they'd be treated and thought of better, but so far none had shown any interest. Considering Doug Finch's recent visit, interest was more than building from the other side. That's why the sheriff was on his way out there now—to warn them. If he happened to find new evidence while doing so, all the better.

A group of shirtless, tanned men stood in a large circle next to a bright green motorhome adorned with strings of colored lights and surrounded by a riot of rose bushes. As his squad car drew closer, they turned toward him and scowled. He was used to it. Romanichal weren't the biggest fans of *muskers*, their word for police. Several seconds later he pulled into the short driveway in front of the motorhome, shifted to PARK, and turned the car off.

The engine barely went silent before the men approached as a group. Despite his troubled stomach, Bowens put on a broad smile and exited the vehicle. He kept his hands well clear of his weapons as he stood up and closed the door.

"What's this now?" a shirtless older man at the front of the group asked, tattoos twitching beneath olive skin as he flexed his considerable muscles and strolled around the front of the vehicle. He stopped a few feet from Bowens and crossed his arms, making sure his large biceps were fully in view. His name was Robert Keet, but his friends and family called him Bobo. Bowens was neither.

"Good afternoon, Mr. Keet."

The posturing man frowned, snorted, and spit a glob of phlegm on the asphalt inches shy of the police car. "It was."

Bowens laughed, the sound empty even to his ears. "I'm sure. Listen, I'm not here to cause trouble. Just the opposite."

Another man stepped forward, his thinning hair lacquered enough with gel that it stood straight up like rows of desiccated cornstalks. Bowens believed his name was Ollie. "If that's so, then turn around and head back to town. And when ya get there, make sure you tell Doug Finch not to show his face here again if he wants to keep what's left of it."

"Yeah!" a young gypsy followed, his dark hair sticking out from his head as though it had been shocked that way. A tattoo of a woman in a bikini winked at him from the gypsy's neck. "Tell 'em they come back here they'll regret it."

"Now now." Bowens hitched up his belt. "No need for talk like that."

Bobo horked up another wad of phlegm and spit it near the sheriff's shoes. "The hell there ain't. He come here demanding we give his kid back. We told him we had nothin' to do with whatever happened to his little 'un. Like we don't have enough kids o' our own to deal with. He wasn't satisfied with that and decided he were gonna check for himself. We uh...told him otherwise. Forcefully. So maybe instead of botherin' us, you should roll that car around and go pester him. You know, do your job and go after the real troublemaker."

Heat roiled through Bowens's chest, and he had to grit his teeth to keep from giving the gypsies a blistering tongue lashing. "Mr. Keet, I've already spoken with Mr. Finch. I informed him that you and yours weren't suspects, and that it would be in his best interest to let me handle things."

"And how's that going?" Ollie ran a calloused hand through his spiked hair. "Closing in on the napper are ya?"

Another burst of heat hit Bowens, and sweat broke out on his forehead. "That's none of your damn business."

Bobo took a step closer to Bowens. "We all got children, Sheriff. That makes what you do our business."

"Then keep a close eye on them," Bowens replied, his right hand inching toward his holstered gun.

A sneer split Bobo's face like a jagged crack in concrete. "Oh we are. Trust me on that. Now let me return the favor. If I were a betting man, which I am—"

The crowd of men burst into sudden laughter. It must have been an in-joke, but Bowens didn't care enough to ask about it.

Bobo chuckled and gave his cronies a flashy smile before turning a stern gaze on the sheriff. "Anyway, like I was saying. If I were a betting man, I'd put my money on that old witch Estera being behind all this. Her or that retard son of hers."

As soon as her name hit the air, all the anger ran out of Bowens like a drain was unplugged, and in its absence he felt sick. His face tingled as blood drained away, and he grabbed the open squad car door to keep his suddenly wobbly legs from dropping him to the ground.

"I uh…," he said, looking around for a cogent thought to appear. "An old woman like that, I… There's no way."

Ollie and Bobo looked at each other and tiled their heads as though they were conversing, but not a word passed between them.

"You feelin' all right there, Sheriff?" Bobo asked with a raised eyebrow.

Bowens nodded, but his hold on the door was so tight his knuckles were white as bone.

The corners of Bobo's mouth turned down. "I only ask 'cause you got a little gray around the gills when I mentioned Estera."

Bile lurched up Bowens's throat in a violent surge, and he scurried backward to avoid puking all over the car door and window. As he reached out to grab the lights atop his car and steady himself, the gypsies backed away from him as a group.

Ollie lifted his right arm up and pushed his fist forward with his index and little fingers pointed outward, the kind of gesture that would have been common at a metal concert as kids headbanged and sang about rocking the devil. "He's been hexed!"

The other gypsies followed suit immediately, each with their horn-shaped hands out, some adding a spit or hiss to the mix. Bowens had no idea what any of it meant, but at the moment he had more pressing concerns, the greatest of which being to drop trou and shit out everything he'd ever eaten. His stomach was a beast inside him, and he feared it wouldn't rest until he was dead on the ground, dry as a husk.

"You people need to calm down now," he said, using every last bit of his fading will to pull himself together. "It's nothing."

Bobo kept one horned hand toward him while he used the other to wave his people back. "Oh it's somethin', you damn fool. Somethin' bad, and it ain't gonna get any better. Not for you at least. She may be a gypsy, but she ain't one of us. She's old school. Get out of here before the evil she's put on you spreads. You hear me, Sheriff? Go!"

Bowens's stubborn side wanted to shove his badge in Bobo's face and tell him just who the fuck was boss around here, but the bubbling cauldron that was his bowels overrode that and led him back toward his driver's seat.

"I'm going," he told them as his ass touched vinyl, "but not because of you. I've got other places I have to be. If I have to come back here, next time I won't go easy on you."

Bobo snorted. "Whatever you got to tell yourself."

Bowen fumbled around for a retort, but all he could think of was "I will!" before slamming his door closed. He pulled the transmission lever down and hit the gas, but instead of backing up the squad car lurched forward. The gypsies scattered away as he cursed, grabbed the lever again, and this time shifted it into the proper gear. It wasn't until he was back across the creek bridge that he dared look in his rearview mirror. The gathered men were obscured by trees lining the road bend.

What the hell was that about? he asked himself. *I went there to do my job, and I end up running away like a kicked dog. Why is this happening to me?*

There were clues, he knew it, clues that he should be able to see and piece together, but his brain was too much of a mess to do more than string one whole thought together, and at the moment he felt lucky to be able to do even that. He was being undone from the inside out.

Maybe I should give Doc Givens a call. Yeah, that's a good idea. Unless he tells me I have stomach cancer or some shit. That would be even worse. Maybe… Maybe I should tackle one problem at a time. I should focus on the missing girls. That's what's really important. But first I should go home and rest. Shit, shower, and rest. That's what Momma would have told me to do.

A loud fart reverberated against the car seat as Bowens turned left onto Matheson Road. Quickly he rolled the window down next to him as his eyes watered from the fumes.

Chapter Twelve

Maya took her last french fry, dragged it through a small puddle of ketchup, and then shoved it in her mouth, but she took little pleasure in it. Normally fast food helped ease her mind when she was troubled, and nothing made her feel better than a greasy burger with a side of equally greasy fries, but not this time. Not after what she'd just experienced.

"So…" Taylor said, the word dragging itself from her mouth, "wanna talk about it?"

Maya glanced at the passenger seat and watched Taylor take a huge bite out of her burger. Mustard and ketchup smeared her lips like clown makeup. When the girl swallowed, the giant lump of chewed up meat and cheese slid down her throat without any trouble. A bite like that would have choked a lesser person, but the girl, despite her small size, was a champion eater.

"Your brother took big bites too."

Taylor closed her eyes and held up a hand shiny with grease. "Please stop. I can't… I'm not ready to deal with that just now. I already cry my eyes out when my brain slows down too long, and it won't take much to get me crying right here, so just…not right now. Okay?"

Maya nodded and looked away. She couldn't stand to see the pain and loss in Taylor's eyes. It made her sadness seem thin. What were a couple of days compared to a lifetime? If anyone had the right to be maudlin, it wasn't her.

He was only the beginning, a cold voice whispered in her head. *So many more will die.*

"Shut up," she replied, not realizing she had spoken out loud.

Taylor coughed loudly. "Excuse me?"

We will do great things, you and I. All the world will weep.

Images flashed through Maya's mind. Fire, blood, and darkness exploded across her inner eyes, a vision of what had been and might be again. Maya grabbed the sides of her head and pressed her palms against her temples. "Stop it! Get out of my head!"

"Who get out?" Taylor leaned over and grabbed Maya's shoulders.

Resist, if you like, the Dark God Demael said, its snake-like words slithering through her brain. *It changes nothing. We are joined, the two of us, and soon we will be one. You should feel honored. Godhood is just a dream for many, but for you it will be a reality. Accept the future. It is inexorable.*

"No it isn't!" Maya shouted, her fists leaving her head to pound on the Trailblazer's steering wheel.

Taylor shook Maya's shoulders like she was trying to awaken a deep sleeper. "Snap out of it, Maya!"

The dark voice laughed, the dry rattle of it signaling the end of the world. Fortunately the laugh faded with each second until eventually her mind was hers alone again. Relief settled on her like a cool rain. She patted Taylor's hands at her shoulders. "Thanks. I'm okay now."

"Okay from what? Ever since this morning when you tried to find the source of this town's trouble you've been a little off, and then there was that strange shit with the reporter. I've been quiet because I figure you know your business, but it seems like it's getting worse. So spill it, sister."

Maya wasn't sure where to start, or what she dared to admit, but after a few silent seconds she opened her mouth and let it all flow out of her–the nightmare from the day before, the moving shadows, the voice in her head, everything. It felt like she unloaded her entire soul in the course of a couple of minutes, but instead of feeling unburdened, the litany of events drove home just how screwed her life had become.

"Holy shit," Taylor said, her burger all but forgotten between her black-lacquered fingers. "So even after Ky... Even after all that, the Dark God in that mountain is still a threat to the world?"

"It seems so."

Taylor sighed and used a napkin to clean her face. "So…what do we do? Do we leave Mayfair and–God forbid–go back to Stillwater? Do we get you an exorcism? What?"

It was Maya's turn to sigh. "I don't think location has anything to do with it. Its body might be locked away, but its mind, its essence…that's the real problem. As for what I can do about it…that part I haven't worked out yet. It might come down to an exorcism. I don't know. Trust me, no one wants this ancient asshole out of my head more than me."

"Well, if worse comes to worst, don't worry," Taylor replied as she tossed the napkin into the bag the food came in. "I'll put you down. One bullet, behind the ear. Make it quick."

Maya laughed, but there was a steeliness in Taylor's eyes that unsettled Maya's stomach. To cover her unease she said, "Let's hope it doesn't come to that."

Taylor nodded and winked at her, but then raised her hand and mimed shooting a pistol. No, Maya definitely didn't feel any better now that things were out in the open.

"So, what do we do now about these kids and the dolls? What's our next step?"

Having already asked herself that same question, Maya took a sip from her Styrofoam cup of Diet Coke and turned the SUV's ignition to ON. "I want to go see where the kidnapped girls were taken from. I might be able to pick something up, an impression maybe. Might even get a psychic bead on where they were taken. Worth a shot anyway. We'll start with the first girl's house."

"Sounds like a plan." Taylor snapped her seatbelt closed before diving into her fries.

After opening her notepad, Maya pulled out her phone, activated the GPS app, and plugged in the address of the first kidnapping. It took a few seconds for a route to be calculated. As with all small towns, everywhere was close to everywhere else, so the finalized route was a short one—barely four miles.

Hating to use it because she now understood where it came from, but knowing she had to since lives were at stake, Maya breathed deeply and called her amplified psychic powers to work. Hunting for a psychic needle amidst miles of haystack would be no easy feat, especially since Mayfair – despite its meager size–was an old town, at least by American standards. And, like all small towns, every inch of it was soaked in history. Most people experienced that history through the peeling paint on the post office that looked as out-of-date as it actually was, through the sway of picket fences too long in the ground and in desperate need of replacing, through the rust embracing every last piece of exposed metal. Windows coated with dust that could never truly be cleaned. Electric poles that leaned like drunkards. It was a history written in grime, love, and neglect.

Maya saw all those things, but she also saw the secret history of the town's inhabitants, the things they'd done when no one was looking, and now she was able to do it with a clarity she'd never known before. In a vacant lot she saw the shadow of a building burned to the ground by Confederates who'd rather see slaves dead than freed. She watched as young lovers snuck away in the dead of night, hopeful to get away before her father caught wind and ended their secret relationship with a shotgun blast. Through a dilapidated apartment window she saw a father rape his youngest daughter while the eldest looked on, glad it wasn't her turn that night. People loved, people hated, all of it woven into the fabric of the town yet visible only to the few whose sight extended beyond the physical world.

"Destination ahead on the left," the GPS app's voice said in feminine yet mechanical tones.

As the Trailblazer drew even with the pin marker on her phone, Maya pulled over onto a leaf-covered shoulder and parked. The house across the street looked unassuming, a craftsman home surrounded by oak trees and cyclone fencing. An old but well-kept station wagon sat on a cracked driveway next to a small pink bicycle tipped over on its side. A dented mailbox stood at attention next to the end of the driveway, its door open to reveal several envelopes. It was a stock photograph of suburban living.

"You see anything?" Taylor asked, a heightened pitch in her voice indicating there was more to her question than the words implied.

Maya nodded. She saw quite a bit, and none of it was good.

"Something supernatural definitely happened here. Normally the aether is calm and quiet, but this place looks like a powerful presence came through it and churned the currents into a frenzy. It's enough to give me motion sickness. Can't you feel it?"

A pale face shook side to side next to her.

"Be glad. Whoever or whatever it was that took Cassidy Finch was as powerful as it was evil. Today's a sunny day, but I see shadows everywhere, pools of darkness that will probably linger for weeks. Evil like this leaves scars that don't heal easily or quickly."

Taylor shivered despite the warm light falling through the window next to her. "Can you tell what we're dealing with? I mean, is it some evil spirit? Or a wizard? Or a...a creature? Hell, was it aliens?"

"I wish I knew," Maya replied, meaning every word. "It's like nothing I've ever seen before. Ghosts I've dealt with, but this is... It feels human for the most part, but a human who's consumed by evil and has great power. It could be magic, but I've never tangled with that before."

Taylor looked down at her hands folded in her lap. "I uh… I have."

"You did?" Maya asked, her eyebrows crinkling together. "When?"

Taylor nodded, her aura suddenly expanding around her like a murky cloud. "It was years ago. I was just a young gay girl trying to fit in, you know? Eventually I became friends with some Goths. Imagine that." She gestured at the black Cure concert tour t-shirt, black jeans, and black thickly-soled boots she wore. "When they started playing with magic and witchcraft I figured it was just a game. You know, a little childhood rebellion. At first it was fun, but after a while a few of them started taking it really seriously. I mean hitting up book stores and the 'Net for old grimoires and stuff."

"Grimoire," Maya replied. "That's what they call a witch's spellbook, right?"

Taylor's shoulders hunched inward as though she wanted to shrink and disappear. "Yeah. Somehow they managed to get their hands on some actual spells. I was content to just look at all the symbols and diagrams, but they went further…much further. I was done when they tried to summon a spirit. One minute everything was silent, and the next it's like the air was screaming, and all the candles were blown out at the same time. It was scary as hell, and I ran. After that night I made friends with other kids and tried not to think about it."

It was a lot for Maya to take in. "I had no idea."

Taylor glanced over at Maya, probably afraid she would see disappointment or mistrust in her eyes, but instead Maya shrugged and threw an arm around Taylor's shoulders.

"You've got nothing to be ashamed of," Maya said as she squeezed her friend. "You wouldn't imagine the strange stuff I got up to when I was your age. At least you could move on from it. Mine's kinda built in."

A deep red blush spread across Taylor's face, the color made more intense by her bony pallor, and nodded, then she leaned over and kissed Maya's cheek. "Thanks. Really."

A fist suddenly hammered against Maya's window. "Hello! Excuse me! Who are you? What are you doing here?"

Maya jerked around to find a woman dressed in a house robe standing next to her door. The woman's hair was a mess, her face lined with wrinkles, her blue eyes red-rimmed and watery. When she brought a cigarette up to her lips, her hand shook. A dark aura covered her like a shroud. Even if Maya hadn't had her second sight she would have known who it was beside her. She rolled her window down and put on her most sympathetic smile.

"I'm sorry, Mrs. Finch. I didn't mean to cause you any alarm." Maya kept her voice as soft and calm as possible. "Do you mind if I step out of my vehicle?"

The frazzled mother looked at Maya as if she were a snake coiled up in tall grass, then looked at Taylor. After a few moments she sighed and backed away from the SUV. Maya gave Taylor a "stay put and be quiet" look as she unbuckled her seatbelt, opened the door, and stepped out.

"So who are you?" Mrs. Finch asked again. She took a quick, shaky drag on her cigarette. When she exhaled she waved at the smoke cloud to disperse it. "I've never seen you before."

"I'm Maya," she replied, extending her hand. "Maya Gallows. I'm an investigator."

The mother looked at Maya like she was a wild animal likely to bite her at any moment, but the extended hand couldn't be ignored for more than a few seconds before she overcame her reservations and shook it. "And what do you 'investigate,' exactly?"

Maya nodded. "I specialize in the...unusual."

Mrs. Finch barely had a chance to take another drag on her cigarette before a derisive snort shot from her nose in twin blasts of smoke. "Then you've come to the right place."

"So it seems." Maya reached into her purse and withdrew an audio recorder. "Do you mind?"

The mother glanced at the recorder and shook her head as she shifted her tear-strained eyes away. "I already said all there was to say, but whatever."

Maya pressed RECORD and set the device on the roof of the Trailblazer so it was out of sight but still able to hear them.

"First let me say how sorry–"

"Everybody's sorry," the mother said with a withering stare, the words spit out like they tasted foul. "Everybody cries, says they know how I feel, says they can't believe what happened. And then what do they do when it's my turn to cry? They go home and tend to their own lives. I've lost my daughter, but all they lose are a few tears and a moment of their time. Sorry means fuck all to me."

The venom in the mother's voice surprised Maya, who'd expected sadness instead. Perhaps sadness could only last so long before it became something else. For the mother in front of her, it was anger.

"I would never claim to know how you feel, Mrs. Finch. All I can do is imagine, which is bad enough. To live through it isn't something I would wish on anyone. When I read about what was happening here, I knew I had to try and help."

The mother looked her up and down, an appraiser examining a new item. "Help? And what exactly can you do that Sheriff Bowens can't? You a Fed or something, like that X-Files show?"

"No, nothing like that," Maya replied, using all of her willpower to not laugh or snort. "I'm just a civilian. I have a blog, and I investigate the strange and unusual."

"You mean you're one of them ghost hunters." The mother's eyes squinted together and her lips twisted into a frown. "Sorry to disappoint, but nothing is going on here because of no ghosts."

The disdain was easy to hear, but Maya thought she detected a hint of bait in the mother's words too. "Then what do you think is happening?"

The mother pursed her lips and spat on the ground. "It's those damn gypsies! They've taken my baby girl, and I know they're going to sell her off into white slavery or something! And the sheriff ain't doing a damn thing about it!"

"Gypsies?" Maya hadn't expected to hear that word. "Here?"

Another glob of spit landed in the dirt. "Here, there, and everywhere! Damn gypsies are spreading like cockroaches. And now they're taking our babies!"

"You seem awfully sure. Do you have any evidence?"

"I don't need no damn evidence!" The mother's aura turned from gray to red in a flash, as though she'd spontaneously combusted. Maya pulled back instinctively. "Everyone in town knows what's happened! Them gypsy trash have stolen our kids and the sheriff ain't doin' a damn thing about it. I hope it's 'cause they paid him, because he's gonna need the money, and soon. My husband will see to that."

The threat wasn't implied or subtextual in the least. "I can't imagine that violence will—"

Mrs. Finch poked at Maya with her finger like a dagger. "You lose a child, and then tell me what you'd do! I don't know if my baby is alive or dead! Me and the rest of this town are tired of waiting for the sheriff to get off his fat ass. You want to blog something? You'll get something worth writing about soon enough. Now if you'll excuse me, I have a son to feed. Goodbye."

The mother turned and was nearly back across the street before Maya could do more than blink, the woman's blood-red dark aura swirling like a storm around her.

"Well that just happened," Taylor said, leaning toward the open driver's window. "Gypsies huh? I didn't know they actually still existed."

Sighing, Maya opened her door and slid back into the SUV. "Gypsies live all over the world, including here in America, and they're usually hated by everyone around them."

"So do you think the mother's right? Are gypsies behind the children and the dolls?"

That's the million dollar question, isn't it? Maya asked herself. "I don't know. The easy answer is yes. We've all heard stories of gypsies putting hexes on people and dabbling in the occult. And hell, we've all seen *The Wolf Man*, right?"

Taylor grunted as she finished eating her fries. "Just because it's the easy answer doesn't mean it's the right one."

And there it was, a truth Maya couldn't deny. "You have a point. I find it hard to imagine that an entire group of people would be behind these kidnappings. Still, though, I wouldn't be doing my job if I didn't at least give them a look-see."

"Then I guess we'll have to go check them out." Taylor grabbed Maya's shoulder and gave it a rough shake. "Right, boss?"

"Ow!" Maya replied as Taylor let go, then laughed. "Right you are, my young apprentice, but before we do that we have another stop. It's high time I met the sheriff. Whatever it is that's going on here involves him in some way, that much I can tell from what others have said. If he's obstructing the investigation willingly, that's one thing, but if he's been influenced—supernaturally speaking—then that's a whole other thing. I can't do much about the former, and I can't promise I can anything about the latter, but knowing is half the battle. Right? Right."

"Then get driving, boss." Taylor buckled up and patted the dashboard with heavy thumps. "Time's a-wasting."

Chapter Thirteen

Boden's long, gnarled arms ached as they swung the axe up and down, the rise and fall as steady as a metronome. *Thwack!* One length of wood became two. *Thwack!* Two became four. *Thud!* The axe settled into the chopping block as he bent over and grabbed another piece of sawed wood. Branches and smaller pieces of tree trunk sat in another pile, patiently waiting for him to work his way over.

Despite the ache and monotony, Boden was as happy as he could be. The spread of land behind the house was mostly as God intended, with very little of the natural landscape cleared away, and he was perfectly at home. Sometimes he felt like he was supposed to be a tree–he was tall like a tree, his limbs as thick and knotted as a tree's branches, his back bowed but unbroken, just like a tree in a storm–but through a twist of fate he'd been born to his mother. At night, when the house was quiet and nothing stirred, he wished fate would twist back.

When he was a child he'd adored his mother and loved spending time with her. Her magic had been simple back then, focusing mostly on earth magic, which meant plenty of days spent in the woods gathering flowers and wild herbs. And the nights were even better, especially those with a full moon. Watching her dance between trees and splash through streams with gentle incantations flowing from her lips was to behold something beautiful, something pure. The stars never shown as brightly as her eyes did on those nights.

But then Momma got sick, and nothing was the same after that.

As he set the fresh log on the chopping block, Boden suddenly heard distant voices. They were indistinct at first, the words like water burbling over river stones, but every second brought them closer, and even though he still couldn't make out what they were saying, their anger was clear enough.

Oh no. Momma!

All thought of firewood disappeared from Boden's modest mind as he lifted his axe and shambled toward the house. By the time he reached the living room, the knocking on the door became pounding. As he reached for the door knob he made sure his grip on the axe was tight.

"What's going on?" he bellowed as he opened the door and brandished his axe. "What do you want?"

The group of men standing on the front porch jumped back, their eyes moving back and forth between him and the large weapon in is hand. They didn't look as if they wanted to tangle with either. But, after a moment of hesitation, one of them stepped forward and raised his chin in defiance. Boden wasn't overly familiar with the other gypsy families in the area–Momma didn't want to have anything to do with them–but he knew the man stepping toward him well enough.

"Boden, lower that axe," Bobo said, flexing his muscles and puffing his chest out. "We ain't here for you. You're a good boy, staying with that momma of yours like ya do, and I respect that, but bad things are happening now that's causin' us trouble, and we won't have it. *I* won't have it. So put that axe down and step aside."

Deep in Boden's brain, in the part that wasn't hampered by the sluggish lumps that made up most of his gray matter, Boden knew what Bobo was saying, knew what was happening, and knew that he should let the men in so they could try to stop the evil Momma was committing. But that part was alone and unable to do anything. The rest of him was committed heart and soul to his momma, and he would die before he let anyone hurt her. So, instead of lowering the axe, he choked up on the handle and got ready to swing.

Suddenly a hand touched his right arm from behind, and the subject of their anger stepped into view. When Boden glanced over and saw the look in her eyes, he knew the gypsy men were about to learn what it really meant for bad things to happen.

Estera hurt. Aches and pains were part of life, especially when old age settled into the bones, but for her pain was more than a nuisance, it was constant and crushing. Every joint burned, every muscle trembled. And her chest…that hurt worst of all. The cancer that had begun as a tiny aberrant cell conquered more and more of her body every day, and the pain of it went straight to her bones. Ironically, the pain of trying to stop her death hurt her even more. Three times she'd reached into her torso, and three times she'd cracked her rib cage and taken a rib out. Closing that wound and healing the break took more and more magic each time.

If I don't find the right child soon–

Pounding on the front door drew her up from her bed, ending her thought before it could reach its sorrowful conclusion. As she stood up she heard the door at the back of the house open and heavy footsteps thud their way to the front. She had no idea what was going on, but her sensitivity to changes in the aether made one thing clear–trouble was brewing. She didn't panic, though, didn't flinch. She'd been expecting it. The greater mystery was why it had taken so long.

After sliding a course robe over her shoulders, Estera hobbled to the stairs and walked gingerly down to the ground floor. A raised voice met her halfway down. Her lips curled into a sneer, but that didn't mean she was unhappy. Just the opposite. Putting that puffed up jackass in his place would do wonders for her mood.

"You're a good boy," Bobo said, as though his stupid words mattered to anyone outside of his gaggle of sycophantic toadies, "staying with that momma of yours like ya do, and I respect that, but bad things are happening now that's causin' us trouble, and we won't have it. *I* won't have it. So put that axe down and step aside."

When Boden's hands tightened around the axe handle, love fluttered through her heart like a sickly bird. Beyond him stood Bobo and what looked like a dozen other men, including his chief flunky Ollie. Her sneer deepened as she touched Boden's arm and shifted him to the side.

"Well now," Estera said, her eyes flicking between the gathered men before landing on the ringleader. "Robert Keet, what's got you away from your weights and suntan oil today? Not work, certainly. Never known you to do a real day's work in your life."

Bobo's chest flexed as he returned her sneer. "Estera Kalderash, as sweet as ever."

"And you're still a liar." Moving slowly, Estera reached into a pocket of her robe and closed her fingers around the charm within it. "Now that the pleasantries are out of the way, tell me what you and your lackeys are here for before I turn all of you into newts."

A chuckle rumbled through the gathered men, Bobo and Ollie laughing the hardest of them all. "You don't scare us, woman. You may have that brainless sheriff under some kind of spell, but we ain't so easily manipulated, so save your threats."

Estera's hand clamped down on the charm in her pocket so tightly the metal bit into her flesh. "Threats? I haven't even begun to threaten you. Keep that sharp tongue wagging, though, and I'll cut you with it. And that, *Bobo*, is a promise."

"Shut your mouth, you old crone," Ollie said, stepping forward to stand next to his master. "You don't have—"

Ollie suddenly stopped talking and grabbed his throat, which had turned an alarming shade of red. The color change continued up to his face and down across his chest.

"I'm sorry, what was that?" Estera asked. She raised her left hand, and above her palm hovered a flame. All the men stumbled backward, even Bobo, leaving Ollie to fall to his knees as sweat suddenly covered his body. "Mayhap next time you'll address me with a bit more respect. That is, if you don't want to burn to a crisp from the inside out."

Ollie clutched at his burgundy throat and blood filled his eyes. He opened his mouth to scream, but instead of sound a jet of fire leapt from his throat. He then fell over and clawed at his chest.

"Estera, that's enough!" Bobo said from the lawn just beyond the porch. "You're killing him!"

She continued to watch Ollie writhe in pain for a moment, then flicked her eyes up to Bobo. He and his minions took another step backward.

"Yes, I am. He means nothing to me. None of you do. I could kill all of you as easily as slaughtering a rabbit for dinner. You belittled my powers, thought I was just some dabbler in witchcraft, but now you know better, yeah? You'll show me more respect?"

"Yes!" the men replied, their voices tripping over each other to be heard.

Seeing the fear she'd created on their faces filled Estera with a savage glee. With all the flair of an actor on the stage, she withdrew her right hand from her robe pocket and held the charm toward the men. They gasped at the sight of the horned man etched on its silver surface.

"Then let me give you one last lesson!"

With a flick of her wrist, Estera tossed the charm into the flame over her left hand. The charm spun on its edge, and together they became a blur of silver and red. She then said, "*Āga laga rahā hai!*"

The flame above her hand exploded, sending tendrils of flame shooting at the men. They were engulfed within seconds, each one lit up like a scarecrow put to a match. Howls of pain filled the air, and one by one they dropped to the ground. Some rolled to put the flames out, and some batted at their bodies, but all of them continued to burn.

"Momma!" Boden said behind her. "This ain't right!"

Irritation made her upper lip curl. "Boy, I'm teaching a lesson here. Go inside or be silent."

"But Momma!"

She hated the plaintive tone in her son's voice, and hated even more the weakness that sat at the heart of him, but even so she figured she'd made her point well enough. Pulling the spinning charm close, she said, "*Thaṇḍī havā uṛā*," and then blew out the flame. Within seconds all trace of fire disappeared. Not a single person was singed, not even their clothing. All that remained was bright red skin and thin wisps of smoke drifting up from their clothes.

"You fuc–" Bobo started to say as he got back up on wobbly legs. "I mean... Hell, I don't know what I mean. This– You– I didn't –"

"Think?" Estera smiled like a cat watching the mouse run for cover. "No, you didn't. You should start, though, because I only give lessons once. Now go back where you came from and never come this way again. So far as you and yours are concerned, I'm just a story you tell to your water-headed children to scare them into being good."

Bobo's eyes were bloodshot and his body shook, but there was some defiance left in him. "But what about the missing kids? The town wants to blame us for it."

"What happens to the children of this town is not your concern," she replied as she rubbed the charm in her hand. Little by little she grew taller, and her shadow loomed over the gathered men. They stared at her with eyes shaking in their sockets. "I exist in a world far darker and stranger than any you can imagine, communing with Gods, beholding and mastering beings beyond your understanding. You pry into that world at your peril. Now go before I change my mind and burn you all to cinders!"

She amped the illusion spell with her last words, and to the men before her she appeared to grow ten feet tall and sprout deer antlers from her skull, shredding her robe in the process. All of the men, even Ollie who'd returned to normal and no longer belched flames, scrambled backward until they could turn and run down the tree-shrouded driveway as though the Devil Himself chased them. As they turned right at the end, she couldn't help but laugh.

"Good riddance," she said as she returned the charm to her robe pocket and went back to the house. "I don't think they'll be a problem anymore."

Boden grunted and stepped clear of the front door. She glanced at him as she passed by, and his face was set in a look of fear and disappointment. She knew as his mother she should take him in hand and help him understand, use love to show him what she was doing and why, but during her life she'd learned many hard lessons, and one of the hardest had been to never need anyone. Not for help, not for company, and certainly not for love.

"Come on, boy," she said as she crossed the threshold. "It's almost time for dinner, and we have things that still need doing."

Nodding, Boden followed after her and closed the door behind them. The lock made an audible click when he threw the deadbolt. She nearly laughed. If anyone needed security, it certainly wasn't her.

"Yes, Momma."

It seems like everyone learned a lesson today, she thought. *Good. Now if I can just get my hands on whoever invaded my rest. They're out there somewhere, and come hell or high water, I will make them pay for their rudeness. Pay dearly.*

Chapter Fourteen

The drive from the Finch home to the sheriff's building wasn't a long one, but after refilling the Trailblazer's gas tank, Maya asked Taylor to take over the driving. The day had been far more taxing than she'd anticipated, and it probably wasn't going to get any easier once they sat down with the sheriff. She used the brief time it took to get to the sheriff's building to rest and center herself. It wasn't the easiest thing to do as the SUV rattled over a mountain range of potholes and bumps, but it was her only option since she wasn't in a position to roll out her yoga mat and play a CD of calming nature sounds.

When they pulled into the parking lot, Maya had to stifle a laugh. The sheriff's department building was the epitome of government spending–plain brick walls, lots of ninety-degree angles, and no style or decoration to speak of. Pure function: that was the government way. Three sheriff's cars were parked on the side of the building, but no one was parked in the general lot, so Taylor was able to stop the Trailblazer directly in front of the building, which–judging by the fist pump she gave herself–Taylor viewed as a personal victory.

After making sure she had her audio recorder and the battery level was good, Maya opened the passenger door and left the vehicle. Taylor locked the doors after them and set the alarm, then handed the keys back. After taking a few short steps, they were through the building's doors and looking for someone to assist them.

The interior of the sheriff's building was just as spartan and cold as the exterior, if not more so. Beige file cabinets sat against off-white walls with dingy yellow linoleum beneath it all. The only spot of color was a small potted plant sitting on the corner of a gray desk. Hovering over the plant was a heavily powdered face topped by white hair that had a slight purple sheen to it. A name plaque reading BETTY WHITFIELD sat next to the plant.

"Can I help you?" Betty asked, her face set to resting bitch and her voice flat as a robot's.

Maya wasn't sure if the offer was genuine, but decided to push forward and act like it was. "Yes, my name is Maya Gallows, and I'm a journalist. I'm hoping to be able to speak with Sheriff Bowens."

Betty's thin, white eyebrows inched up her forehead. "And what is this regarding?"

"His kidnapping investigation."

The receptionist's brows lowered as her mouth settled into a thin line like a crack in granite. Maya didn't know if the expression was because of her, or a sign of how Betty thought about the job the sheriff was doing.

"I'm sorry, Miss, but Sheriff Bowens isn't here, and I don't know when he'll be back. If you'd like to leave a message and your contract information, I'll make sure he gets it."

Next to her, Taylor snorted and shook her head. "That's a brush off if I've ever heard one."

"Young lady." Betty's face somehow became more severe than before, reminding Maya of her second grade teacher, a stern woman named Mrs. Crouch. The old woman had looked like someone created her face on a lump of rock using heaping amounts of the gaudiest makeup possible, and not once did a smile ever grace her lips.

Her face is probably too scared to smile, Maya thought with a suppressed chuckle.

Taylor blanched and looked down. "Sorry."

"Mm hmm," Betty replied.

"Mrs. Whitfield, is there a place we can wait for him?" Maya hoped if they did, it wasn't facing her desk. She had no desire to relive primary school.

The receptionist tilted her white-haired head to the left with an audible creek from her neck.

Maya turned to follow her gesture. When she saw a collection of hard, plastic chairs she was glad she had ample padding. *Taylor's narrow ass is going to be sore though.* The fact that tall potted plants separated the chairs from the reception desk made her sigh in relief.

"Thank you. We'll try to wait quietly."

Betty's right eyebrow rose up her forehead like an icy comet. "Please see that you do."

Half of Maya was scared silly of the receptionist, and the other half wanted to fall down laughing. In the struggle between the two reactions, she settled for a tightly controlled smile followed by a nod.

Taylor grabbed her hand and pulled her to the waiting chairs, her smile less controlled and her eyes dancing with laughter. When they sat, Maya gave her a stern look.

"Don't!" she whispered. "Cruella will hear you!"

That was all Taylor needed. Her young, girlish laughter bounced off the walls of the sheriff's department like giant, golden bells.

Maya hunched down in her seat, mortified of Taylor's actions and scared she was about to join her.

Deputy Jimmy Fuller's head jerked up at the sound of laughter so quickly he felt several of his vertebras pop. "Ouch," he said as he rubbed his neck. He looked over at the front entrance area where it seemed like the sound came from, but the potted plant Betty watered every day at noon— he appreciated her dedicated and methodical care for it— blocked his view. Laughter wasn't something he was used to hearing in the sheriff's building, especially laughter so light and fresh and feminine. To him it sounded…pretty. And definitely not local. He'd remember a laugh like that.

His curiosity getting the better of him, Jimmy locked his workstation and stood up from his desk, feigning a back stretch in case someone was looking. No one was. He then picked up a random case file from his top drawer and made his way toward Betty's desk in long, slow, casual strides, just a deputy going about his duty.

As he neared the waiting area he was caught by the subtle smell of jasmine wafting through the air. If laughter was out of place here, pleasant perfume was practically alien. The notes of cream and subtle fruitiness teased the nose rather than assaulting it, so he immediately appreciated the person wearing it. Too many people–men and women both– thought they had to bathe in the scents they wore, and it always irritated him when he had to be in their funky presence for more than a few seconds.

Breathing deeply, Jimmy continued around the tall plants. From the corner of his eye he caught flashes of color that usually weren't present in the waiting area, but he didn't stop to take a longer look until he came to Betty's desk. The old woman lowered her paperback book–tawdry romance novels were all she ever read–and glanced up at him over the rims of her rhinestone-encrusted bifocals.

"Can I help you, Deputy?" she asked without a hint of helpfulness in her crusty voice.

Jimmy looked down at her and shook his head. "Nope, just taking this file to where it needs to go."

Betty coughed like an old pickup trying to start. "And where might *that* be, *Deputy*?"

"Uh…" He noted sweat popping out on his forehead and upper lip. Wiping it off on his uniform shirt with the back of his forearm, he glared at Betty, saying with his eyes, "Would you kindly shut up?" He then looked over at the waiting area to see if their conversation was reaching that far.

Betty either couldn't read his expression or didn't care to, but when she followed his gaze across her desk she shook her head. "Bless your idiot heart," she said in low tones, raising her book back to her face.

Jimmy heard her, but he didn't *hear* her, so after a quick shrug he tapped the file against her desk and said, "Well, that should do it. Thanks, Betty." He then straightened up and made his way back the way he'd come.

But this time I'll stop and ask if there's anything I can do. Just a cop being helpful. That's me.

Rounding the plant separating Betty's desk from the waiting chairs, Jimmy adjusted his gun holster and slapped on his best ah-shucks smile. When he saw what greeted him he stopped so suddenly his shoes squealed against the linoleum.

Oh boy, he thought as his heart lub-lubbed in his chest. *Oohhh boy.*

Seated in the waiting area were exotic creatures from a distant land. On the right was a teenage girl with dark hair streaked with white wearing some band's t-shirt and black jeans. She was pretty, but she was way too young for him. The only Goth kids he knew were the ones he'd seen in high school who'd been beaten up by some jock or another. The girl in front of him shared their sense of style, but there was something about her that made her seem stronger, more sure and capable.

The person on the left, however, was entirely his type, and thankfully well clear of her teen years. Curly dark hair, light brown skin, blue eyes, full lips... She was a conundrum in the best possible way. He was in love instantly. As he slowly drew closer, he also noticed she was the one wearing the jasmine scent. He shocked himself at the power of his reaction to her. She was gorgeous, of that there was no doubt, but there was something else about her, something beneath the surface. He was drawn to her like the moon to the Earth.

"Excuse me," he said when he stopped in front of them. His voice sounded shaky in his ears, and he hoped it didn't carry. "Can I help you ladies?"

The brown-skinned woman looked up at him, a smile pulling at the corners of her lips. "That depends. Are you Sheriff Bowens?"

Never before had Jimmy wished he could trade places with the sheriff, but at that moment he would have traded vital organs for the chance. "Sadly, no. I'm Deputy James Fuller." He pointed at his badge and the name tag above it. "Sheriff Bowens left a little while ago to look into something. He might come back here, or he might just head home when he's done. If I can help in any way, I'd be more than happy to."

"Oh brother," the girl on the right said with a roll of her raccoon eyes. "Here we go."

Jimmy withered inside, but when the woman next to her gave her a sharp "Sshh!" and punched her arm, he recovered a tiny bit of his dignity back.

"Don't mind Taylor. She's young and stupid."

"Uugh," Taylor replied, her eyes rolled back so far all he could see was white.

"My name is Maya." The beautiful woman extended her hand. "And you said your name is James?"

Jimmy gulped as he grasped her hand. His palms had a habit of sweating when he felt stymied or nervous, and he felt plenty of both at that moment. "Yes, ma'am. Sheriff's Deputy James Fuller." He gave her hand a firm-but-not-too-firm handshake, then let it go. Her skin was as smooth and warm as it looked.

"It's a pleasure to meet you, Deputy Fuller."

Jimmy put everything he had into a smile. "The pleasure is all mi—"

The front door suddenly opened behind him. Jimmy could tell by the heavy steps who entered the building, and he groaned. *Not now, of all times. Can I ever get a break?*

The deputy was cute, in a Barney Fife sort of way. When he first walked, by she'd noticed him trying to look at them with his peripheral vision. That wasn't anything new for her. Being an attractive woman–Maya knew she was attractive, but there was a difference between knowing and caring–she was accustomed to people looking. Being of mixed racial heritage, she was even used to people staring. If the stare was accompanied by a smile rather than a frown, she didn't even mind it. And Deputy Fuller was definitely smiling. She didn't think he knew it, either. His aura was a subtle pink shimmer with occasional flashes of white, a good sign.

"My name is Maya. And you said your name is James?"

When she extended her hand she wondered what he'd do. Some men avoided touching her, some had handshakes like limp fish, and some took her hand like it was made of crystal that would shatter at the slightest touch. More often than not, unfortunately, when a man shook her hand he treated it as an opportunity to show her how manly and strong he was. Those men never got a chance to touch her again.

"Yes, ma'am. Sheriff's Deputy James Fuller."

He hesitated a moment, but then shook her hand. His palm was a bit damp, but his grip was firm without being painful. She gave it four stars out of five.

"It's a pleasure to meet you, Deputy Fuller."

The deputy's aura widened and its pink hue deepened. "The pleasure is all mi–"

Suddenly the air pressure changed as the front door opened. Maya couldn't see who entered the building, but when James's aura dissolved into weak gray wisps, she didn't think it was Santa Claus bearing gifts.

"Betty," the unknown person behind the deputy said in a weary voice, "remind me to institute a gypsy hunting season."

James's mouth fell open, and behind him the receptionist cleared her throat loudly. "Ahem hem!"

Maya wasn't sure what else was communicated behind the deputy's back, but a few seconds later a new person walked around to the waiting area. Ice filled Maya's veins.

"Is there something I can do for you?" a large black man said, his sheriff's badge winking in the overhead fluorescent lights. Above it was written BOWENS. The man looked like he was well into his fifties, but his stomach hadn't started to spread over his belt just yet, and there was more pepper than salt in his hair and moustache. Physically, he looked like what she expected a sheriff to look like. If he hadn't been sheathed in a murky aura that churned around him like spilled oil, Maya wouldn't have looked at him twice. But he was, and the awfulness of it was too much to look away from.

Maya stood up with all the casual grace she could muster, but she felt her knees shaking like a new-born foal. "I was hoping I could speak with you, Sheriff Bowens." She extended her hand, and it took all of her will to keep her fingers from trembling. She hoped he would decline the offer.

"I guess that depends on what you want to talk about." Bowens looked at her hand as if she was trying to give him a dead fish, but after a second he reached out and shook it.

The world fell out from under Maya's feet, and if she hadn't known better, she would have thought she'd somehow been ejected into space. Her skin was ice cold, her lungs emptied of all air, and vertigo spun her head over heels. Worse than all that, though, was the darkness. At first it felt empty, achingly void of anything, but all too quickly she discovered she was wrong. It wasn't empty at all. Things crawled within it, creatures with names no human tongue could utter. She sensed power in the darkness, shapeless yet alive and filled with wicked intelligence. It was a darkness carved from Hell itself, made from the hearts of the wicked and the fallen. A scream gathered in her chest.

"Hey, are you all right?" Bowen's asked. He took hold of her other hand and guided her back to the seat she'd just vacated.

The last thing Maya wanted was the sheriff touching her more, but when she fell into the seat she was grateful he hadn't let her fall. Taylor and Deputy Fuller also stepped in and helped her sit down.

The deputy dropped to one knee beside her. "Do you need some water? I can get you water."

"No, I…" Maya pulled her hands away from the sheriff and rubbed her face. As soon as their skin separated she felt better. The world returned, her stomach settled, and the overwhelming feeling of hopelessness that had begun to creep over her evaporated. After a few seconds she felt almost human again. "I'm okay. Thank you, really, but I think I just…stood up too fast. Sometimes it makes me light-headed."

Taylor pursed her lips and shook her head, but then patted her arm and took the seat next to her again. The sheriff and Deputy Fuller continued to stare at her, worry etched across their foreheads in deep lines.

"Are you sure?" Bowens asked. "If you need something to eat or drink, say so."

Shaking her head, Maya took several deep breaths and smiled. "No, really, I'm okay."

The two officers gave her one final looking over before nodding and resuming casual stances.

"You can go on back to your work now, Jimmy," Bowens said with a hitch of his belt. "I got this now."

The deputy's mouth settled into a subtle frown, but after a few deep breaths he said, "I'm glad you're okay," and then walked back the way he'd come. His aura was still mostly white and pink, but now it had a bit of gray in it. Maya was glad that whatever was going on with the sheriff hadn't spread to him.

"Why don't you two follow me to my office," Bowens said.

Maya wasn't sure what expression he wore because the thickness of his aura was actually beginning to obscure his features. "Thank you, Sheriff."

Together Maya and Taylor stood up and followed the sheriff as he walked past Betty's desk–the old woman didn't raise her head an inch when they went by–and took a short walk down a hallway until he opened his office door and waved them in.

The office was sparse and impersonal. Aside from a framed picture on his desk and a few plaques on the wall, it could have been anyone's office. The only item in it that caught her interest was the computer sitting on the corner of his desk like a giant beige bullfrog. *That thing is older than I am*, she thought with a mental chuckle. And, just as with the deputy, Bowens's dark aura hadn't leeched beyond him to taint the room. Not yet, anyway.

"Okay," he said as he sat down and straightened his tie, "you said you wanted to talk? What about?"

Maya opened her purse and pulled out the recorder. "I'd like to ask you some questions about the missing children."

Bowen's aura, already thick and dark, exploded outward until it filled the room with midnight. Maya drowned in the darkness, felt it enter her mouth and nose like sewage water. Her skin prickled from the sudden chill, but then her flesh went numb and she felt nothing. Vile evil was without her and within, consuming her totally, and all she wanted to do was run screaming, but she couldn't feel her body anymore, and her throat was choked with black. Death felt as close as her next heartbeat.

I told you you weren't ready for what was coming, Demael whispered in her head. *I warned you. You have the blood of ancients, but you're still just a child, and you can't hope to deal with the power arrayed against you. Which is why you're about to die. Such a pity.*

No! she raged silently. *Auras can't kill! This can't be happening.*

Which proves just how little you know.

I knew enough to help stop you!

A long, slow chuckle rumbled through Maya's skull. *Indeed you did, child. But can you stop what surrounds you now? Can you save yourself before it's too late?*

Maya's lungs burned and her head pounded, but she pushed all that aside and tried to stop the onrushing black before it crushed her. Focusing her mind and will, she imagined her lungs, imagined the evil aura filling them like swamp water, and pushed against her chest with mental hands. The black didn't budge. She pressed harder. The water became tar, clinging to her. She pressed down with all her strength, pushing her chest until she feared it would collapse. Slowly her lungs contracted, pushing the tarry black back up her throat.

Feeling a faint glimmer of hope, she reached for her mouth and nose and pulled at the aura. As the clumpy ethereal substance detached from her face, she opened her eyes, but still all she could see was blackness.

This isn't real, she told herself. *It's only an aura, a metaphysical projection of mind and emotion. That's all. I'm not blind or drowning. All I have to do is open my eyes. Open them and see.*

As her thoughts guided her psychic ability, a light shone from her eyes as she pushed herself through the murky aura. The black sizzled wherever the light touched, and for a moment Maya thought she heard a woman scream. Seconds later the black was burned away, and she found herself sitting as she had before, Taylor and the sheriff not the least bit aware of what had happened.

Perhaps there's hope for you yet, Demael said. She wasn't comforted by his words.

"So then you can't tell us anything?" Taylor asked. The young woman then looked over at her with a curious expression on her face.

Bowens, now without any trace of an aura around him, nodded. "Yes. Like I said, I can't comment on open investigations. Once we have concrete information to share, our public relations department will disseminate that. I'm sorry I can't help you any more than that."

Maya looked at the sheriff intently, studying every inch of the man she could see, even with her mystic eye, but he was as clear of corruption as a newborn babe. She'd never experienced anything like it.

"We're sorry too, Sheriff Bowens," she said, turning off her recorder and putting it back in her purse. "And I'm sorry to have wasted your time."

Bowens stood up behind his desk with a broad smile. "Not at all. In fact, I feel strangely better after this little chat. Not sure why. I'm not one to look a gift horse in the mouth, though." He looked around as though he wasn't quite sure where he was, but then smiled again and extended his hand. "If you ladies need anything unrelated to the case, please feel free to call. Now, if you'll excuse me, there's no rest for the weary."

Maya smiled as she stood up, but it was as fake as his was genuine. She reached for his hand wearily, still unsure of exactly what had happened, but when their skin touched she didn't feel anything untoward. No blackness, no chills. It was a plain old handshake. "Will do, Sheriff. Thanks again."

Once the pleasantries were exchanged all around Maya led Taylor out of the office to the front door. As she entered the building's front foyer she saw Deputy Fuller standing at his desk, a quizzical look on his thin face. She offered a brief wave, and he returned it, a goofy grin on his lips.

"So are you really okay?" Taylor asked as they entered blessed daylight. "You zoned out in the sheriff's office. I covered for you though. Did something else happen?"

Maya let her face warm in the sunshine for a moment, then rummaged in her purse for her keys. "You wouldn't believe me if I told you."

Taylor laughed. "After what happened at home, there's nothing I won't believe."

"Let's get in the car first," Maya said. She hit the unlock button on her key fob. The Trailblazer's lights blinked.

"Okay." Taylor went to the front passenger door and opened it.

Once they were seated and the engine was warming up,

Maya pulled out her recorder, hit REW, and then pressed PLAY. Taylor's voice wafted from the recorder's tiny speaker, and then Bowens's, but that was all. She frowned and rewound the recording again, then increased the volume. Background hiss accompanied Taylor and Bowens. After a few seconds a strange warble was heard.

"What was that?" Taylor asked. "It sounded like someone screaming."

Maya played the sound again, and then again. After one more time she said, "I think so too."

Taylor tilted her head and took the recorder in her hands, then closed her eyes and held it against her ear as she played the sound. When she handed it back she nodded. "I didn't hear that in the room though. Was that you?"

"No," Maya replied, shaking her head. "I thought I heard it when…well, I'll explain later. Anyway, I was hoping the recorder caught it. Now I know I'm not totally crazy."

Taylor laughed. "Not totally, no. Do we have another stop to make, or are we going to get something to eat? Please say we're done and I can shove lots of food in my mouth. Please."

It was Maya's turn to laugh. In her ears it sounded off, not quite true, but after her experience in the sheriff's office she was glad she could laugh at all. "Yes, we are definitely done for the day. I've had as many brushes with the supernatural as I care to. What do you want to eat?"

"I don't care." Taylor clicked her seatbelt in place and pulled out her phone. Her fingers flew across it in a mad rush. "But if you see a Taco Bell, make a run for the border."

"Taco Bell," Maya echoed. "Okay. I think I saw one a few streets back. Cheese and beef-like product, here we come."

As they left the sheriff's building in their rearview mirror, Maya breathed a sigh of relief. The Dark God had been wrong. She hadn't died. She was stronger than it wanted to admit. She could do this. She could save these girls. For the first time that day, she actually felt confident. It was a nice change.

Chapter Fifteen

Screee!

Estera ran a whetstone across the blade of her large knife.

Screee!

She turned the blade and ran the stone down the other side.

Screee! Screee!

The knife and stone ground each other several more times, then she set the stone down and picked up a dish towel. After running the knife under a stream of water she dried it off and looked at the knife's edge. Light winked off the sharpened metal. Now she was ready to start.

Scallions and green garlic sat on her wooden cutting board. When she placed the knife against their outer skin, the sharp edge sliced through without a hint of resistance. Powerful aromas burst up and flooded the kitchen. Her eyes watered and nose twitched, but she wouldn't have wanted it any other way.

Stufat de miel was her favorite meal. Grandmother Vertina had made the lamb stew for her often as a child, and Estera made sure she learned how to make it before Thanatos carried the old woman to the next world. She'd studied every aspect of the dish, made copious notes, but try as she might her stew never quite tasted as good.

Next, a rack of lamb ribs fell before her blade, each chop bloody red and delicious looking. She opened a cabinet and withdrew a large pot. After being put over a lit burner, she tilted a bottle of olive oil over it for a few seconds, then scraped the meat and sliced vegetables inside it as well. The smell of garlic and cooking meat filled the air like the world's greatest perfume, now accompanied by a delicious sizzle.

After sautéing the ingredients for several minutes, she picked up a measuring cup and placed it under the faucet.

Once the cup was full, she turned the water off and lifted the now-heavy glass over to the pot just a few feet away. A sudden wave of pain slapped her in the face so intensely she cried out. The measuring cup shattered when it hit the floor. She fell with it but was able to catch herself before she planted her face in sharp glass shards. After that, everything went black.

Boden brought his axe down on the day's final log, two halves flying apart from each other with explosive force, when Momma's scream cut into his ears. He ran for the kitchen door before the split pieces of wood hit the ground.

Inside he found Momma lying face down on the kitchen's hardwood floor. Water and broken pieces of glass surrounded her. Smoke and the heavy odor of burning food clogged his nose. He quickly turned off the stove's gas burner, and then he went down to his knees to kneel next to Momma. After turning her over he found she was unconscious, but the rattle in her chest as she wheezed in and out frightened him. Luckily he didn't find any cuts or wounds from her fall.

What's goin' on, Momma? he asked himself, wishing like hell that he could ask her instead. Ever since she'd instructed him to get that first girl for her, things hadn't been right. She was aging like someone in a movie when it was sped up. Now she was being attacked by someone or some…thing, and as powerful as she was, it didn't seem like she was winning the battle.

The worst, though, was knowing there wasn't anything he could do to help her. She had power, not him. He wasn't good for anything that didn't require strong arms. She'd said so before, many times, but now he understood just how useless he was.

No, not useless. Not entirely.

Using those strong arms, Boden lifted Momma and carried her to the living room, where he set her down on the couch. He put a pillow under her head, then recalled something he'd seen on TV once and put a pillow under her feet too. When she was as comfortable as he could make her, he went to the restroom and grabbed a wash cloth. He held it under a stream of cold water and wrung it out before going back to Momma and putting it on her forehead.

"Come on, Momma. Wake up."

He rubbed her face with the cloth, the wrinkled skin so pale in comparison to the tan he got from working outside.

"Momma, you're stronger than this. I've never seen you fear nothin'."

Boden folded the wet cloth into a rectangle and laid it flat on her forehead. *Her tea always seems to make her feel better,* he thought. *Maybe I should get her some.*

Intending to do just that, Boden stood up and turned toward the kitchen. When Momma sat up like the couch was spring-loaded and yelled, "No!" he nearly jumped right out of his dilapidated boots and screamed.

Estera was surrounded in darkness so complete she thought she was dead and her soul had been cast into the void. There wasn't an up or down or direction of any kind. Nothing touched her, nothing moved. There wasn't even a sense of time. The black was just…it. In all her dealings with demons and forgotten gods, never had she felt so helpless, frightened, or alone, because the feeling of magic that had always been part of her life was gone. Not that she could have cast a spell anyway since she didn't have air to speak or components to manipulate.

After a period of time that could have been a few seconds or a few years—she had no idea which—sounds echoed in the darkness. Indistinct at first, she pushed her panic down and hoped the sounds would become clearer.

Eventually they did. They were voices.

The black exploded in a bright flash so sudden she held up her arms to shield her eyes. Of course it didn't help—she had no arms, nor did she have eyes. She floated in the black because she *was* the black. And that was when the truth finally struck her.

I'm in my own spell. Someone's using my magic against me. But how? And who?

As the blackness pulled away, she found she was sitting at a desk, though she had no control over her body. She spoke and moved, but none of it was her doing. It also wasn't her voice she heard, nor her hands when they came into view. When her eyes drifted past a picture on her desk she recognized the faces in it and understood more of what was happening. But it wasn't enough. Sheriff Bowens was a buffoon, an easy to manipulate tool. Someone else had to be behind this attack.

Sitting on the other side of the desk were two women. One was young, her hair like a peacock and her eyes like a raccoon. Estera sensed a small bit of magic about her, but that was all. The other woman was older, a black bitch far too pretty for her own good, skin like a fawn and eyes…her eyes…so blue and…looking right at her. Estera felt a jolt coarse through her body. The black woman wasn't looking at the sheriff, oh no, her too-damn-lovely eyes were looking at Estera, staring straight through the physical world and into the dimension of magic beyond it. And there was something else about the woman, something familiar. Then it hit her like a bolt of lightning.

So, Estera mused, tumblers in her mind finally falling into place, *you're the source of my woes today. First you attack me in my bed, and now my kitchen. But how? You aren't old enough to be a threat to me. You barely have any power…at…all…*

But that wasn't true, and Estera knew it as soon as the words formed in her mind. The woman in front of her might be young, but she had considerable power, and the longer Estera stared at her, the more she realized how terribly she'd misjudged the situation.

Suddenly a dark cloud erupted from the woman, filling

the sheriff's office. In the cloud Estera saw raven wings, funeral tapestries, claws, tentacles, and a thousand other images, each worse than the one before, and she felt battered by it all. Here was power equal to hers, if not greater. But how? HOW?!

Suddenly the darkness reached for her with claws long and sharp, and they encircled her throat in a tight grip that burned her very soul. She tried to pull away, but she was locked in place, a passenger in the sheriff's body, tied to him through the spell she'd cast to keep him on a leash while she searched for the right child. Through her own magic she was damned. The irony wasn't lost on her.

And that's when she knew what she had to do. Using every bit of will and concentration she had, Estera searched for the magic she'd implanted into the sheriff. Once she found it she took hold of the eldritch thread in her mental hands and pulled, pulled, PULLED! When it finally tore apart, the release of energy hurled her out of Sheriff Bowens's body. Once again she was drowning in black.

Boden looked into Momma's deep brown eyes, and they stared straight back, but there wasn't any life in them, no thought. But she'd spoken! He knew it, he'd heard it.

"Snap out of it, Momma!"

He'd seen people slap unconscious people awake, but the idea of striking her was too abhorrent to even contemplate, so instead he took her by her shoulders and shook her.

"Come on, you need to stop this right now!"

Her head lolled from side to side. He shook her again, harder this time. When her eyes didn't react, he rattled her back and forth like a misbehaving animal that didn't want to do what it was told. Her teeth smacked together with a loud *Clack!* If he kept the shaking up he worried her head would pop off and roll away. When her eyes finally blinked and then turned his direction he exhaled a massive sigh of relief.

"Oh thank God, Momma. I was so 'fraid you was badly hurt."

Momma shook her head and rubbed her neck. "If you kept shaking me like that I probably would have been."

Boden felt his face glow red in shame. "I'm sorry. I didn't know what to do."

"If there was a list of the things you don't know," Momma replied as she slowly swung her legs around so she could sit upright, "it'd be a hundred miles long. Ain't your fault, though, boy. You just are what you are, little as it is."

The unexpected affection made Boden's face even warm, so he stood up and turned away. "So you're okay then, Momma?"

A quick yet gusty sigh fluttered the back of his shirt.

"No, I'm not okay. I'm a damn sight from okay. Somebody out there is messin' with my magic, and if I don't figure out a way to put a stop to it, they'll put a stop to me. And we don't want that, do we boy?"

Boden turned back to his momma and looked at her sternly. "No, Momma, we don't."

"Damn right."

Momma sat still for nearly a minute, her nose crinkled and her mouth turned down in a frown, all sure signs she was hip-deep in contemplation. Boden knew better than to interrupt her when she got that way. When she finally stood up, her eyes gleamed with a terrible light.

"You'll have to feed yourself tonight, boy. Momma's got some work to do."

She was already halfway to the front door before he digested what she'd said.

"Wait, what? Momma? Are you leavin'?"

Momma grabbed the doorknob and looked back at him over her shoulder. "Yes, boy. There's things I need to take care of before they're the ruination of us. And no, I don't need you going with me. I can handle this just fine on my own. Got me?"

Boden nodded.

"Good. I'll be back when I'm back. Don't wait up."

With that said, Momma opened the door and left. The door closed after her on its own.

It was a long night after that. She'd said he shouldn't wait up for her, but of course he did. Momma wasn't well, and hadn't been well for longer than he'd realized. He was her son, though, and he'd wait for her until the sun went out and the sky boiled away. That was the depth of his devotion to her.

Even if she was becoming a monster.

Chapter Sixteen

"I know it means I have no taste," Taylor said from her motel bed as she shoved a chip dripping with cheese and ground beef into her mouth, "but I don't care, I love Taco Bell. Mm mm good!"

Maya hoisted a double-decker taco and took a bite. "Haters gonna hate, Taylor," she said around a mouthful of refried beans and masticated tortillas. "Always remember that, my young Padawan."

Chewed up nachos exploded from Taylor's mouth. "Dammit, bitch! Don't do that! Now I've wasted all that deliciousness." She snorted and wiped her mouth clean, then pulled at her shirt to dislodge the chewed up bits onto the comforter beneath her. When that was done, she levelled a steady gaze at Maya. "I understand why he fell for you, ya know."

Maya didn't have to ask who she was talking about. Kyle's spirit seemed right there in the room with them, and her heart ached for the thousandth time that day. "You do?"

Taylor's eyes were red as she nodded. "Yeah. And it wasn't because you're so pretty. I'm sure that's what caught his eye at first, but it's not what kept him interested. You both are…I mean, were…geeks. When he left to join the Army he didn't take much with him, so I stole a lot of the DVDs and CDs he left behind. I felt like I…ya know…that we…"

And that was it. As soon as the first tear sparkled above Taylor's eyeliner, Maya shoved her food to the side and leapt to cradle the young woman against her. Taylor grasped her as if her grief was a tornado that could tear them apart. Feeling the same pull, Maya laid Taylor's head on her chest and rocked with her on the cheap motel bed. Both women cried loud and hard. After a few moments Maya pulled at the bed sheet crumpled across her lap and used it to dab their cheeks. When Taylor sobbed, Maya sobbed with her and held her tight, her fingers stroking Taylor's hair and brushing her cheeks. Her chest felt like the sun had set on it; Taylor's face was so hot, but she needed that heat, needed to feel that her pain wasn't alone, that *she* wasn't alone. For the first time since her father died, she remembered why misery loved company.

"I'm so sorry," Maya said, following her words with a kiss to the top of Taylor's head. "I feel like what happened is my fault. If I hadn't gone to Stillwater, maybe he wouldn't have stayed. Maybe he would have taken you from your parents and just left."

Taylor sat up and wiped her runny nose with the back of her hand. "Don't think stuff like that. You don't know what would have happened. How do you think I feel?" The young woman's face turned bright crimson as more tears poured down. "If I hadn't been such a baby and begged him to come, he wouldn't have been there to begin with."

"Sshhh," Maya replied, pulling the girl back. "You can't think stuff like that either, okay? If I can't blame myself, neither can you. All we can do is remember him, remember the reasons why we loved him. He saved the goddam world, and no one but us knows it. That right there fucking sucks. Everyone alive today should know his name. But they don't, and they never will. I'm so glad I got to have him in my life, even if it was only for a couple of days. He was a good man, Taylor, a damn good man, and I will always hold him inside me."

"I wish I'd had more time to know him too." Taylor brushed her nose against Maya's shirt, but she didn't mind. "He was a great brother when I was young, but then he was gone and all I had left was the stuff he left behind. When Mom and Dad were out, I'd sneak in and look through his desk, read his school yearbooks, sometimes even wear his shirts. It was all I had, and I held onto it as hard as I could for as long as I could. He *was* a good man, and he was a good brother too. I'll never stop missing him and wishing we'd had..."

Maya leaned against the headboard and hugged Taylor tightly. "I know, baby... I know... More time. In the end, time is what matters most, because we never have as much of it as we need."

"Please don't ever make me leave," Taylor said, the fear in her eyes like a living thing as she looked up. "Please don't. I lost a brother already, and I don't think I could stand losing a...a sister too."

What little control Maya had over her emotions left her in that moment, and the rain falling beneath her eyes was a storm of pain and love, each wrestling to dominate the other. "Oh sweetie, you can't mean that. I'm not–"

Taylor pulled away and stared directly in Maya's eyes. "Don't tell me what I mean. You're like a sister to me now. If anything good came out of...what happened, it's you. You're my only family now. You and Morgana. We're it. Period. End of discussion."

"I'll never ask you to leave," Maya replied, the sadness inside her abating to the love she felt in Taylor's arms, in the soft, ruddy glow of her aura. "I've never had a sister before, but if I could have asked for one, I'd had asked for someone just like you."

With those words said, the pain and sadness in the room slowly faded like fog burned away by the morning sun. They still shed tears, and they stayed on the bed holding each other for a while longer, but both of them felt better than they had since fleeing the submerged town of Stillwater. They were unburdened of the grief they'd held inside, shared their affection for each other, and forged a new relationship. By the time Maya let Taylor go and stood up, she was glad the dam had finally burst. Pain shared was pain lessened.

"Whew! Talk about an estrogen moment!" Taylor's laugh had an embarrassed hitch in it. "If we were guys we'd have to talk about football or hot chicks now to make things less awkward."

Maya chuckled and nodded. "Fortunately I'm not a guy, so there's no shame in my game." She then glanced at her bed and the tacos scattered across it. "I have lost my appetite, though. Getting emotional always upsets my stomach. I think I'll take a shower instead."

"Sounds like a good idea." Taylor picked up her container of nachos, grimaced, and tossed it back in the plastic bag it came in. "I might take one when you're done, so don't hog all the hot water, m'kay?"

"No promises." Maya flipped open her small suitcase and grabbed a fresh pair of underwear and a nightshirt. Her shampoo and other toiletry items were already in the bathroom.

The Verdant Inn's showers were cheaply made and lacked anything even close to a frill, but none of that mattered when the hot water started pouring. Today had been one of the strangest days of her life, and considering just how strange her life was, that was saying something. There was no better way she could think to end it than with lots of lather and hot water. Slowly the kinks in her muscles worked themselves loose as she soaped up her plastic loufa and scrubbed her body down. Away went the strange visions, down the drain spiralled the ominous visitations. It was ten minutes of watery bliss before she reluctantly turned the faucet knob off.

A rough, white towel waited for her on a shiny rack bolted to the wall above the toilet. She took one, threw it on the ground to act as a bath mat, then took another and slowly ran it over every inch of her body until she was as dry as the cheap cloth could get her. After stepping out of the shower, Maya stood before a steam-covered bathroom mirror. Seeing only a brown blur for a reflection, she put her towel against the mirror and rubbed a clean swath across it.

A demon stared back at her.

"Ah!" she cried out, stumbling backward.

The figure in the mirror was covered in broken, blackened flesh, as if it had crawled from the fires of Hell itself. Blank white eyes shown from the seared face, and impossibly long, sharp teeth filled its mouth. She thought the vision was only a picture, a still image created by her frazzled mind, but when the demon turned its head and glared down at her that hope died.

Scrub all you like, my child, the Dark God said around fangs coated with blood, *but you will never be clean again.*

Rage exploded in Maya's chest like a bomb, and against all her better judgment she leapt at the mirror and pounded her closed fists against it. The demon, as if knowing her mind better than she did, reached *through* the mirror and caught her fists in its hands. Searing pain tore through her skin. Maya tried to pull away, pull back, but instead of getting free she pulled so hard the demon came through the mirror after her.

"No!"

Demael smiled as its sudden weight forced Maya further back from the mirror until she hit the bathtub. The impact buckled her legs, dropping her in the shower tub. The demon landed on her, its cracked flesh sizzling and painful. She burned beneath it, her skin scraped beyond raw. The worst, though, was the laughter. The demon cackled harder the more she struggled.

You are weak! it said, its insides glowing between the cracks in its charbroiled flesh. *You are pathetic! Without me inside you you'd already be dead! You aren't worthy of your own life, or of the power that is your birth right!*

She burned in the bathtub, the scent of scorched skin and burning hair clogging her nose like smoke. She pushed against the demon, but it weighed down on her like a mountain, like grim death come to take her. She screamed and reached out for something–anything–to help her. Shower gel squirted at the dark figure when she grabbed the bottle and squeezed it. Her razor skittered off the edge of the tub and slid uselessly away. The shower curtain became entangled around them, the plastic pressing against her face, choking her.

Stop your struggling, Demael said, its chapped hands curling around her throat. *Accept it. Let go. Your time is done, and mine is just beginning. I had hoped we would usher in the new age together, but you are unworthy of such a gift. So die, child! Die!*

The skin around Maya's throat burned, sending shooting pains through her body, but having the life strangled from her lungs was what drove her to lash and twist and buck. The weight of the world pressed down on her. She reached out, pushed, pulled, grabbed, and twisted whatever she could reach, but it wasn't until the overhead shower faucet released a torrent of cold water that any of it had an effect.

Suddenly the weight lifted off her, and the plastic shower curtain curled and turned black where ever its blistering flesh touched it. As she sucked in air she saw the demon stagger backward, steam rising from its skin where the water touched it. After a few moments, its skin turned from charcoal to ash.

This is the second time you've wounded me, the Dark God said. As it spoke, ash broke off from its skin, revealing something beneath. *None have ever dared defile me.* Light brown skin peaked out from the gray around it, the under-skin fresh and clean. *Yet you dare. Twice.* As gray flakes fell Maya saw that the demon was actually a woman. *And both times you hurt me. Perhaps you are stronger than I thought, Maya Gallows.* As the last word left its lips, so fell the final bits of ash. What it revealed shook her to her core.

"No, that's a lie!"

The demon smiled, its lips her lips, its eyes her eyes. Every inch of the demon was an inch of her reflecting back

I told you we are one now, it replied with a lick of its gory fangs. *Fight all you like, but in the end it won't matter. No power in this world can stop me, the least of which being you. Accept me now, and you will rule as my Angel of Destruction. Deny me, though, and I will burn you alive from the inside out.*

Maya couldn't take any more of the Dark God's words. She heard them in her ears and inside her head at the same time, felt them resonate through her as if she'd said the words herself. Lashing out in terror and anger, she launched herself forward, grabbed the demon wearing her face, and slammed it against the mirror over the bathroom sink. The large pane shattered as if a bomb went off behind it, throwing her backward once more, this time showered in jagged glass pieces. When her head hit the tile wall, the world swam before her, and then she blacked out.

"Maya!" a voice said from a great distance away. "Maya, wake up!"

Feeling like she was at the bottom of a well, Maya shook her head but instantly regretted it when nausea overwhelmed her. She turned her head just as every bit of her recently eaten dinner rushed out of her with a loud, "Hork!"

"Oh, man!" the voice said, Maya now recognizing it as Taylor's. "So gross! Here…uh…let me try this…"

Cold water sprinkled against Maya's face like ice chips, clearing the darkness and cobwebs from her mind. She sat up quickly as her breath hitched in her throat. Leaning over her was Taylor, the young woman's make-up covered face runny like a painting left out in the rain and her dark hair a rat's nest. Over the girl's shoulder Maya saw that the bathroom mirror was intact, and a quick look around told her that her Dark God twin was gone, if it had ever been there at all.

"Holy shit," she said. When he put her hand against her chest to feel her heart she noticed she was still naked. That would normally have embarrassed her, but cuts from a mirror that never actually shattered worried her more. The worst, though, were the very real burn marks on her arms and neck. They were the only proof the Dark God had been there.

Taylor's eyes fell on the burns too. "Oh my god, Maya, what happened? Who did this to you? And *how*?"

Maya didn't reply until she was on her feet and stumbling out of the bathroom. As she told Taylor what happened, the young woman cleaned her cuts, which proved to look worse than they really were. By the time Maya finished, even the burn marks were fading. Naked and terrified seemed the worst of it.

"This is so fucked up, Maya," Taylor said as she got up and retrieved Maya's night clothes. "Maybe it's right. Maybe we aren't ready for this."

Maya took the underwear and slipped into it, though not out of any sense of modesty. Taylor had already seen everything of her there was to see, and frankly the girl was too much her family now for something like that to be awkward anymore. After the shirt was on, she shook her head. Wet curls flung water droplets across her comforter.

"Going home wouldn't solve anything. We're here to stop someone from kidnapping little girls, and that's what I'm going to do. Demael will be in my head no matter where I am, so it might as well be here."

Taylor tilted her head as if Maya was a strange creature that had just crawled out of the swamp, but then she nodded and offered a weak grin. "Okay, Sis. I got you. But do you think you can take a metaphysical day off tomorrow? I don't know if my heart can take another possession or whatever it is that keeps happening to you."

"*You* can't take it?" Maya asked, a smile on her face for the first time in what felt like years. "Bitch, I'm the one who's getting jumped by gods and whatever the fuck is out here preying on kids! Don't even go there."

Taylor laughed and threw back the blankets on her bed. Pieces of cheese and a few jalapeños flew to the thick green shag carpet. "All right, you have a point. Now let's get some sleep. If I look like shit tomorrow, it's on you."

"As if that was possible," Maya replied, sliding into her

own bed. "Good night, Sis."

Turning off the light that shone between their beds, Taylor yawned and settled in. "Good night. Don't let the demons bite."

Maya chuckled, but it was a sound she didn't feel. Her life had always been clouded by the supernatural, and fear was as much a part of it as anything, so much so that she'd started to forget how terrifying her abilities could make her life. Stillwater had been a wakeup call, a reminder, but at least that had been a threat outside herself. Now she carried the terror with her, a dark disease of horror and fire. *How do I fight that?* she asked herself.

She waited long into the night for answers, but none ever came.

Chapter Seventeen

For the first time in weeks Alvin Bowens had no trouble falling asleep. Once upon a time he'd been a champion sleeper, able to nod off just about anywhere at any time, but when the kidnappings started his peaceful rest went the way of disco. But, after speaking with that strange woman in his office earlier, a weight had lifted from his chest, and no sooner had he laid down in bed next to his wife Charlaine and put his head on his pillow than he drifted into carefree slumber. An unconscious smile curled his lips.

Alvin was a kid again, bellowing with joy as the roller coaster ripped through turn after turn, the sound of screaming people and metal grinding against metal filling his ears. Next to him sat his father, a bear of a man who'd died from heart failure just days after his son graduated high school. They smiled at each other, knowing this was a moment they'd share forever, and then held on tight for the loop-the-loop coming quickly down the track. When they hit the first upward curve Alvin felt himself lifting from his seat.

That's not right, his dreaming brain said. *I was pushed downward, not lifted.*

But in the dream he *was* lifted, and the higher they went into the loop the further from his seat he rose. With the rollercoaster's bar across his lap he didn't fear he'd be thrown from the ride—that was just stuff kids talked about to make the rides more exciting—but as the cart flipped over and started down the other side, Bowens was ripped out of the cart and sent spiralling into the air.

Deep into the dream as Alvin was, he didn't hear the locks on his front door disengage, didn't hear it open and the house alarm chirp before it turned back off, nor did he hear the footsteps that slowly lumbered up the stairs. But, when the shuffling stopped at the foot of his bed and was replaced with strange whispers, his sleep smile disappeared.

Now Alvin stood in darkness, yet he could see himself as clear as day. He wasn't a kid anymore, and his father was back in his grave. Alvin wore his sheriff's uniform, service pistol at his hip and his shoes worn in but polished to a dull shine. The silence was as thick and cloying as the black around him.

"Hello?" he said, unsure why but somehow sure he was heard. "Is there anyone here?"

The darkness didn't respond, didn't part to reveal a hidden world beyond it.

"I'd like to go back to th–"

Suddenly a sound rumbled through the void. At first it was indistinct, just a soft bit of noise, but with every second it got louder, until finally he heard it clearly enough to realize the sound was someone speaking, but in a language he'd never heard before. The voice was neither male nor female, young nor old. The more the strange words entered his mind, the more uneasy he became. After half a minute he was ready to claw his ears off.

"What do you want?" he shouted, his voice weak.

Again no answer, but just as he was ready to grab his ears and pull, pain raged up his arms and legs. He held his arms up and watched in horror as his shirt sleeves were ripped open by an invisible force, followed immediately by his black skin. Flesh and muscle split apart on all four limbs, laying bare blood vessels like pulsing red vines around bloodied bones. He screamed in agony as he stared at his exposed innards, his mind leaping between terror and wonder, when suddenly something yanked his blood vessels free from his upper arm and held the veins aloft in invisible hands. The image of a marionette barely had a chance to form in his mind before he was yanked forward. Agony raced up and down his body as his arms and legs were moved by the puppet strings that were his veins, his legs pulled one way while his arms went another. Blood glistened as it dripped and pooled around his wrists and ankles before falling in wet *plops*.

The loudness of his screams was nothing compared to the laughter dropping down on him like hail. He looked up in agony, sure he'd see some distant puppeteer pulling his veins, but instead he saw a face so large it was like a storm cloud hovering directly over him, its eyes black pits of nothingness. His veins rose toward it, eventually slipping into its mouth like bloody noodles. The face laughed around the bloody strings, but then teeth like old tombstones clamped down and started chewing.

Bowens stood in a shower of his own blood, every moment an eternity of pain as he was jerked back and forth like a dog toy, a plaything for a beast beyond mercy. Suddenly he was yanked into the air, and he stared in horror as the laughing, chewing mouth drew him up. Within seconds he would be in that monstrous maw, and he knew instinctively that would be only the beginning of his misery. The mouth then smiled in agreement. The teeth chomped closer, and closer, and closer, spraying carnage with every chomp until Alvin was drenched in his own gore. Death wouldn't even spare him from the agony laid before him. When the tombstone teeth came for his head, the last thing he saw was a black, forked tongue, waiting like a snake to wrap itself around him and tear him to shreds. His throat ruptured from his screams, coating his esophagus and mouth in thick, hot blood.

And that's when he woke up. He could still feel blood filling his mouth, still feel his flayed open skin. His screams, though, had ended. He looked down at his body to see if blood soaked the sheets he'd twisted up in his sleep. When he saw that his arms were whole, relief washed over him, but then he looked past his legs and his terror returned full bore.

Standing at the foot of his bed was a woman clad in a dark robe, her back bent and her face twisted. Words he couldn't understand fell from her thin lips, and she sprinkled some sort of dust on his exposed body. He attempted to move his legs so he could stand up and demand to know what was going on, but his body refused to obey him. Even his mouth wasn't his own. He could only watch in horror as the strange woman spoke, her words exiting her mouth in a glowing mist He was paralyzed, helpless, and afraid. Fortunately the woman didn't seem to have any interest in Charlaine.

As the last of the woman's dust flew from her fingers, she looked at him with dark eyes and sneered. "You got away from me, but whoever that bitch is that done it doesn't know who she's dealing with. Now you're back under my control, and this time it'll stay that way, you hear me? Now get back to doing what I told you to do and make sure no one gets in the way of me doing what I have to do. I don't care who it is. Anyone asks about me or gets too close, and you're gonna kill them, period."

Every word was a nail pounded into his skull, driving her commands further and further in his psyche.

"And if you fail me," she said as she reached down and wrapped her bony fingers around his ankle, "*I'm* gonna kill *you*. Am I lying?"

Alvin regained enough control over his body to shake his head slightly.

"Damn right I'm not. Now, go back to sleep and forget this ever happened." The woman pulled out a small metal coin and blew across it in his direction. As her breath washed over him, all he could think of was getting back to work and settling some people's hash, then his eyes grew heavy, and before he knew it he was out cold again, sleeping the sleep of the just.

Chapter Eighteen

Maya woke up feeling dreadful. Her joints ached, her muscles felt like she'd run a marathon, and when she rolled over to check her alarm clock her back protested like an old man with kids on his lawn. Meanwhile, in the bed next to her, Taylor slept like an angel.

It was 6:41 in the morning. Weak light spilled between heavy green curtains. Slowly Maya stood up and walked to the window. Through the exposed sliver of glass she saw thick strands of trees beyond a parking lot that was empty save for her Trailblazer. Nothing moved or stirred. Just another calm morning in South Carolina. People could be forgiven for not recognizing that evil stalked the small town when birds chirped and cool breezes stirred the air.

Maya turned to the bathroom, her bladder urgently sending distress signals, but when she saw the mirror through the open door she couldn't help but stop. Hackles rose on her back at the memory of what had happened the night before. Without thinking, she rubbed at her bandaged arms. One of the Band-Aids came loose, revealing unmarked brown skin beneath it. She pulled away two more Band-Aids, each one eliciting a hiss of pain as the adhesive fought to hold onto her. The skin beneath those was also unblemished.

So were those just figments of my imagination, too? Like the evil mirror version of me? And the burns? And the mirror breaking? Jesus, at some point I won't know where reality ends and the Dark God's torture begins.

After a few seconds of hemming and hawing, her bladder won out, so Maya went to the bathroom—careful to leave the door open just in case—and lowered her underwear to around her knees. When she finished, she hustled out of the cold, tiled room before her gooseflesh became permanent.

Next to the alarm clock was Maya's smart phone, its charging cord still plugged in. She settled on the bed, unplugged the phone, and activated the screen. A text message from Alan waited for her. He wanted to know how things were going. She hit REPLY and wrote, "You wouldn't believe me if I told you." She then hit SEND and opened her Facebook app. The notification icon showed there were several comments waiting for her to read, but she wasn't in the mood to act like life was normal. For most other people, normal was all they ever knew, but for her it was as rare as a Bigfoot sighting, and the pretense of normality was something she just wasn't up for at the moment.

A text bubble from Alan popped up. "You forget–I know you. I believe everything you say, because I've been there too often when shit got real. Need some help? I'm off work for the next couple of days."

Maya chewed at the inside of her cheeks. Part of her wanted desperately to have her old friend with her. The more strange things became, the more important it was that she had people around to ground her. But, with Demael lurking in her mind somewhere, she didn't want to put him in potential harm's way. Having Taylor with her was risky enough.

"Thanks, but we're okay. We're big girls."

An icon in the corner of her text app pulsed as Alan typed a response. The wait wasn't long.

"Okay, I trust you. Take care of each other, and let Taylor know Morgana's first day at the new job went well. Call me if you change your mind or need anything. L8r d00d."

She almost smiled. "L8r." After closing the text app, she scanned Twitter for a moment, then shut her phone's screen off.

"You have to be the loudest touch screen typist I've ever heard," Taylor said, her unexpected voice causing

Maya's heart to skip a beat. "I'm amazed you haven't broken it."

"That's rich," Maya replied. "I've seen the way you abuse your phone. Poor thing gets treated like it owes you money."

Taylor laughed and slowly pushed up from her pillow, her hair and makeup an unholy mess. "It's youthful exuberance. Don't hate."

The fit of laughter that came over Maya took her breath away. She literally feared she would die of asphyxiation from not being able to breathe in, but after a few lightheaded seconds, she forced herself to stop and draw in air. Her vision swam from tears and giddiness.

"I'm still young," she replied, her voice shaky. "Young-ish, anyway."

Taylor shrugged her shoulders and gave her a lopsided grin. "Heavy on the ish."

"Kiss my ass."

Running a hand through the rat's nest on her head, Taylor reached for her own phone and plucked it from the charging stand she'd brought with her. "Hardy har. So, what's on our agenda today? I'm hoping there's more of those pancakes in our future."

That was a good question, one Maya hadn't given a lot of thought to yet. The previous day was still too much on her mind. "I dunno. After what happened at the newspaper I doubt we'd be welcome back there to ask more questions, and I don't think Sheriff Bowens likes having us here poking around. We could go to the library and look into the area's past, see if kids have gone missing before, maybe dredge up some skeletons in the town's closet. Or we could drive around and see if we can find those gypsies we've heard so much about. Does that sound like fun?"

Taylor looked up from her phone with a raised eyebrow. "Are you serious? Hell yeah! My Spidey sense went off like a five alarm fire when I heard there were gypsies around.

Maybe we'll even get to see a gypsy wedding!"

"Dare to dream," Maya replied, her eyes rolling. She despaired for the youth of the country and the terrible television they were exposed to. "But, yeah, I think we should at least do a drive by of the gypsies, get a look at them, test the vibe. See if anything jumps out at me."

"Just not literally." Taylor's fingers were a blur as they worked her phone's touch screen. "Or figuratively, for the matter. After yesterday I'd be happy to have a simple, non-terrifying day."

Maya understood exactly what she meant. "Me too, but simple and nice won't save those girls or–if worse comes to worst–bring them justice."

The young woman's phone beeped, she laughed, typed something, and then shut the device off. "Thanks, Debbie Downer. But you still didn't answer my question."

"And what was that?" Maya replied, at a loss for what question she might have missed.

"Am I gonna get some pancakes in me or what?" Taylor cried out, rubbing the sleep rumpled shirt over her belly. "Meesa hungry!"

Another bout of laughter rocked Maya's stomach. "Not looking like that you aren't. Take a shower and put on some fresh clothes, and then we can talk. *Capeesh?*"

Taylor glared at her and twisted her mouth in indignation, but when she turned to look into the mirror attached to the motel dresser her eyes widened. "Holy shit, I look like warmed over death. Yeah, I definitely can't go out like this. I have a rep to maintain."

"I bet you do," Maya replied with a chuckle. "The bathroom is all yours."

Clear brown eyes glanced Maya's way as Taylor stood up and opened her suitcase to withdraw underwear and a toiletry bag. "And is it…uh…safe?"

Maya hadn't expected that question, so it took her a moment to respond. "It's safe, at least so far as monsters are concerned. It isn't the bathroom that's haunted—it's me. You should be just fine."

Taylor turned her skeptical expression to the bathroom. After a few seconds she sighed and walked away from her bed. "If not, I'm gonna haunt your ass. Seriously. You will never know peace again. Just so we're clear."

"Crystal." Maya winked.

"Good. Now, if you'll excuse me, I have a miracle to perform. Beauty like this isn't easy."

Truly glad to have the young woman with her, Maya smiled and leaned against the pillows situated between her and the headboard. When the sound of falling water entered the room, she closed her eyes. Taylor took pride in her appearance, and she wasn't above taking an hour or more to make herself ready. Maya then drifted into a light, easy nap. Considering how much they had to do that day, she didn't feel badly about getting in a little more sleep.

Boden yawned and scratched his ass as he stood before the second floor bathroom toilet, emptying his bladder for what seemed like hours. When the last drops finally trickled out, he tucked himself back into tighty whities that weren't all that tighty or whitey anymore. He then gave his crooked face a quick check in the chipped mirror hanging over the bathroom's pedestal washbasin and decided his beard could wait a couple more days before he put a razor to it. His teeth were coated in morning gunk, but he would brush them only after he'd had breakfast first, just like Momma had taught him.

Ready to get the day started, he went back to his room and pulled clothes from the chest of drawers sitting on the wall opposite his bed. Just like his underwear, the rest of Boden's clothing had seen their best days years before. He even had a pair of overalls old enough to remember life before the new century. Boden didn't mind, though. He didn't care about fashion or style. If his clothes were in one piece–relatively speaking–that was all he needed.

Properly dressed, Boden left his room and took the stairs down to the ground floor. His steel-toed boots hit each riser with a heavy, resonant *thud*. Momma liked oatmeal for breakfast with a side of bacon cooked until it was a fly's fart from burnt, so when he hit the landing at the base of the stairs he turned left toward the kitchen, hopeful the bacon in the fridge was still good. He'd let bacon stay too long in the past, and the smell of it had almost been enough to put him off it for good.

Almost.

As he walked past the entryway leading to the living room he caught sight of Momma sitting on the couch, and his large feet nearly tripped over each other when he suddenly stopped. Even when she was younger, Momma had never been a morning person. He often wondered if that was why she'd practiced earth magic–so much of it had to do with the moon and stars. He, on the other hand, loved mornings. He enjoyed the peace, the stillness. So, when he found Momma already awake and dressed, it threw his mind for a loop.

The fact that she was wearing the same clothing he'd seen her in the day before didn't make it through the thick bone of his skull.

"Momma? Why you up so early?"

Boden didn't see Momma's face until he came around the couch, but when he did his blood turned to ice. Momma was furious. Tired, too, judging by the dark bags under her eyes, but furious all the same.

What have I done? he asked himself. *The day's barely started and I'm already in trouble. Oh no.*

"Up?" she replied, her eyes sliding over to glare up at him. "Boy, I ain't even gone to bed yet. I told you I had business to take care of."

"Yeah, but that was last night." The muscles in his shoulders and back relaxed a tiny bit. Whatever had her so upset didn't seem to have anything to do with him. That didn't mean he wouldn't still pay for it, though, if he stumbled into her ire accidentally.

Momma sighed and shook her head. "Yeah, well, things went a little longer than I thought they would. Damn bitch has got some power, I'll give her that."

"What damn bitch is that, Momma?"

"Don't use that language, boy," she replied, her eyes narrowing for a moment. "And don't you worry about her. If I catch sight of her again I'll make sure she gets what meddlin' bitches like her have comin' to 'em. But enough about that, we got work to do."

That brought Boden up short. "We do? But what about breakfast? I was about to make you some oats and bacon, just like you like."

Momma's eyes softened as she graced him with another glance. "You're a good boy, but we ain't got time for that. Not anymore. Today has to be the day."

All thought of breakfast disappeared from Boden's mind, replaced by sadness over what they were about to do. "Does it have to, Momma?"

Her nostrils flared when she stood from the couch. "Don't question me! I know my business. Today is the day I get what I've worked so hard for."

"Yes, Ma'am," he replied, his shoulders sagging. "I'll go get that finder stone and head ou—"

Momma shook her head. "Don't bother. I'm going with you. I don't know if it's you that's been screwing up, or that stone, but it don't matter now. Like they say, you want something done right, you do it yourself."

"Yes, Ma'am."

Momma checked her robe pockets, then grabbed her dark walking stick and headed for the front door. Unseen hands opened it for her when she tapped her stick on the hardwood floor. The world beyond their home was only just beginning to stir. Boden followed after her, hopeful the peace of the morning would last a little while longer, because something inside him said that by the end of the day, peace would be a long ago memory replaced with chaos, fear, and blood.

Chapter Nineteen

"So then down Saul Road for a mile," Maya said, her finger following a black line on a laminated map, "and then I turn left on Shelley?"

The convenience store clerk shook his head. "No, right. Turn right. That'll take you around a bend. You'll see a group of mobile homes clustered together. That's where their section of town starts."

"Gotcha, right." Maya grabbed a pen from the counter and made a note on the map. "I can't thank you enough. How much for the map?"

The clerk—a young guy with zits cratering his face and hair like limp copper wire—shook his head. "No charge. I live to serve, milady." He bowed his head like he was a squire meeting a noble woman.

Maya couldn't help but smile. "That's sweet. Thank you…" She looked at the badge sown onto the clerk's smock. "Darren. You've been a great help."

Darren smiled back at her, then swept the hair hanging in front of his face to the side in a grand gesture probably intended to be suave. "You're welcome. If you…uh…you know, if you need anything else or uh…might want someone to show you around town…I'll be here until three o'clock. It would be my pleasure."

The clerk's aura, which had been a neutral gray, suddenly infused with yellow and red like a sunrise painting the undersides of clouds as it broke into the sky. She was flattered. "I don't know if I'll need a personal escort, but if I do, I know right where to come. Thank you again."

Darren smiled as his bangs slid down over his eyes again. "No problem. Is there anything else I can help you with? Free smokes or candy or anything? The cameras are all busted, so you can take whatever you want. I don't care."

"Mmmm," Maya replied, the conversation now hitting

the inevitable awkward phase. "No, I'm good, but I appreciate the…uh…offer." She picked up the map and walked toward the entrance. "Maybe I'll see you around."

The door chimed as Darren said, "I hope so."

Maya gave him one last smile before returning to her Trailblazer. Taylor sat in the driver's seat. Maya got in next to her, locked her seatbelt, and handed the map over.

"The guy inside said if we follow the directions I marked down, we should get where we're going in about ten minutes."

Taylor activated her phone's map app and compared it to the laminated one in her hand. After a few seconds she nodded and put her phone into the cup holder beside her seat, backed out of the convenience store parking lot, and headed for Saul Road.

"You didn't get any snacks?" the young woman asked. "No drinks or candy?"

Maya burped and tasted maple syrup. "How can you be hungry after that stack of pancakes you just devoured?"

Taylor echoed Maya's burp, but with more bass in it. "That was just first breakfast. I'm talking about second breakfast."

"If only we all had your metabolism," Maya replied, more than a little jealousy slipping into her voice. "And you're not a hobbit, so you don't get second breakfast. Now look out, there are kids ahead."

A few blocks down the road swarmed with kids, as well as yellow buses and a dozen minivans. A street sign notified them that they were entering a school zone. Taylor raised her foot off the gas and coasted to a slow roll. More than a few parents stared at them through narrowed eyes.

"I'm glad I don't have to do that anymore." Taylor pointed at the kids gathered before school's main entrance.

Maya opened her mouth to offer a sarcastic reply, but as she looked around her eyes passed over a large man standing next to a small woman dressed in dark clothes. It was a fleeting glance, and her conscious mind was already forgetting what she'd seen, but a deeper part of her went cold and tried to hold onto the sight.

I saw something, she told herself. *I didn't, but I did.*

"Hey, do you see those…um…?" she asked, pointing over her shoulder even as she began forgetting them again.

"See who?" Taylor followed Maya's gesture. "All I see are trees."

"Yeah, me too," Maya replied, but that didn't feel right. It didn't feel exactly wrong either, though. She started to turn and take another look, but a sudden pain shot through her head like an ice pick, and the end of her nose suddenly felt wet. She brushed her fingers across her nostrils and they came away bloody.

As if sensing she was being watched, the small, dark woman turned her head and stared directly at Maya. When their eyes made contact, the pain in Maya's head intensified, and suddenly the dark woman turned into a giant raven, her black wings spread wide. Maya felt drawn into the darkness, compelled to fall in and never stop.

"Oh my god!" Taylor said. "Your nose! You're bleeding all over yourself!"

Maya heard the young woman speak, heard her words, but they barely registered. Her vision swam before her, her head was as light as a balloon, and nothing made sense. As she swayed in her seat, Taylor pulled over and held a wad of fast food napkins against Maya's nose. The smell of french fries still clung to the paper. The wad was so large it obscured her vision, so she closed her eyes and sank into her seat.

After a few moments Taylor pulled the napkins away. They were soaked with blood. Maya looked for the two figures now that she could see again, but they were gone.

"So I'll assume this isn't a normal nosebleed," Taylor said as she folded the napkins over and pressed the clean side against Maya's nostrils.

Maya grunted, blood trickling down her throat. "No."

"Yesterday's fun continues then. Anything to do with those people you thought you saw?"

"I… Fuck, I don't know. I don't seem to know anything anymore."

"So you're not sure you saw what you saw?" Taylor asked as if she was questioning a lunatic.

Maya gave her a scowl. "No. And don't look at me like I'm crazy."

"Well, we can either drive around looking for them, or we can keep on going like we were. You tell me."

Maya thought about both options, weighing their merits, but in the end it wasn't a choice at all. "I hate feeling so unsure. Let's… Let's just keep going. The universe could end up leading us right where we need to be."

"Sounds hokey to me," Taylor replied with a grin as she shifted the Trailblazer into D and pulled away.

Minutes before, Estera watched the children approach like a shark eyeing a school of fish. Her fingers twitched, pulling at her robe and brushing her unruly hair back. Somewhere amongst them was The One, her first step to immortality, and she could barely refrain from diving into their midst.

"Sense anything yet, Momma?" Boden asked, his shadow falling over her.

Holding back a sigh, Estera shook her head. "If I had, you'd know it already."

Boden sniffed and shuffled his giant feet. "Yes, Momma."

"Now be quiet." Estera resumed her scanning of the school children. The spell she'd cast wove its way through the gathered children, sniffing amongst them like a bloodhound. For many long minutes she felt the spell move this way and that, touching child after child before moving on. Suddenly she felt a tingle at the back of her neck. The search spell had caught a scent.

A dark smile slowly spread across Estera's face, her feral grin full of crooked teeth. She prepared herself to cast another spell, one that would draw the child out, but before she could get through the first incantation pain radiated through her body as if someone had punched her in the gut. She nearly doubled over, but then she watched in fascinated horror as her misdirection spell waivered.

Has my enemy found me? she wondered as she rubbed her temples. *So soon?*

She pulled the hood of her robe down and turned her eyes from the school to the area around her. It only took a few seconds for her to spot the Trailblazer and the black woman looking around like a security camera on high alert. As soon as her sight fell on the woman, she locked eyes with Estera. Sparks practically flew between them.

Not wanting to be caught off guard again, Estera held out her right hand with her index finger and pinky held high while her thumb held her middle and ring fingers against her palm. "Pain, interloper," she hissed as she directed her gesture at the black woman. "Pain!" Dark energy swept from Estera to the Trailblazer, and a second later she felt it hit its mark. The Evil Eye was an old spell, but it still worked. The black woman jerked away from the window and put her hands to her head.

"It's time to go," Estera said with a wave to her son.

"It is? But we don't have the girl yet, Momma."

Irritation clawed up Estera's back. "Like I don't know that! I didn't say we were giving up, just that it's time to get away from here. My enemy is nearby, and I don't have the strength to spare for a full-on fight. We withdraw…for now."

Boden stepped in behind Estera and the two backed into the wooded trail they'd taken to the school. "When we gonna deal with this enemy you keep talking about?"

Estera ducked under a low branch and then reached into one of her robe pockets. After a few seconds her fingers closed on cold metal. She took it out and eyed the badge closely. BOWENS was etched on it in precise letters.

"Oh, we don't need to waste our time on her," she said, her hold on the badge tight. "The authorities will deal with her." She pulled the badge to her face and whispered words to it, then ran her thumb around it in a clockwork motion. When it grew warm in her hand, she knew her spell had taken effect. In the dark recess of her hood, Estera smiled. Her path to immortality would now be problem-free.

Chapter Twenty

"I think it's just around this bend." Taylor steered the Trailblazer around a cluster of trees. "Yep, there it is. Look."

Maya looked up from her notebook, her tight handwriting filling line after line with notes about what they'd discovered. Sure enough, a group of mobile homes greeted them as they rounded the trees, just like the convenience store clerk had said. The homes looked nicer than she would have thought–she scolded herself for assuming the worst–and the cars parked in front of them were nice too, if a bit gaudy with flashy colors and shiny chrome bits everywhere.

"Uh oh," Taylor said. "Looks like we have some trouble."

Before Maya could ask what kind of trouble and where, her searching eyes landed on a large group of men, one half facing off against the other, arms gesturing wildly on both sides. Their collected auras were a seething black mass.

Taylor slowed down until the SUV was nearly at a stop. "So, do you want me to get closer, or should we go? In case it wasn't clear by now, I'm a lover, not a fighter."

Maya chuckled. "I'm not much for fighting either, but my gut tells me this is where we should be. There are answers here, I know it. Just... keep driving slowly, and once we're past them pull off to the side of the road and park."

"I hope you're reading your gut right then," Taylor said, her eyes focused on the arguing group of men ahead, "and not misinterpreting Taco Bell indigestion." The young woman offered up a burp as an example.

For all Maya knew, Taylor could be right. Her intuition was strong, and usually correct, but the power of double-decker tacos should never be underestimated. Still, even from as far away as they were, Maya sensed something strange about the men, something off, and if she played the situation correctly they might lead her straight to the person she was searching for.

"I hope not either. Now drive, my young apprentice, and be mindful."

When Taylor laughed, Maya smiled to herself. Tension hung thick in the air, and she felt like a bow being drawn across taut strings that could snap at any moment. Laughter lightened the mood, and for that, Maya was grateful.

Deputy Fuller sat across from Sheriff Bowens in his office, staring at a man he'd known for years, yet he felt like the man opposite him was a stranger. Gone was the fire that often lit his eyes like an internal furnace, gone was his ornery energy, and in their place was a person who seemed…empty. It was as though a vampire came along and drained the sheriff dry of everything that made him who he was, leaving him a shadow, a wraith.

What happened to you? Jimmy asked himself.

"Are you listening to me, Deputy?"

The question brought Jimmy out of the daze he hadn't known he'd fallen into. He coughed and straightened up in his chair. "Yes, Sheriff, of course. Sorry. It's…uh, a bit warm in here."

Bowens frowned, his moustache brushing his nostrils. "It's going to get a lot warmer if we don't increase our citation revenue. That's why I need you out there on the road catching speeders instead of going off on unapproved stakeouts."

"Understood, sir." Jimmy wanted to defend his actions, but he knew the sheriff didn't want to hear a word about it, and all he'd do by pushing things was lose himself a job.

Bowens nodded and patted his desktop, his way of closing out the conversation. "Glad to hear it. Now get on out—"

The sheriff's mouth closed in mid-sentence, and his eyes

took on a thousand-yard stare. He didn't move a muscle.

"Sheriff?" Jimmy asked. When Bowens didn't respond, he held up his hand and waved it in front of the sheriff's face. Nothing happened.

"Come on, Sheriff, wake up now." He tried waving again, and when that didn't get a reaction he tapped on the sheriff's hands, softly at first but then escalating to heavy knuckle thumps. Again, nothing happened.

Jimmy stood up to come around the sheriff's desk, but before he could take a step the sheriff spoke, his words soft, almost a whisper, as if said as if in a dream. "Yes, of course. Deal with the enemy. I can do that. Yes. Immediately. Very good."

A few seconds after he finished speaking, the sheriff shook his head and looked around as if he was lost. Jimmy could see Bowens working to remember the last few minutes, and when he did, he looked up at his deputy with an angry expression. "What are you still doing here? Get going! Find us some lawbreakers before the bean counters in Columbia decide we're a waste of resources."

Jimmy nodded, but before he turned to leave he said, "Are you okay, Sheriff? You seemed like your mind went somewhere far away for a minute there."

Bowens frowned again as he rose from his chair. "Don't you worry about me, Jimmy. Worry about yourself. Now get going. Meanwhile I have business of my own to deal with." The sheriff reached for his gun belt and hat, both items hanging from the coat rack behind his desk."

"You expecting trouble?" Jimmy had his hand on the office door knob.

Bowens stared at him with eyes like obsidian. "Every minute of the day, Jimmy."

Jimmy looked at the sheriff one last time before turning the knob and exiting. No, he wasn't the same man he used to be. Ever since the kidnappings started he'd changed, and for the worse. Something was definitely going on, something

Jimmy didn't have a clue about, and it irked him. He didn't like being in the dark. It was one of the reasons he'd become a police officer. Unfortunately there wasn't anything he could do about the sheriff without asking a lot of questions that would probably get him fired. Unless the sheriff or someone else wanted to let him in on what was going on, in the dark was where he had to stay.

"Stop here," Maya said as the Trailblazer slowly rolled past the group of arguing gypsy men. She rolled her window down as the wheels came to rest, and what had been muted voices suddenly became full on yelling.

"Oh that's bullshit!" one man yelled, his gelled hair glistening in the sun. Sequins outlined the shape of an ornate cross on his black shirt, each one winking brightly. "She's just an old woman who likes scaring people."

"Well she scared the hell out of me!" the man opposite him said. His hair was thinner and had gray in it, but he was tall and strapping.

A short man with his head shaved and tattoos all around his neck laughed. "That ain't hard to do, is it, Bobo?"

Auras that were already dark suddenly turned inky black, and Maya felt the oncoming violence like a tingling of the skin before a thunderstorm struck. Knowing it was foolish before she even moved, Maya opened her door and stepped out of the Trailblazer. Behind her Taylor cursed before shuffling to follow after her.

"Hey, hello?" Maya said, hoping she wasn't about to jump in a meat grinder. "I was hoping I could speak with you."

Taylor huffed as she stepped in next to her. "What the hell do you think you're doing?" the young woman whispered, a smile wide on her black lips.

Maya took her hand and gave it as reassuring a squeeze as she could manage, then let it go and stepped closer to the crowd of men, all of whom were looking at her like a green-skinned alien had dropped in their midst.

"Hi, my name is Maya Gallows." She tried to make eye contact with as many men as she could, a smile on her face that was pleasant without being too friendly. "I don't mean to intrude, but—"

"Then why the fuck are ya?" the man with the graying hair said, his aura dark and pulsing with red flashes. "I don't know who ya are, lady, and I really don't care. Get back in your car and get the fuck outta here. None of this concerns you."

His aura practically lashed out at her, dark tendrils laced with crimson, and it shocked her so much she nearly cried out. Never in her life had she seen an aura like that. Auras were supposed to be nothing more than psychic shadows, but somehow the man's aura had gained a life of its own. *That can't be good*, she thought with a mental grunt.

Ignoring her increasing desire to run, Maya kept her pleasant expression on her face and said, "Don't be so sure, sir. I'm a journalist looking into the kidnappings, and—"

"And you were told the gypsies had something to do with it," the younger man with gelled hair said. "For fuck's sake, when are the assholes in this town going to stop blaming us for every bad thing that happens to them?"

Maya waited for his aura to lash out as the older man's had, but his stayed around his body like it was supposed to.

"They're never gonna accept us, Sonny," the older man replied, his chest and neck flushed beneath his shirt. "Ever. And you know what? This time they might not be wrong."

A roar rolled through the men standing opposite him, the thundercloud of anger pervading them growing larger.

"Here we go again!" a faceless voice yelled.

"That old bitch ain't one of us!"

"Don't be her patsy, Bobo!"

Maya stepped closer to the older man, his aura whipping around like a tree in a storm. "Is your name Bobo?"

He turned dark eyes on her and sneered. "Yeah, what of

it?"

"What did you mean when you said they might be right?"

The younger gypsy barked out a merciless laugh. "He means she gave him a good scare, and now he's here with his tail between his legs telling us to leave her alone."

"She?" Maya asked, a gong ringing in the back of her mind as puzzle pieces shifted and began locking together. "She who?"

Bobo shook his head and opened his mouth to speak, but behind him several of the men started shoving each other, and one of them bumped into him, sending him falling in her direction. He was too big to stop on her own, but instinctively she reached out to catch his flailing arms.

That's when everything exploded.

As soon as her skin touched his, she felt plunged into chaos. His aura reached for her, wrapped tendrils around her, and her mind reeled at the attack. In them she felt anger, pain, and terror. Her sight went dark, and suddenly she saw a man on fire, felt flames growing inside her, but beyond that she saw an old woman cackling like something out of a horror movie, her skin wrinkled and gray yet her teeth bared like she wanted to eat everyone in front of her. Her hair was wild, and lightning crashed in her eyes as terrible energy swirled around her. She was the eye of the storm, the dreadful winds at her command. She had terrible power, power she took pleasure in using to hurt and control and kill. Maya felt tiny compared to the woman in Bobo's vision, a leaf torn apart by the storm.

And that was when she recognized the old woman. *She was the one standing by the school*, her racing mind said. *She's at the heart of everything!*

As if that recognition was a switch waiting to be flipped, Bobo pushed away from her and threw himself into the fight behind him. What had at first been a tussle between a few men had grown into a full brawl. Fists flew, feet kicked, and teeth bit. Taylor grabbed her arm, but before they could move the fight swirled around them, surrounding them. A fist came out of nowhere, hitting Maya on the right side of her face, and she fell to the ground with a ringing in her ears and terrible pain lighting up her entire body.

Suddenly a police siren wailed, the sound of it cutting through the clamour of fighting men. Maya had never been so thankful in her entire life.

Sheriff Bowens sat behind the wheel of his squad car, driving through the town, waving at citizens, stopping at all the appropriate corners and intersections, like a man going about his usual business. But he wasn't. The smile on his face was painted there, his hands pulled by invisible strings. The sheriff was as much a passenger in his body as he was in the car, but he didn't notice. She had seen to that. What little control he had was more than happy to sit back and go along. It hurt less that way.

As he neared Shelley Road, his subconscious stirred. He'd been here before. Oh yes, he'd been here before, more than once. He'd driven this same stretch of road just yesterday, as a matter of fact, and it hadn't gone very well for him. He'd left shaken, disturbed. And here he was again, but this time he came on a mission. He'd been sent...by her. The part of him that had given in took comfort in that, but the part that still remembered what it was to be an officer of the law took no comfort whatsoever. The two halves struggled as he turned around the bend. When the crowd of fighting men came into view, the lawman rested control. The other side, though, was still there, skulking in the dark recesses of his mind. So long as it stayed there, he would do his job.

With a flick of his hand Bowens turned on the lights atop his car and activated his siren. Normally that was enough to disperse a roughhouse crowd, reminding them they lived in a world of law and that the dispenser of that law was among them. Several of the gypsy men did just that, their heels and dirty backsides all he could see of them, but a dedicated group continued to punch and kick and yell. For them he had other incentives.

His bumper was ten feet from the crowd when he stopped, unlocked his shotgun, and opened his door. As soon as he was clear he pumped the gun once and sent a blast of buckshot booming into the sky. As thunder carried through the crowd, he was glad to see it did the trick. After a final few punches, everyone stood down and slowly backed away from each other. When they turned to look at him, the blank expressions on their faces sent a chill through his heart. They looked like zombies, mindless creatures out for nothing but blood. After a few moments, they shook their heads as a group and then cast their eyes around in shock.

"What in the hell?" Bobo asked, his chest and hands bloodied. "How… Sheriff?"

Seeing that the situation was under control, Bowens leaned the shotgun over his right shoulder and walked toward the men. The gravel crunched under his boots the way he wished these gypsy assholes' faces would. "I told you not to get into any trouble, now didn't I?"

Bobo stared around like a sleepwalker who'd just woken up in the middle of nowhere. He nodded in reply, his head moving slowly.

"Then why do I see all this shit going on? Do we have a different understanding of the word trouble?"

"No, I…" The older gypsy shook his head again, then looked at his hands. The way he reacted to the blood and busted knuckles was like he'd never seen them before. He turned this way and that, searching for something, until he inhaled sharply and said, "It was her. She did it." His finger pointed behind him, his hand unwavering.

Bowens stepped to the left a few feet. On the ground several yards away was that black woman who'd come into his office asking questions. When his eyes made contact with hers, his control slipped away so easily that he didn't realize he was being directed again.

"God Almighty," he said, his left thumb hitching onto his belt.

"It's true!" Bobo ran over to the sheriff, his face drawn and eyes wild. "She came here, and…wanted to ask questions…and then… She's hexed! She brought that woman's evil into our community. That damn wit–"

Bowens sighed as he swung his shotgun and hit Bobo across the back of the head. The gypsy dropped like a sack of dog shit. His friends gasped and instinctively came to his defense, but Bowens levelled his gun on them.

"Take one more step, any of you, and they'll be picking your brains out of the blackberry bushes for months. Now, by all rights I could have the lot of you thrown in jail right this minute, but I've got other fish to fry, so it's your lucky day. Pick up your boy here and take him on home, then get in your own homes and stay there. If I come by and see any of you goddamn gypsies outside your doors, I will shoot first and come up with excuses later. Am I understood?"

Bobo's friends nodded, their faces hard and dirty, but he could tell they knew they were getting off light. It took a couple minutes for all of them to file off, and while they did he looked at the woman…Maya, she'd said her name was. It seemed she'd been roughed up a bit since he'd last seen her. Her pretty face had several scratches on it, and a large bruise was already forming a lump next to her right eye. Her clothes were dirty, and her curly brown hair was a mess, but aside from that, she seemed okay.

"You're just going to let them go?" the woman's young friend asked as she stood up.

Bowens nodded. "Yep."

"But you're a sheriff, for fuck's sake! A…a man of the law! You should be arresting them!"

Already tired of hearing the young girl talk, he poked her in the chest with the barrel of his shotgun and said,

"Miss, you'd do well to shut the fuck up right now. This ain't your business. Now I'd suggest you get in that SUV there and hightail it on out of here before I start to feel threatened and have to blow you away in self defense. I'll only say it once. Go."

The girl glared at him, and then bent down to get her friend.

"Ah ah," Bowens told her, his gun swivelling toward her head. "Leave her."

A protest rose to the girl's lips, but before it could go any further Maya said, "It's okay, Taylor. Go on. This…isn't something you can help me with. Go back to the room and wait. Please."

Taylor looked at her friend, then looked at the sheriff, tears swimming in her wide eyes.

"Please, Taylor. Do it for me. I'll be fine. I promise."

The look on Taylor's face said she didn't believe her friend for a minute, but after a few mute seconds she sighed and walked away. She glared over her shoulder at him the entire way, but he didn't give a shit. All he wanted was for her to get in her vehicle and go.

"So are you going to arrest me, Sheriff?" Maya asked, still sitting on the ground.

He walked over to her, dropped to his haunches, and sneered. "I thought I'd kill you instead. Which would you prefer? A shotgun to the face? Or maybe you'd like a pistol shot to the back of your head? Either way means the same to me. You've made enough trouble around here."

"I'm not the one making trouble," she replied.

She reached out toward him with a shaky hand, and he started to move away before realizing there wasn't anything she could do to him. He had two firearms with him and years of experience in dealing out justice. All she had was a pretty face, and hell, it wasn't even that pretty anymore with the knicks and bruises. If she thought her gentle touch could persuade him to change his mind, let her try.

Her fingers brushed the tips of his boots, and she stared at him as if she expected him to react somehow. He laughed, but after a minute the laughter died and a cool breeze blew past him, taking some of the stuffing in his head with it.

"You're a good man, Sheriff," she said, her words strangely distorted. "I know it, deep down. You're a good man, and no one can take that away from you."

Warmth touched his cheeks and curled around his heart. "I am?"

She nodded, her exotic blue eyes staring into his. "Absolutely. Good and true. Like Marshal Dylan."

Yeah, he thought. *I am good. One of the heroes. So then why was I going to shoot her? That…that doesn't make any damn sense. Still, I do have a job to do.*

"Like Dylan, yeah." His knees cracked like old wood burning in a fireplace as he stood up. "I guess I was letting the excitement of the moment get the better of me. That doesn't usually happen." He shook his head and took several deep breaths.

"So does that mean I can go?" the woman asked, her hand still on his boot.

He backed away from her, and as he lost contact with her some of the earlier darkness crept back in, but not as far as before. "No, Ma'am. I still have to take you in. You started a fight, after all. Can't let rabble-rousers wander the streets."

Maya looked down at the ground while using the back of her arm to wipe her lips clear of blood. When she looked back up at him she peered intently into his eyes. He could almost feel her in his head, rummaging around, and he nearly let the black take over again when she gave him a lopsided smile and nodded. "I guess it could be worse."

"That's a good girl," he said, a little wobbly on his feet. "Now stand up slowly and put your hands behind your back."

She sighed but did as instructed. Metal cuffs locked

around her wrists seconds later. He put his hand on her shoulder to guide her to his car, and as his hand settled on her skin, he felt another gust of that cool wind, and again he felt more himself. By the time he had the back door of his car open and was helping her in, he wondered what in the hell he was even doing. Nothing made sense.

"It's okay, Sheriff," she said as she settled on the lumpy bench seat, her arms behind her back and her head hung low. "It's not your fault."

At first he wanted to laugh, but then he ducked down and looked at her. "Are you sure?"

She nodded, her thick, dirty hair bouncing against her cheeks. There was a great depth of sadness in her eyes, but he didn't know if that was for him, or for herself.

Wishing he understood what any of it meant, Bowens shut the door and then slid behind the wheel. After locking the shotgun in place, he headed back the way he'd come. Lots of faces looked out at him through lots of windows, all of them appearing as confused as he was. In the rearview he looked at Maya. Part of him still wanted to pull over and empty a magazine into her chest, but at the moment most of him just wanted to go home and go to bed.

Maybe I'll wake up and this will all have been a dream. That would be nice. Everything will be back to the way it used to be, and none of this weird shit will have ever happened.

He gave Maya one last look in the mirror, even going so far as to smile at her, but she didn't smile back. Instead she shrugged and turned to look out the window next to her.

Oh yeah. That would be great.

Chapter Twenty-One

The sound of children playing reminded Boden of the one and only time he'd been to the ocean. The crashing waves, the birds wheeling in the sky crying out to each other and diving for bits of food thrown to them from the beach. He'd loved the feel of the salt in the air and the wet sand between his knobby toes. In a life that hadn't known very many pleasures, it was a memory he cherished.

And here was the sound again, this time coming from children as they played and jumped and threw themselves down slides, swung on ropes. They sounded just as carefree as the seagulls, just as wild. But unlike the birds, these children were hunted, and the predator waiting to devour them stood by his side in the treeline.

"Oh, look at these little morsels," Momma said, her withered hands curled around her walking stick in a ravenous clutch. "One of them will do nicely. Very nicely indeed."

Boden hated hearing his Momma speak like that. They were children, not food or something to be consumed. He understood what Momma needed, and because of his love for her he would do everything he could to help her, but that didn't mean he liked it. And he didn't.

"They look so happy," he said aloud, intending the words mostly for himself.

Momma coughed, the sound full of snot. "Little lives with little purpose. Through me, though, one of them will find the greatest meaning of all."

Hoping she was right, Boden shook off his misgivings as best he could and turned his eyes back toward the playing children. Dozens ran hither and yon, most of them in groups, but some were off by themselves. Those he feared for most, especially the girls. But, scattered amongst the children were teachers, each one watching the little ones around them with an especially cautious eye.

"Damn their suspicion," Momma said, noting the same thing. "I suppose it's what I deserve for not getting the child personally from the start. Still, this will require the use of more magic than I was planning on, and my old body can't do what it used to. Nothing to be done about it though."

Boden watched as Momma removed several items from the pockets of her robe–shiny dust that looked like silver powder, tufts of fur, and a small, white feather–and held them between her cupped hands as she whispered strange words over them, the sound of which set his teeth on edge. After several seconds, a dim light shimmered through her fingers. She then plucked a hair from her head and dropped it into the small, glowing ball. As soon as the hair disappeared, so did the light, but he noted a faint glimmering trail lead away from her when Momma waved her hand toward the playground.

"This shouldn't take long," she said, her eyes seeing what his could not. Her head turned left to right, right to left, and back again. After a few minutes, she stopped and smiled. "And there…she…is."

Boden followed Momma's gaze to a solitary girl sitting on a plastic horse perched atop a giant spring. He gasped at how much she looked like Momma. Same long, dark hair, same sharp cheekbones, same sunken brown eyes. They weren't mirror images, but the resemblance was closer than with any of the previous children.

"What a pretty thing she is, too." A toothy grin spread across Momma's weathered face as she reached back into the folds of her robe. This time she pulled out a small, blue, oval, clay object. A tiny mouthpiece sprang from one end of it, and several holes dotted the top, with various markings etched into the hard blue glaze covering it. "Now let's bring her to us."

Momma brought the instrument to her lips and blew gently into the mouthpiece. A bright note vibrated through the air, but when her fingers fell across the holes and moved up and down, the tiny flute went silent, though the hairs on the back of Boden's neck rose as if charmed to life. On the playground, the young girl looked up sharply.

Unfortunately for Momma, so did a nearby teacher.

"Zoe!" the woman shouted to the girl on the horse, her plaid skirt flapping in the breeze. She put a hand on her head to keep her pinned hair from catching the wind too and pulling apart. "Come on, sweetie! The bell's about to—"

As if that was its cue, a loud clanging berated the air, and as one the children all turned and pelted toward the school. Zoe was slower to move, her attention focused instead on the trees bordering the playground.

"Come along, Zoe!"

The teacher looked expectantly at the girl until she turned to face her and nodded.

"Okay, Mrs. Henley! I'm coming!" Zoe got down from the horse and skipped toward the distant entrance door her fellow students filed through.

Mrs. Henley nodded, then turned to go the same direction.

Momma hissed and raised her tiny flute. "It's now or never."

Again a sharp note slipped into the wind, and again the girl turned as if called. When the flute went silent despite Momma's fingers moving and lungs blowing, Zoe changed direction and skipped toward the trees. Less than a minute later she stood before Boden and Momma, her face slack and eyes droopy.

"Oh, yes," Momma said, her thin fingers brushing the girl's hair behind her ears. "There's power in this one. She will do perfectly. Pick her up, boy, and…"

Zoe was already cradled in his arms when Momma's voice trailed off. "Something wrong, Momma?"

"Of course there is," she replied with a hiss. "Trouble is all I seem to have lately. Damn sheriff seems to be slipping the leash. This should fix him up. If not I'm just going to kill him and be done with it. With sweet Zoe here, our time in this town is just about over with anyway. Now give me a minute."

Momma dug around the collar of her robe for a moment, eventually pulling out a shiny metal badge hanging from a leather string. After making a small cut on her palm with one of her jagged fingernails she spread blood across the badge in a bright red swath. She then spit on it and used her thumb to spread the mixture until the badge was covered in pink wetness. Waving her uncut hand over it, she said, "*Efectua licitare meu.*" A sickly green glow briefly overtook the badge, but then the glow faded, and with the glow also went the blood and spit. The badge looked brand new.

"That should hold him," Momma said as she tucked the badge away beneath her robe again. "If it doesn't, his wife will be a widow soon enough. Now let's go. There's lots more work to do."

Hating what he did even as he did it, Boden followed Momma away from the school. In the distance behind them, Mrs. Henley called out in terrified confusion as another young girl disappeared.

Maya's heart beat like a rabbit chased by relentless hounds, but that didn't stop her from being surprised at how close the interrogation room the sheriff put her in resembled the rooms she'd seen on endless TV shows and movies. Flat gray walls broken only by a door on one wall and a wide mirror on another surrounded her, with a camera in the upper corner facing her and another recording the back of her head. There was even a metal handle on the table in front of her for cuffs to be slipped through, presumably if she got rowdy. She felt like she was on a Hollywood stage, but the man glaring at her from the other side of the table was entirely real, as was her danger.

"So, you're an investigator," the sheriff said, his eyes as dark as the aura curled around him. "But you don't work for any agency, and you don't have a P.I. license."

Maya sighed, tired of answering questions that had nothing to do what was really going on. "No, I'm a journalist. Investigating is just part of what that entails."

"Uh huh." Bowens glanced at the open notepad on the table, but there wasn't anything written on it. It was as though questioning her was simply going through the motions. "And who do you write for?"

"Myself. I'm a blogger."

"So you're not even freelance? You just write for yourself? Can't pay much."

"Unfortunately not. Not yet anyway."

"And is that why you're here? You looking for a payday?"

The venom with which the question was asked took Maya aback. Every word he spoke made his dark aura twitch, the usually smooth energy field agitated and getting more so with each moment.

"I'm not sure what you mean."

"Of course you do. You came to this town looking to make a buck off the pain and sorrow of the poor parents who've lost their children. How do you live with yourself?"

By the time the sheriff finished speaking, his aura was riled up like a ball of snakes, each black tendril snapping at her. She was reminded of the older gypsy from earlier, and again was shocked at how the auras of these men reacted to her. Hoping to break through to the man buried in the blackness, she leaned against the table and stared him in the eyes, willing her mind to reach out to his. The darkness fought her, its energy like a hurricane blowing against her, but she pressed on, pushing and pushing to break through.

"What are you doing?" the sheriff asked, his brown face ashen. "Answer the question."

She ignored his words and kept her psychic self pressing

forward. The harder she pushed, the more his brown face drained of color. Even his short black hair turned gray along his brow. But even so, she felt the wall between them crack, and she knew if she worked harder that crack would widen until he was free of the dark influence of that strange, little woman. Using all the strength she had, she gritted her teeth and pushed ahead, imagining she was a battering ram. But, as she slammed her mind against his defenses, a sudden burst of black energy filled the aether, repelling her attack and nearly sending her backward in her chair. Bowens jerked on the other side of the table, his head thrown back and hands twitching.

"Sheriff, are you okay?" she asked, so unsure of what was happening.

When his head lolled back to face her, blood dripped from both his nostrils. Without a word he took a handkerchief from his back pocket and held it to his nose, then got up and exited the room. The look in his eyes, though, was pure hatred. The door locked automatically behind him with a loud *click*.

Unsure if she'd made matters better or worse, Maya hung her head and waited for what came next. With her arms stiff cuffed and the room locked, there was nothing else she could do.

Deputy Jimmy was ready to pull the hair out of his already thinning head. He liked order and consistency, to the point where like no longer applied and it became a need. It was one of the reasons he joined law enforcement. Laws were there for order, to keep society functioning properly, and when someone tried to bring chaos to that order, he devoted every ounce of himself to putting them away so that order could resume once more. He expected that same love of order in the people he worked with, that same level of consistency, but Sheriff Bowens was actively wrecking all of that for him, and it drove the deputy mad.

"Okay, I know the sheriff's been a little off lately," Deputy Harold Dunn said as he wiped barbeque sauce from his mouth, "but this is nuts. Do you have any idea who that was he rushed into the interrogation room? And why?"

Jimmy nodded, for once too flustered by other things to be bothered by Dunn's slovenly ways. "Her name is Maya. She was in here yesterday. Journalist I think. She sat with the sheriff in his office for a bit. When she left I didn't figure I'd be seeing her again."

"Journalist?" Dunn picked up a plastic cup of iced tea and took a long swallow. Condensation dripped from it onto his shirt like a light Spring shower. "What, is someone outside this town finally interested in these kidnappings?"

"Could be," Jimmy replied. "I didn't catch much."

Dunn laughed as he used his napkin to clean off his cup, then used the moistened bit of paper to scrub his fingers clean. "Yeah, probably too busy tripping over your own tongue to ask many questions." He gave Jimmy an exaggerated wink. "I'll give it to you, she's a looker, no question about it, even with that shiner. Still, that begs even more questions, such as who gave it to her."

Jimmy could only agree. He had questions aplenty, and the drought of answers irritated him terribly. *I have half a mind to go up to Sheriff Bowens and demand to know what's going on*, he thought. *And dammit, I think I will, just as soon as—*

The door to the interrogation room burst open, interrupting him in mid thought. Through it stormed the sheriff with one hand held up to his face and…

"Was his nose bleeding?" Dunn asked, the voice of the obvious.

"Looked like it."

"Christ on a cracker. Maybe she popped him. Sad to say, but that would be a hoot."

Jimmy wasn't sure about all that, but he did know one thing—he wanted answers. His training told him to go right and follow Bowens into the bathroom to get them, but his gut told him to go left and talk to the woman in Interrogation Room 1 while he had the chance. After a brief internal battle, he stood up and turned left.

Maya felt tears heat up the backs of her eyes. She was confused, scared, helpless, and certain that terrible things were happening in the town just outside the Sheriff's Department building. Crying seemed like the only sensible thing to do given those circumstances, but she refused. No one–not the sheriff nor the old witch pulling his strings– would get the satisfaction of seeing her break down. Bad enough her nose had started to run and she couldn't wipe it.

Me. Handcuffed. This is insane.

Just then the electronic lock to the room beeped and the door opened. Instead of seeing the sheriff and his rabid aura re-enter the room, she saw the lanky deputy from yesterday. He looked nearly as confused and flustered as she did. And, even better, his gray and red aura was behaving normally. As soon as he was through the threshold, he closed the door and leaned over the table toward her.

"I'm sorry, I don't remember your name, but I need some answers, and for some reason I feel like you're the only person who can give them to me. So…please tell me what the hell is going on."

Relief washed over Maya, and for a moment it made her lightheaded. "Finally! Someone who isn't under the influence of that bitch."

"Influence of…who?"

Knowing she had to speak quickly, Maya said, "Listen, there isn't a lot of time. I know who has been kidnapping those children. It's an old woman, wears dark robes, has a walking stick of some kind. And a guy was with her! Had to be nearly twice as tall as she was. He reminded me of Sloth from The Goonies."

The deputy held up a hand, stopping her before she could keep talking. "Woah, wait a minute. How do you know this? What evidence do you have?"

"I saw them," Maya replied, alarms going off in her head like a bank robbery. "They were there near the school. And she's come at me before! First when I drove into town, and then a couple more times, but those she came at me through other people, like the sheriff and the gypsy guy. Bobo I think his name was. She wants these kids for some sinister purpose, and I think if we don't move fast enough another little girl is going to die."

The deputy gave her a puzzled look, even going so far as to tilt his head like a dog seeing something it didn't understand, but there was also recognition in his eyes, an understanding, even if it was limited. "Okay, I know who Bobo is—every person in this office does—and I think I might remember the other two you mention, especially Sloth, but what do you mean she attacked you? And through the sheriff? You're not making much sense."

"Deputy, if we had the time to go into it, I'd love nothing better than to explain who I am and what I do, but we don't. You probably wouldn't believe me if I did. All I can ask is that you get out there and look for that woman. She needs another child, and she's going to get one. You have to stop her."

For a moment the deputy's face looked pained, as if he didn't know what to do and the indecision was killing him, but after several agonizing heartbeats he nodded. "Okay, I'll go take a look."

A thought suddenly struck Maya square in the forehead, but she knew to voice it would only complicate matters, so instead she simply held her hand out as far as the metal restraints allowed and put her most thankful expression on her face. "I can't thank you enough, James."

He looked down at her offered hand, the shiny cuffs so bright against her skin, and after half a second's worth of thought took it and gave it a squeeze.

Without warning him, Maya clutched his hand and

pulled him close. Unprepared, the deputy leaned over quickly until his face was mere inches from hers, and she stared into his eyes with all her will. "Find her, Deputy. See her. Don't be fooled by her tricks. *See* her." Her communication went beyond mere words, though. Using her developing psychic abilities, she planted in his mind the memory she had of the woman and her hulking son. Along with that she tried something new–implanting some of her psychic vision in him so that the witch's aversion spell wouldn't work on him. She had no idea if she succeeded with any of it, but she hoped like hell she did as she released his hand.

"Hey!" he said as he jerked away and stood up. "I can hear you from here, and I get it. I'm leaving right now."

Maya exhaled heavily and nodded. "Okay, yes, please. Again, thank you."

Suddenly the door beeped again, and when it opened Sheriff Bowens appeared, his face clear of blood but his expression one of surprise at finding the deputy in the room.

"What in the hell are you doing, Jimmy?" he asked, his aura still black and writhing, but now pulled back to encase him in darkness.

The deputy turned sharply. "Sorry, Sheriff. I…uh… I thought I heard something strange, and I came to investigate. Everything's fine though."

"Good, now get the hell out of here." The sheriff jerked his thumb at the door.

Jimmy gave his superior a "Yes, sir" nod and headed for the door. As he went past the sheriff he looked back over his shoulder at Maya and winked.

Once the deputy was gone, Bowens glared down at Maya. "And you, get up. You're going to a holding cell."

"So I'm under arrest?" Maya asked, daring his wrath. "For what?"

"For whatever I say." Bowens's nostrils flared as he reached down and grabbed her by the upper arm. "Keep your mouth shut or I'll just put you under the jail rather than in it and save myself further trouble."

Maya wanted to jerk away from the sheriff's touch. He felt slimy, corrupted. She knew, though, that the line separating him from fully becoming the witch's puppet was a fine one, so she let him lead her out of the room without another word. She'd done all she could. Now she would have to wait.

Chapter Twenty-Two

Jimmy couldn't have picked a worse time to go looking for two people with a kid. School had let out just minutes before he got in his car, so now the streets were full of children and parents heading home every which way, and with the weather turning colder, most of them were bundled up and hunched over.

Talk about a needle in a haystack, he thought with a sigh.

Figuring the best place to start was the last location that old gypsy woman and her son were seen, he drove for the elementary school–the very heart of the storm. Making his way between buses and endless lines of minivans wasn't easy, but eventually he made a complete circuit of the building and grounds. For that effort he was rewarded with nothing.

Well, where do I go now? he asked himself. *Better yet, what am I even doing? What, I meet a pretty girl and suddenly I'm doing whatever she says? How stupid is that? There's no reason whatsoever to trust her. Yet I do. Guess that makes me the crazy one.*

Crazy or not, he did believe her, so he kept driving, steering on instinct rather than trying to come up with a logical route. Side street after side street he went, whim and fate turning his tires. The sun was cradled along the tree tops as he crept through the intersection of Cooley Road and Sigler Street. Jimmy glanced left, glanced right, and then wiped his head back to the left. At the far end of Cooley was a hobbled figure in dark clothes shuffling next to a man nearly twice her height. At first he hadn't noticed them, but somehow they'd registered enough to warrant a second look. Jimmy pulled a pair of binoculars from a case strapped to the passenger seat and aimed them at the retreating figures. A length of black hair fell from a small body held by the taller walker.

That's them! And dammit she was right, they've kidnapped

another child. This ends here and now.

Jimmy backed up, turned on his lights, and swivelled left. It only took seconds to catch up with the slowly walking couple. When he was within two car lengths he hit his siren. They stopped after a few halting steps but didn't turn around.

"Halt and face my vehicle," he said into his loudspeaker handset as he turned on the small spotlight secured to his car door and aimed it at their backs. The two stayed motionless. "I said turn around. Now."

After a few seconds the mother and son finally shuffled around. Jimmy opened his door and stepped out to stand behind it when he got a better look at who the tall man was holding. Sure enough, it was a young girl, her long dark hair falling over his arm. Her eyes were closed and she didn't move. He unbuttoned his holster and rested his right hand on the gun sitting snug inside it.

"Who's the girl?" he asked, subconsciously thickening his voice.

No answer came.

"Answer me! Who's the girl and why do you have her?"

For a moment silence reigned, but then the old woman tilted her head to look up at her son, and words passed between them he couldn't hear. After several seconds of that the hulking son turned back around and went on the way he'd been going before. Jimmy drew his gun and yelled, "Freeze!"

Sloth didn't freeze. He didn't even hesitate.

"I said freeze! Now! Or I *will* shoot you!"

The old woman, her face lost in the gathering shadows of late afternoon, tsked at him. "Deputy, I know you mean well, but don't threaten my boy."

Jimmy pulled back the hammer of his pistol and aimed it squarely at the man's swaying back. "It's not a threat. It's a promise. Take one more step and I will put you down!"

The man didn't stop, but his ancient mother stepped

over and placed herself between her son and Jimmy's gun. She then held out her hands, pinkies and thumbs extended with the others curled in while strange words dripped from her mouth. An odd chill suddenly overtook the deputy, turning his breath to fog.

"Turn around, Deputy," the old woman said. "Drive away, and I promise you won't remember a thing by the time you reach the end of the road. Keep that gun aimed at me, though, and it will be the end of you. *That* is a promise."

The defiance both people displayed stoked a fire in his belly, the heat of it burning away his chill. "Move, ma'am, or I will shoot you, too. Don't think I won't."

The old woman chuckled, her wrinkled face like a skull. Behind her, her son was at the end of the block, the child in his arms nearly gone from view.

Screw it. I gave them both ample warning. They forced my hand.

Regretting he had to do it, Jimmy checked his aim one last time and then pulled the trigger. He steeled himself for the expected blast of noise and lead, but instead all he got was a cold *click*.

The woman laughed with a sound like old leather cracking.

Jimmy pulled the slide on his gun, looking for a jammed bullet, but found nothing, so he readied the gun and pulled the trigger again. *Click*.

Now walking toward him, the old woman laughed even harder. He wanted to put his hands over his ears to block out the sound. Instead he tried to shoot a third time. *Click*.

"Screw this," he said to himself as he holstered the useless gun and pulled out his baton. When he looked up to face the old woman, she was no longer in front of him. He turned his head left to right, scanning the trees and ditches, but she was nowhere to be found. Suddenly a terrible burning pain filed his chest. When he looked down he saw a hand protruding from his sternum holding a still beating heart. Blood dripped from the hand and from the ragged hole it had punched through.

"I warned you, Deputy," a cold voice said behind him in a hiss. "Now you pay the price. On the bright side, your heart will give me the energy I need to finally deal with that bitch. I smell her stink all over you. She's why you're dying now, Deputy, but don't worry, I'll be dealing with her shortly. Now die."

Thankfully by the time the old woman jerked her hand back through his chest he'd lost all feeling in his body. He dropped to his knees, then fell over onto his side and bled the last of his life away. The last thing he heard was the sound of teeth tearing into wet meat. Then everything went black, and Deputy Jimmy Fuller passed into the final darkness.

The metal bench was as hard as a rock beneath Maya's butt, but aside from the concrete floor and stainless steel toilet there wasn't anywhere else to sit in the gloomy holding cell, so she sat and wondered how she was going to get out of her current predicament. Sadly she didn't have a lot of options. With the sheriff under the influence of that witch, there wasn't much chance she would be released or given a phone call, and the only person who knew where she was, was Taylor, not that the young woman could do anything about it. Her only hope was the deputy.

"Help me, Obi-Wan Kenobi," she whispered to herself.

A dark chuckle tumbled through the holding cell. "I don't know who that is," a craggy voice said, "but if you mean that deputy you sent after me and my boy, then prepare yourself for disappointment. He's dead."

The words seemed to come from everywhere and nowhere at once. Maya looked all around the cell, but it was empty save for her and the dust bunnies. Suddenly, impossibly, a figure stepped out of the shadows. It was the old witch, her furrowed face covered in gore, and in her red-stained hand was a chewed hunk of meat. Maya knew what it was immediately, and her gorge surged up her throat. Quickly she leaned over and vomited on the floor. More dark laughter shook the air.

"I guess I should thank you," the witch said. "It's been a long time since I tasted the heart of a strong young man. I'd forgotten just how delicious they are, and how full of energy. I feel so much better now."

Without thinking Maya leapt up from her seat, the cuffs holding her in place shattering into a million metal pieces. Part of her marvelled at the sudden display of power and wondered how she'd done it, but the rage created within her by the witch's words quickly pushed everything in her mind away. Maya extended her hands and ran toward the old crone, intent on choking the life from her flabby neck. She barely made it two steps before the witch clenched her empty hand into a fist and swept it downward. Maya felt invisible fingers grab her and shove her back onto the bench that ran the length of the cell.

"Why is it the young who always want to rush into death?" The witch chuckled as she popped the last bit of heart into her mouth, her blood-slicked lips smiling as she chewed. After a final swallow she waved her fingers around her face, and the streaks of blood disappeared. She did the same for her hands. Now no one would ever know she'd just made a meal of a human heart, and not just any, but that of a brave man who only wanted to make the world a better, more orderly place.

Maya would have vomited again if she'd had anything left in her stomach. "You goddamn monster."

The witch wagged a finger at her. "Sticks and stones, young lady. Then again I've been called a lot worse in my time, and by better. Besides, I didn't come to fight. Firstly, I came to thanks. I've got a long night ahead of me with powerful magic to wield, and that deputy you sent after me has added to my strength. So, thank you."

Maya struggled on the bench to get free, but the witch's

spell might as well have been titanium bands around her legs and it pinned her arms to her side. The only part of herself she could control was her head, so she snorted up a wad of phlegm and spat it at her. "Fuck you, bitch."

Standing in the shadows, the witch's aura had been impossible to see, but as Maya swore at her, writhing darkness exploded all around, filling nearly half the holding cell, vicious flashes of crimson swirling through it. The witch stormed away from the shadow and made her way directly to Maya, whom she slapped with the back of her withered hand. Fireworks exploded behind Maya's eyes from the force of the blow, and small cuts on her face and lips split opened, dribbling thin streams of blood.

"You're a fiery one, I'll give you that," the witch said as she licked the back of hand clean. "And that's good, because it means when I swallow your soul I'll gain that much more power."

"Is that why you kidnap little girls?" Maya asked with numb lips. "You like to hurt them too and then steal what little power they have?"

The witch laughed and shook her head. "Oh no no. I don't harm a hair on their precious heads. Just the opposite. Why would I damage them when it's their body I want? Their souls I try to lure out with the dolls so that I can then move my soul in. So far I've not found a vessel strong enough to accept me, but today I found just the one. She's perfect. Tonight I finally get to taste the immortality I've spent decades struggling to find."

Like tumblers in a lock, things fell into place in Maya's mind. "So that's your goal. You want to live forever, and you'll kill as many innocent children as you have to to make it happen. How pathetic."

The witch grabbed Maya's face in a cold, iron-like grip, her ragged nails biting into her skin. "Easy for you to say when you're young and healthy and pretty. Everything I have, I worked hard for, and when working wasn't enough I fought tooth and nail. I've spent decades collecting spells and books and relics. Decades! And why, just so my body can betray me when I've finally attained true power? No ma'am, not if I have anything to say about it. I plan on shaking the pillars of heaven, little missy. Someday the world will be mine, and I will dominate it for the rest of eternity."

"Oh Jesus," Maya replied, jerking her head back from the witch's grip. "What is it with you dark and scary types always wanting to rule the world? You're all just clichés. You make me sick."

Another backhand rocked Maya's head to the side, and then the witch took her head in both hands, her thin fingers were like snakes in her hair.

"Luckily for you I'm about to kill you, so you won't have to worry about it much longer. Now let's crack you open and see what's inside."

The pain that split Maya's head felt like the witch was literally tearing her skull apart. It was as if an axe was buried in the middle of her forehead. She screamed in pain and horror.

"Oh, yes! Cry out! Tell me how much this hurts."

Maya glared at the woman in front of her, and the grin that slithered across the witch's face was terrible. Old nails broke the skin of her face, and the witch licked every bit of blood from her hands. She shivered in pleasure.

"I've never tasted power like this. You surprise me. It's...ancient, buried in your blood like something out of time. It's primal, and now it's all mine."

Maya's throat was torn from screaming, and blood dripping down her forehead obscured her vision, but deep down a spark flashed in the dark, and strength she didn't know she had roared forth. Gritting her teeth, she glared at the witch and imagined a blast of light searing her wrinkled face off. No sooner was the image in her head than it was made manifest. For a brief moment the holding cell was filled with blinding light.

The witch clawed at her own face, as though hornets swarmed her, and staggered backward. After shaking her head for a moment, she rushed back at Maya and grabbed handfuls of hair. "How dare you! I hope you enjoyed that, because now I'm gonna make this hurt."

The witch reached into her robe, pulled out a knife that shimmered in the overhead lights, and reared back to maximize her swing. Maya, hoping to save her own life, dug down for the power she'd just used, hoping to knock the witch out, or at least wear her down, yet when she reached for the power she found nothing. But, as she panicked to find something–anything–a new power found her, and in her panic she took it. She suddenly felt invulnerable, as mighty as a god, and she giggled as she sent another bolt of power at the witch. But this time it wasn't a shimmering column of light; instead it was a beam so black it was beyond color, beyond understanding.

The witch flew backward with a scream. "What the hell are you?" she asked from her knees, smoke rising from her robes. She staggered to her feet, her dark eyes wide and mouth agape. "I've never felt anything like that."

Maya rose as well, her body humming with power. "It doesn't matter who or what I am, bitch. All that matters is I'm going to kill you and finally bring this town some peace. Now come and die."

Psychically reaching out, Maya felt her mind grasp the witch. The old woman was helpless for a moment, her feet sliding across the concrete floor, but then she uttered a series of incoherent words and Maya's telekinetic hold broke. The witch scuttled backward to the shadows from which she'd come.

"I don't need to know what you are," she said as darkness closed around her. "Soon I'll be in a new body, and my power will be at its fullest. After that I'm going to hunt you down, and the torture I'll put you through will be legendary. I'll draw every ounce of pain I can from you, drain every drop of blood, and when you're breathing your last breath I'll heal you and start all over again. This is far from over."

And with that she disappeared.

Maya, her chest heaving and her head swirling, growled for a moment, but then she threw back her head and laughed. The laughter didn't last long though, and as it tapered off, so did her newfound power. In the silence that followed, she wept.

Chapter Twenty-Three

It took all of Boden's will to not break into a run after Momma told him to go while she dealt with the cop. He'd feared that eventually the authorities would catch on to what they were doing, so when the car pulled up behind them with lights flashing and the megaphone squawking, for him it was just the other shoe finally dropping. But Momma said she would deal with it, and if anyone could, it was her.

Shadows grew long as he carried the newest girl home. He'd never seen her before, but gold letters dangled from a chain around her neck spelling ZOE. Up close, the resemblance to Momma was even more striking. She was an adorable little girl who weighed nothing in his arms, her eyes closed and brow untroubled.

Let this be it, he thought, a prayer to any god that might be listening. *Please let her be the final child we take. I don't know if I can do this again.*

After several twists and turns, Boden made it back to their house. Holding Zoe in one arm, he used the other to unlock the door and open it, then relock it once they were inside. The wooden stairs leading down to Momma's casting chamber groaned as he trundled down in his heavy boots. Her altar sat in the middle of the chamber like a massive, dead heart cut from black stone. Once the child was laid on top of it, he took twine from a shelf and secured her wrists together. As he held her ankles to secure those too, she stirred, so he wrapped the twine around as quickly as he could and then tied it all together. When he backed up and stood beyond her head to check his handy work, her eyes opened. Her expression went from serene to panicked within moments. She turned her head back and forth as if searched for something—anything—familiar. When she couldn't find any, tears spilled down her cheeks.

"Hello?" she said, her voice tiny and fragile. "Is anyone

there?"

At first he didn't respond. He hadn't when the previous children woke up and began crying out, but something about her compelled him to speak. "I'm here."

Zoe gasped and tilted her head up to look at him, and he dreaded her reaction because it was always the same. First she gasped, and then she whimpered, "Oh my God, what are you? Please don't hurt me."

"Ssshhhhhh, you're okay." He tried to make his voice soothing, but the little girl squirmed even harder on the altar. If she didn't watch out she would wiggle off and hurt herself. "Stop moving or you'll fall."

That brought the child up short, and she immediately became still. "Fall? Where am I? Where's my mommy? I'm scared."

A hard, cold lump formed in Boden's throat, and for a moment all he wanted to do was untie the little girl and tell her to run as fast as she could. But he didn't. As bad as he felt about what was going to happen to her, he loved Momma more, and Momma needed her.

She's counting on me, he thought, the weight of responsibility heavy on his shoulders.

"Just be quiet," he said, softening his voice as much as he could. "Please. It'll be over soon."

"Over?" Zoe wiggled again as she tried to free herself, but when she realized that was hopeless she slumped against the altar. "What are you going to do to me? Please don't hurt me. I never hurt anyone. I'm a good girl. Please, just let me go."

The scales in his heart that weighed his compassion against his responsibility slowly began to tip. He didn't know if it was her tears, or her pleading, or the fearful look in her eyes, but Boden suddenly felt less than sure about what they were doing. How much was a life worth if it cost so many more to keep it? He'd never asked himself that question before, but now he couldn't avoid it.

Before his mind could go more than a few steps down that road, though, the air swirled as if something quickly moved through it, and from one of the shadows in the stone basement Momma appeared. Her robe was dishevelled, as was her hair, but it was her eyes that caught his attention most. In them was something he'd never seen before.

Fear.

"Is she ready?" Momma asked, her words rushed as she went to one of her shelves and gathered the items she'd need for the spell to come.

"Who's that?" Zoe asked, her head whipping around again.

Boden nodded and stepped away from the girl. "She is, Momma. She's awake though, and cryin'."

Momma gave him a sour look when she approached the altar. "Let her cry all she wants. Don't matter now. You hear that, little girl? It's too late."

Zoe shrank within herself and looked away from Momma's baleful eyes. "Please let me go! Please! I haven't done anything."

Momma set her spell components on the altar, her movements quick and fluid from having cast it so many times already. "It's just the luck of the draw, little 'un. Now shut up and say whatever prayers you got. This won't take long."

After sprinkling ash on the painted pentagram on the floor that encircled the altar and lighting red candles that sat at each point of the star, Momma took up her knife and began shouting words Boden had heard before but still had no understanding of. He dreaded hearing them, though, because what came next was terrible.

Suddenly the air in the basement stirred, within seconds becoming a whirlwind with the altar and the child on top of it in the eye of the storm. Souls of the damned soon joined the storm, their cries of centuries' long torment a dark and chilling chorus. "Powers of the ancient realms, I call upon you! Polúmētis, rise from beneath your mountain and grant me your art!"

Dark light flashed from the pentagram casting circle on the floor. Momma nodded in satisfaction and then pulled out her ceremonial knife from a pocket in her robe. She set the sharp blade against her inner forearm.

"Goddess Hekate, I make this offering in your many names–Chthonia of the Underworld and Kleidouchos, Holder of the Keys. Please accept it and give me your blessing."

Momma slashed open her skin in a move too quick to see, and blood quickly dripped to the ground. She turned to the chalice and held her arm over it so her blood wouldn't be wasted on the floor. A small smile played across her face as the chalice filled and bubbled, though no fire burned beneath it. Once she drained enough of herself she waved her wolf bone wand over her arm and spoke in low grumbles. Within seconds the wound on her arm was closed, one more pale mark on a limb covered with them.

"Baphomet, Goat of Mendes, bless this child and make her ready, I beseech you." Momma grabbed a hunk of Zoe's long dark hair, cut some free, and dumped the strands into the boiling chalice. Nasty smelling smoke drifted up and was quickly caught by the spiraling wind. The hair was joined by cut swatches from the girl's clothing. From memory Boden knew what came next, and he closed his eyes so he wouldn't have to watch. The sound was bad enough.

"And now I call the witches' three–Abonde, the goddess; Mayfair, the Beautiful Pilgrim; Cernunnos, the Horned One. Guide my hand so I might find new life!"

Symbols on the walls and floor flashed so brightly Boden could see them through his lowered eye lids, and then Momma cried out in a terrible wail of agony. In his mind's eye Boden couldn't help but remember the sight of her thrusting her hands into her own chest, her flesh rent open by her ragged fingernails. He recalled the way her chest moved as her hand plunged into it and searched mercilessly for what she needed. He bit his lower lip and tried not to cry when he finally hear a loud *SNAP* as the needed bone broke free.

"Argh!" Momma screamed, her voice like a wounded animal.

When he opened his eyes, he watched her rise to her feet, her rib bone clutched greedily in her bloody hand. With the other hand she again wove her wand over the gaping wound and whispered. The wound closed, but the look of suffering on her face didn't waiver. After waiting a few seconds, she straightened up as best she could and dropped the rib into the chalice. With her wand in one hand and a shiny medal hanging from the other, she tilted her head back and shouted at the ceiling words he could never hope nor want to understand.

Zoe screamed, her voice joining the foul spirits swirling above her prone body. Sickening green and yellow light floated ghost-like through the air, and the ground shook hard enough to nearly send the chalice crashing down from the dark glass column it sat upon. Above them, the maelstrom of wind and souls picked up speed and spectral voices screamed.

Please let this be the last time we do this, Boden said to himself as he squeezed his eyes shut and put his gnarled hands over his ears. *Please... No more.*

Maya knew something was wrong, terribly wrong, but the exact nature eluded her no matter how hard she concentrated and tried to discern it from the aether. So she paced, back and forth, back and forth, measuring the holding cell by how many steps she took before having to turn around. The answer was twenty-two.

Suddenly the lights flickered and dimmed. Maya whirled around, eyeing every shadow. If the witch was back, she had to be ready for her. "Come on, you bitch," she said low in her throat. "Let's go."

Laughter like the flapping of vulture wings broke the silence. Maya spun to her right, her mind grasping desperately for psychic power, but there was none to be found. She was unarmed. Fortunately it wasn't the witch who laughed at her. Unfortunately it was something worse.

So, the Dark God said, the words issuing from a body made of smoke on the other side of the holding cell's bars. Dark wisps broke free, the beginnings of arms and legs. Seconds later the smoke evaporated, and Maya inhaled sharply when a mirror image of herself was revealed. It was a perfect replica, save for the blood red eyes and rows of razor teeth. *The person who stopped my rise now finds herself trapped in a cage. I'm insulted.*

Fear sent electric shocks throughout her body, but she tried to hide it, to not show the Dark God what he wanted to see. "Yeah, well, pardon me if I don't give a shit."

Fire turned the Dark God's eyes into glowing red spheres. *And then you were nearly murdered by the witch woman. If not for my interference, you would be dead this very moment. Perhaps some gratitude is in order.*

"Gratitude?" Maya approached the bars that separated her from the infernal doppelganger. A moment ago she was nearly on her knees in terror, but now anger kept her on her feet. "You invaded my mind, forced me to see terrible things, attacked innocent people, and you took control of me. And for all that you want me to be grateful? Fuck off and die already."

The Dark God laughed slowly. *It was you who first invaded my mind. You attacked me. You might be able to hide your hypocrisy from others, but you can't from me. I'm inside you. I know you better than you know yourself. You are no damsel in distress. And you are correct—I did take control of you. I had no other choice. You would have been destroyed by the witch had I not. By taking command of your body, I saved us both. And truly, you have to admit it. Not to me, but to yourself.*

Maya's nostrils flared, but an icy chill filled her stomach. "Admit what?"

Demael's glowing eyes smouldered as he stared straight into her soul. *That you enjoyed it.* His words came out in a hiss, a sizzle like blood falling on hot coals.

"I…" Righteous indignation filled Maya's chest, but even as she attempted to give it voice, she knew she couldn't. As much as she hated it, despised herself for it even, he was right. Part of her enjoyed it. The depths of his power had made her tremble, but using it to lash out at the witch had been pure pleasure. To say anything else would have been a lie. "Yes."

The Dark God moved to stand directly opposite Maya. She felt his closeness like a roaring furnace that warmed her skin, yet at any moment could reach out and burn her alive.

And now we do away with all pretences, Maya Gallows, blood of my blood. Let there be no more lies or refutations between us as we go forward. Power greater than any you've ever known is yours. All you need do now is take it.

Maya's hands shook and her heart quaked in her chest as she felt within herself a terrible desire to do just that.

Taylor sat on the edge of her bed at the Verdant Inn, her legs bouncing up and down like a jackrabbit as she stared a hole through her mobile phone.

"Ring!" she shouted at it. "Dammit, ring!"

But it didn't ring. It hadn't rung all afternoon. For the twentieth time she activated her smart phone's screen and made sure she was getting a signal. Four tiny black bars glared up at her, mocking her with their strong connectivity.

She contemplated calling Morgana, then considered Alan, but she didn't open her contact list for either.

What could they do? she asked herself. *Better yet, what do I even tell them? I don't know if she's under arrest, or just being questioned, or anything. This is insane!*

So she continued to sit and bounce her legs nervously,

hoping against hope Maya would call her and say everything was fine. But, when the sunlight streaming between curtain panels started to wane, she decided enough was enough.

"Fuck this. I don't care what she said, I'm going to get some answers."

Taylor grabbed the keys, made sure her wallet was in her back pocket, and left the room. The air outside had taken on a chill, but her worry already had her shaking. The drive to the sheriff's department felt like it took forever, and she'd had to turn around more than once when she steered down unfamiliar streets. By the time she made it to her destination, the sun was nearly gone from the sky.

The gray-haired receptionist was still sitting at the front desk when she walked in. Taylor headed straight for her.

"I need to talk to the sheriff," she said, not caring how her tone sounded.

The receptionist didn't reply. Instead she worked on a crossword puzzle.

Tired of everyone's shit, Taylor slapped both hands on the woman's desk and leaned over. "I'm sure that puzzle is really important work, but my friend was taken by the sheriff for no damn good reason, and I want to see her. If she's under arres–"

"Missy," the receptionist said as she slowly looked up and scowled at her over the rim of her bifocals, "I don't know who raised you, or how, but around here we keep a civil tongue in our heads, especially when speaking with elders. Do you understand me?"

The power of the woman's gaze made Taylor stand up and take a step back. "Yes, ma'am."

The older woman nodded. "Very good. Now, as for your friend, she's in a holding cell at the moment. If you want to know her status, have a seat over there and I will contact Sheriff Bowens. I'm sure he'll be with you as soon as possible."

Taylor detected sarcasm in the receptionist's voice, and

the ember of anger inside her caught fire once more. "He'd better, because my friend wasn't doing anything wrong! She shouldn't be here! I want to talk to her now, or so help me I'll…I'll get an army of lawyers in here suing you for racial discrimination. Yeah, that's right! I'm throwing that card down! So unless you want them setting up an office in your ass, along with all the press that'll go with it, I suggest you get the sheriff out here now!"

"Hey now!" a voice shouted from behind nearby walls. "What the holy hell is going on?"

The door to the sheriff's office jerked open, and through it stormed Sheriff Bowens. The look on his face was angry as she felt, but he was nearly twice her size and the gun on his hip looked bigger than her arm. Instantly she regretted raising her voice.

But hell, if it helps me see her, then screw it. There's something really funky going on in this town, and Maya's the only one who can stop it. So bring it on, Sheriff, and let's see who's madder than whom.

"Can't you just…" Maya didn't know what to say, how to phrase her thoughts. She was scared, so scared of giving into the temptation that coiled around her heart. Yes, dammit, she wanted the power the Dark God offered, more than that she needed it if she wanted a hope in hell of stopping the witch, but she didn't want to be responsible for what else it might make her do, who it would make her become. "I don't know, take control of me again?"

Demael smiled, the Dark God's lips red and full, just like hers. *Yes, but I won't. Not a second time. If you choose to use the power I offer, then you must take it of your own free will.*

I was afraid of that.

"Will I… Will I lose myself? Will I stop being me?"

Her dark mirror smiled wider. *On the contrary, you will be you, but better. Stronger. All the power that sings in your blood will finally be yours. Nothing will be able to stand against you. Imagine all the things you could do if you only had that power. How many killers you could stop, how many children you could save. Nothing will be beyond you. And, when you and I are finally one, the world will kneel at our feet.*

Maya didn't care about ruling the world, but the idea of being able to stop so many terrible people appealed to her. Though the power came from a dark place, that didn't mean she had to do dark things with it. Right? Couldn't some good come from her sacrifice?

She wasn't a fool. She knew she was selling herself a line of bullshit. But, she also knew she was stuck in a cell while all sorts of evil deeds were being done in the darkening world beyond. A child could be dying even as she considered Demael's offer. If there was even the slimmest possibility that accepting his power meant she could save someone's life, she knew she had to try.

"Okay, I...dammit...I accept."

The shadow version of herself nodded and began to fade. *Very well. My power is yours, Maya Gallows. We are now one step closer to achieving our true destiny.* The Dark God disappeared before his final words were spoken, the sound of his voice floating in mid-air.

For a moment Maya wasn't sure what was supposed to happen next, if there was some sort of contract she had to sign, or a ritual, and she was about to ask when suddenly her entire body felt electrified. Every cell screamed, her body vibrated, and for a moment she floated in the air with all her limbs outstretched. Her brain boiled in her skull, strange memories filled her mind, and she feared she would go insane from the influx. But, just when she was sure she would explode, her feet touched down and her body came under control. The power was still there, a black ocean of energy that she could shape and use however she saw fit, but now it no longer threatened to overflow her body and split it open.

This feels amazing! Now I can find that witch, and when I do I'm going to rip her to bloody pieces that I can scatter to the four corners of the Earth. I'll kill her son, too. And then I'll pay a visit to those gypsies and turn all of them to ash. Finally they will all get the justice they deserve.

Ready to test her power, Maya pointed at the cell door like her hand was a gun. When she pulled the trigger, the door exploded off its hinges and slammed against the brick wall opposite her.

Oh yes, this is going to be wonderful, she thought as she walked out of the holding cell, smoke swirling in the air behind her.

"Miss, do you want to get thrown in jail too?"

Sheriff Bowens's moustache shook like a bush with a nervous rabbit hiding inside it, and for some reason it tickled Taylor so much she nearly laughed out loud. Luckily for her she didn't, or the angry sheriff might have shot her on the spot.

"No, sir," she replied. "I just want to check on my friend, make sure she's okay. Has she been given a phone call? Is she even under arrest?"

The sheriff grabbed his tan pants by the belt and hitched them up so high they made a moose knuckle of his scrotum. "I don't have to tell you shit, but if it'll get you out of my hair and quiet this racket, no, she's not under arrest. She is a person of interest, though, and I'm holding her while I investigate, which is perfectly legal. I didn't bring you in with her, but maybe I should have. If you don't get out of this building in the next thirty seconds, I'll correct that oversight."

Taylor's guts tightened at the threat of incarceration, but what the sheriff said didn't make any sense, and the feeling of injustice kept her from being cowed.

"A person of interest? Interest to what? To who?"

Bowens's eyes widened for a second and then shrunk to slits as he raised a finger and aimed it at her face, but an explosion interrupted him before he could say anything.

Alarms blared and red emergency lights activated as the building rumbled. The sheriff immediately drew his gun, and the receptionist shot up from her chair and clutched her pearls, but all Taylor could think to do was try and look everywhere at once.

"What on Earth was that, Alvin?" the gray-haired woman said, her bifocals hanging against her chest by a thin chain.

Bowens shook his head and scanned the area. "I have no idea. You two stay here and I'll–"

"You'll do nothing."

Taylor spun around to look in the direction the words came from. It sounded like Maya yet...not. "Maya? Is that you?"

As the question left her mouth, a woman walked around the corner. Like the voice, it looked like Maya, but not like her, too. She seemed bigger, her presence filling the room as it never had before, but in a way that made Taylor's head hurt and guts tremble. She walked closer, yet Taylor wasn't sure Maya's legs actually moved. She had to blink her eyes to keep from going crazy. When Maya was close enough for the emergency lights to unveil her face, Taylor gasped and stumbled backward. Her friend's eyes were entirely red, two bloody orbs that saw nothing, and everything.

"Stop right there!" the sheriff told Maya, his gun aimed at her.

Maya smiled as she continued to approach, but there wasn't any kindness or humor in the expression. "You don't frighten me, Sheriff. Not anymore." She waved her hand, and the sheriff's gun disappeared.

The receptionist screamed and ran for the door with a speed Taylor wouldn't have thought her capable. Not that she could blame her. Taylor wished she could scream and run, too. But Maya was her friend, her *sister*. She had to understand what was happening, even if every instinct screamed at her to flee. The door shut with a loud bang after the receptionist pelted through it.

"What happened, Maya?" Taylor asked, though she regretted it when Maya turned her crimson eyes toward her.

"I accepted his gift," Maya replied in wistful tones.

"His?" Taylor was afraid she already knew the answer.

Maya looked at her with an expression usually reserved for morons. "The Dark One. Through him I'll be able to do so much good, more than I ever could have before."

"I don't know what you're talking about, lady," the sheriff said as he pulled out his nightstick and walked toward Maya, "but I'm done playing with you. This ends now."

He closed on her quickly and raised his baton high to smash it into her skull, but Maya didn't blink or act afraid for a second. Instead she reached out and touched his forehead. He dropped to the ground like a robot whose batteries suddenly ran dry. The baton clattered to the floor and bounced under a desk.

Taylor felt all the blood drain from her face, and for a moment she forgot to breathe. "Oh my God, Maya! Did... Did you just kill him?"

Again Maya gave her an I'm-dealing-with-an-idiot look. "No, though the world wouldn't be worse off if I had. He's weak, Taylor, and because of his weakness children have died. Should I leave him alive to endanger more?"

"How the fuck do you even ask that?" Taylor trembled from all the conflicting emotions that battled inside her. "You're not a judge or jury, and you're sure as hell not an executioner. This isn't you, Maya. It's him. He's already changing you!"

"He opened my eyes, nothing more. Now, though I hate to leave this *riveting* conversation, there's a little girl out there that needs saving."

Maya turned to the exit and walked toward it without another word. Taylor chased after her, wondering all the while why she wasn't headed the other direction.

Because I love her, dammit. She's family, and I'm not going to leave her like this. Especially with that thing inside her, manipulating her.

"I'm coming with you," she said as Maya waved at the front door, opening it with just a thought.

Maya glanced over at her, her pitiless red eyes sending shivers up Taylor's back, then shrugged. "Your funeral."

Once they were outside, Maya headed for the Trailblazer, which started up even though Taylor had the keys to it in her pocket.

"If you're going, then be useful and drive," Maya said, her tone making it an order. The passenger side door opened as she neared the vehicle, and she got in as though she didn't have a care in the world.

Taylor instinctively became angry. She wasn't used to being ordered around. But one look at Maya simmered her down.

"So where are we going?" Taylor asked when she was behind the wheel.

"Just drive," Maya replied. "When I say turn, you turn. I'll divine where that witch is, sooner or later, and when I do, it's going to be messy."

The coldness in Maya's voice was nearly as frightening as her eyes, so Taylor merely nodded before backing out of the parking spot and turning them back toward town. But, in spite of her fear, Taylor vowed she would help her friend find her way back from where that damn Dark God had taken her.

Come hell or high water, I'll save you, Maya.

She wasn't oblivious to the irony of her words.

Chapter Twenty-Four

Estera wanted to weep from the pain.

"You okay, Momma?" Boden asked behind her.

She hissed and tossed a withering glance over her shoulder. "Shut up, boy! You'll ruin the spell!"

"Please, don't do this," the little girl on the altar said, her words nearly inaudible over the storm of souls above them.

Estera ignored her pleas as she cut the child's cloth and hair and put them in the chalice. "Gods of flame and darkness, spirits of creation, take my offerings and mould from them a mirror of the child before me. Grant me this vessel to draw away her spirit, and it will be yours to do with as you please. This I offer unto you, and this I command!"

The surge of energy that suddenly filled the casting chamber made Estera's hair stand on end, and she wanted to laugh, giddy at the titanic forces swirling around her, forces she'd summoned to do her bidding. She didn't laugh though. The beings at work in the chamber wouldn't have taken that well.

Suddenly a ball of light so bright it transcended color exploded to life above the girl, and all the air in the basement swirled around it like a vortex. Estera's robes fluttered with the wind, and lose bits of dust and paper flew round and round. The wind swirled faster with each moment, and the glowing sphere fluctuated as if it were a star going nova. Estera stared into the sphere, her eyes watering from the strain, but she had to keep all her focus on it or the spell would break, possibly killing her in the process. When the sphere finally disappeared, the wind went with it, and in the silence that followed she stared in mute wonder at the sight before her.

The doll was...perfect. From top to bottom, from dark hair to black shoes, it matched the girl it rested on in every detail. Its eyes shined, and its porcelain-smooth skin was unblemished. The previous dolls hadn't been nearly as exact, so her hopes rose that now they had the perfect one. When she reached out to pick it up, she smiled.

"Oh yes, yes! Finally, perfection."

The little girl's reaction at seeing the doll wasn't as joyful. As soon as her small, dark eyes lit on it she started screaming. "Oh my God! Is that me? Why is that me? What's happening? Let me go!"

Yes, little one, Estera thought with a grin, *feed the Gods, feed the spirits. Scream as much as you want. You only give the spell more power.*

The doll was warm in her hands, like sun-warmed stone, and for a moment Estera imagined she felt a heart beating inside it. "Isn't it lovely?" she asked as she held the doll above the girl's face. "Soon your spirit will join with it, and then the life force in your body will be mine. Isn't that wonderful? Because of you I will extend my life for decades, perhaps even a century. Who knows what I'll learn in that time, what powers I'll gather to myself. I may even rule the world one day, and then I'll have endless cages filled with girls like you, each one a step further into immortality. I will become a goddess, and it will all be because of you. You should be honored."

The way the girl screamed and stared up in mortal terror said she wasn't honored in the least. Estera felt a momentary pang of sadness for her. Not because of the pain she was in, or the horror that racked her tiny mind, but because she couldn't see and appreciate her moment of destiny. Most people sleepwalked through their lives, deaf to destiny's call, and this poor girl seemed no different.

What a pity.

Estera, though, wasn't so deaf. Years ago she'd decided to take control of her destiny rather than wait for it to come to her. When the winds sang and the children cried, destiny's voice joined with them. Now it was only a matter of one final spell before the fates were hers to command. Three times she'd failed, but she vowed that this time would be different. It had to be. Other forces moved out in the world, their purpose cross to hers, and if she failed again there might not be another chance. It was now or never.

"Heed my call again, spirits of light and dark! Once more I summon you!"

The aether churned, a psychic storm as far as Maya could see, and the increased activity made it hard for her to locate the witch. It was like looking for a cloud in the midst of a hurricane. But, as she called forth the Dark God's power, some of the fog dissipated, giving her at least a general direction in which to go.

"Turn right," she said, her eyes closed so she could focus.

The girl next to her–Maya had difficulty feeling affection for Taylor now that she'd ascended to the next stage of her evolution–sighed. "I can't. There isn't a right to take."

"Then do it when there is." Irritation made Maya's neck muscles tense up. How could she have ever loved someone so…limited?

"Well pardon me, Lady Garmin, God of GPS."

Sarcasm was thick in the girl's voice, but Maya wasn't upset by it. She'd risen above pettiness such as that. The disrespect was another matter, though. "Speak to me that way again, and I'll make hurting you last a thousand years."

The girl grunted as she turned the vehicle to the right and headed down a narrow neighborhood street. "That's not you talking, Maya. It's that Demael son of a bitch. Don't let him win."

Maya rolled her bloody eyes. "There is no win or lose. There just is. We are one."

No we're not! a tiny voice said in the distant recesses of Maya's mind. She tilted her head, curious at the inner dissension but unconcerned that it could amount to anything. With each passing moment, the Dark God's influence deepened. Soon there would be no separation, and then her ascension would be complete.

I'll stop you, the tiny inner voice said, the words having all the power of a moth's wings fluttering against a window.

Maya chuckled at the hubris as she honed in on the witch. "She's northeast of us. Head in that direction."

"Uh huh." The Trailblazer bounced over potholes and cracks in the road.

Maya felt anger radiating from the girl like heat, all of it directed at her, but as her anger built to a boiling point it suddenly vanished, and in its place was something Maya didn't expect–love.

"I remember when I first met you," the girl said as she as she turned onto a dirt road. "I had no idea what was going on, but Kyle trusted you, and it didn't take long to understand why. You have this…aura about you. You're smart and self-assured, but I think it's your kindness that drew me in most. You're such a sweet woman, Maya. Don't let that thing take it away from you. Hold onto it."

Maya sneered. What need did she have for kindness? It was a waste of emotion. Kindness kept the weak alive when they should rightfully perish, held the strong back when they should flourish. She felt no need for it.

Yes you do, the tiny inner voice said. *Or you wouldn't be trying to save a little girl.*

"This isn't about a child," Maya said aloud, drawing a strange look from Taylor. "It's about destroying that witch."

You can lie to the world, but you can't lie to me. We're one, remember?

Maya clenched her hands into fists so tight her nails bit into her palms. "No, we're not!"

"Who are you talking to?" Taylor asked with fear in her voice.

Growling, Maya shook her head. "No one. Just drive."

Taylor faced forward and did just that, occasionally stealing glances at her from the corner of her eye. "Yes, ma'am."

Maya's breathing deepened in anger, and her skin tingled. She was losing control of herself. When she'd accepted the Dark God's power, with it had come a confidence she'd never known before, and she'd revelled in it. If allowing the Dark God to join with her meant she never had to be afraid again, she'd been willing because the loss of part of herself was gained back in extraordinary power. Feeling that power at her fingertips had made the trade-off seem worth it. But now...

No, she wouldn't lose it now. Not now, and not ever. She couldn't let her weakness stop her or cause her to doubt herself. There was too much at stake! There were beings moving in the shadows of the world, some who would serve her, and others who would be destroyed. If a child or two was saved along the way, so much the better. But that wasn't her goal. If she had to cut the kindness from her brain with a knife, so be it. Better yet, cut out the old parts of herself that denied the glory of the Dark God. The sooner their souls were no longer separated, the better. She... He had plans. Great plans. And no weak woman was going to stop him.

"We're getting closer," Maya said, the aether more troubled than ever.

"Do I need to turn left or right?" the stupid girl asked.

Maya reached forward with her mind, then behind and around the vehicle. "Neither. Back up. Then head south."

The girl did as ordered, thankfully without saying anything. It was hard turning around on the narrow dirt road, but after several seconds of shifting backward and forward they did it. A side road appeared on their left a minute later, and they turned onto it. The feeling of the witch's power increased immediately.

"Yes! She's down this way. We nearly have her."

Two turns later, Maya's entire body hummed in sympathetic vibration to the witch. When her red eyes spied a dirt driveway nearly hidden by trees and overgrown plants, she knew she'd found her quarry.

"Turn right onto that narrow strip of dirt," she said. "She's at the end of it."

The girl slowed down and leaned forward to see more clearly. "What strip of dirt? I don't see it."

"That's because you have a weak mind and pathetic eyes. If you saw as I do, the radiance of her magic would shine like the moon. It's just up ahead."

Wisely, the girl was silent as she slowly approached the driveway. Branches scraped against the SUV as they turned right, but the potholed driveway was just wide enough to let them in. A hundred yards down was a house surrounded by the swirling glow of a powerful spell, but to normal eyes it was just a dark blob against darker blobs. The Trailblazer's headlights landed on it halfway there.

"Is that it?" the stupid girl asked.

"Yes."

"It's…just a house."

"What did you expect?"

"I don't know, something more…witchy. Like it would be made of candy, maybe lots of pointy towers and cats standing on the roof."

Maya regretted allowing the child to accompany her. "This isn't a child's story. This is real life, that's a real house, and in it she's casting a spell of incredible evil. When you park next to it, just stay in the car. I don't need you in my way like some wandering sheep. The witch could be a threat to me, so I must destroy her before that can happen."

"I don't know who or what it is that you're becoming, Maya," the girl said as she applied the brakes, "but please come back. This isn't you, goddammit. You're caring, and kind. You help people because you know it's the right thing to do, because it's who you are. You do it out of love, not fear, and not hatred. Let go of that bastard. You don't need him or his power!"

"Yes, I do," Maya replied. "I was too weak before, a fool playing with fire, but now I'm strong. I don't expect you to understand this as the opportunity it is. He's more a part of me with every second. We're becoming one, and there's nothing you can do about that."

Maybe she can't, but I can. I'm still here, you bastard! I'm not lost yet!

"Shut up!" Maya smashed her fists on her thighs. "Both of you!"

The mewling girl stared at her with her stupid cow eyes. "Both of us?"

A growl rumbled up Maya's throat as she reached for the door handle and opened it. "Just be quiet and stay here. You're clouding my head. I can't allow that." She then stepped out of the SUV and slammed the door closed behind her.

How does it feel? the tiny voice asked.

"How does what feel?"

A small laugh fluttered through Maya's head. "Fear."

Maya didn't reply. She didn't know how. Instead she scowled at the house and let the eldritch heat emanating from it wash over her. It cleared her mind for a moment, and she seized the opportunity to shut the back of her mind away so she didn't have to hear that damnable voice anymore. Fear? Demael knew no such feeling. For him, all that existed was hatred and hunger. It was all he would need to bring the world to its knees.

Her teeth bared, Maya stomped toward the back of the house. The Dark God wanted blood, needed to feel it drench his new body, and he planned on ripping the witch apart to get it.

So focused was he on his black desire he didn't hear the Trailblazer's door open, and Taylor slip out. What remained of human Maya heard it, though, and in the back of the

Dark God's mind she was glad. Despite all the reasons why she should, Taylor hadn't abandoned her. That gave her hope she didn't know she needed.

Chapter Twenty-Five

As Maya rounded the house, she found a short set of concrete steps leading up to the backdoor. The sensation of power felt closer now. After taking the two steps that led to the door, she grabbed the doorknob and twisted it, not caring if it was locked or not. No lock made by man could stop her. But, as her hand grabbed the metal knob, a jolt of powerful energy surged through her and sent her flying backward. It took her several seconds to catch her breath.

"Well well," she said to herself. "Not quite as stupid as I'd assumed."

Maya's eyes glittered in the night as she used Demael's power to enchant her vision. When she looked at the door, several magical wards were revealed laying over it, making it impossible for anyone but the witch or her retarded son to open it. It was a nicely done spell, and she admired the witch's effort, but it only took a few seconds to find a hole in it. She looked around at the rest of the backyard, searching for something she could use. When she saw the large axe embedded in a tree stump next to a pile of split wood, she grinned, then waved her hand at it. The axe heaved into the air, spun once, and then flew at the backdoor. The door exploded off its hinges from the force of the blow.

With that done, she entered the house. The axe was buried in the opposite wall. Pieces of metal and wood littered the kitchen as though a bomb had gone off. As she stood in the middle of the room, her body vibrated with magical power. She was practically on top of it. When she saw stairs leading down to a basement she realized she was literally on top of it as well. She made for the stairway immediately.

"Come on!" Estera shouted, blood running from her nose

in thin streams. "Get out of that body!"

The whirlwind of spirits surrounding the casting circle continued to howl. The girl, Zoe, laid atop the altar, her eyes open and a howl of her own erupting from her mouth in an endless cry of pain and terror. Above her floated the doll, its flawless face staring down at her like a reflection in a stream, its mouth open as well. Everything was exactly as it should be, everything was perfect.

Then why isn't it working? Estera asked herself in a rage.

"Accept this vessel, child! Place your soul within it and make it yours!"

Estera didn't know what to think or do. She'd read the spell hundreds of times, knew it back to front, used the purest components. The child was a match for her in every way that mattered. She'd made all the required sacrifices. By all rights, the spell should be working. But the girl was resisting; and not just resisting, but succeeding. It shouldn't be possible.

Suddenly a loud *BOOM* reverberated through the wood floor overhead.

"Boden, see what's going on!" she said, shouting to be heard. She pointed at the stairs.

"Yes, Momma," her son replied. He was halfway to the kitchen when suddenly he was blown backward down the stairs. He hit the ground on his head and didn't get back up.

"Boden!" Estera cried. Instinct compelled her to rush to him, but if she did it would break the spell and ruin everything she'd worked for. So she had to make a choice— help her son or continue the spell. In the end, the choice was easy. She turned back to the girl and raised her hands.

"Spirits of death and life, I call on you to move this girl's spirit! Empty her body and fill the vessel with her soul! Do as I command!"

The whirling spirits screamed and tightened their circle. Suddenly a thunderous laugh filled the casting chamber. Estera turned to find the black woman standing outside the pentagram. She looked the same as she had in the holding cell, but there was something different about her, something off.

"Having trouble?" the black woman said with a smile that was too wide to be human.

Estera narrowed her eyes and crossed her arms in front of her, her thumbs, pinkies, and index fingers extended. Her view of the world changed so that she could see beyond the physical and into the aether. She gasped when she looked at the black woman. Instead of a person she saw a towering black shadow with tentacles extending from it in all directions. The black woman it possessed looked small and insignificant next to the massive being. Never in all her explorations of magic and the occult had she come across anything like it.

"I don't know who or what you are," she said, putting as much steel in her voice as she could, "but do not interfere. You try, and I'll rip you to shreds and dine on your bones."

The dark woman smiled like a shark, and instead of backing away she stepped closer. When she neared the spirit vortex she reached forward, plunging her hand into the whirlwind. Its smile vanished as it hissed, and its hand burned as hellborn spirits raged around it, but after a few moments she plunged her other hand in and ripped the spirits apart. Wind and thunder shook the chamber as the storm was rent asunder.

"What was that you were saying?" The woman who wasn't a woman glared at her.

Fear blossomed in Estera's heart, but with it came rage. Her spell was now ruined, her preparations all for nothing, all because of this…beast. She didn't know why it had entered her life, but she knew how it would leave it—in pieces.

What are you doing, you stupid twit? Taylor asked herself, not for the first time. From outside it sounded like a war was raging inside the house, a war fought by beings she couldn't understand using weapons she didn't have. So why was she there, creeping closer and closer to a fight she didn't know how to win?

Because my friend is in trouble, that's why.

Keeping a picture of Maya's face at the front of her mind, Taylor snuck around the side of the house and kept close to the old wooden walls until she neared the concrete steps that led to the backdoor. The entranceway was busted to hell, and when she peeked her head around it, she saw the kitchen was filled with what remained of the door. An axe was stuck in the far wall.

Now there's something I know how to use.

Doing her best ninja walk, she crept across the kitchen to the axe. It took a few pulls, but eventually she wiggled it free from the wall. Having the weapon in her hands helped her feel marginally better.

Loud noises erupted from an open doorway on her right. Using only the tips of her toes, she went to it. Wooden stairs led from the doorway down to a basement. Lights flashed and voices cried out indecipherable words, so she had no idea what was being said or by whom. All she knew was that she had to go down there.

Swallowing her fear as much as she could, Taylor went to the top riser and looked down. The bareness of the stairs combined with the light show going on meant she would be exposed all the way down. She just had to hope everyone down there was too busy to notice her. Holding that hope in her mind like a shield, she took the first step down, then the second, and then the third. After that she was able to see more of what was going on. Her shield trembled.

The basement was lined in stone from the floor to the walls, with strange, glowing symbols etched into the rock. Ancient wooden shelves leaned against the walls like drunks, their mysterious contents dangerously close to tipping them over. A black altar stood in the center of the room, and a little girl laid on top of it with a doll on her chest. Standing before the girl as if she were her protective mother, the witch had her walking stick in one hand and a knife in the other. Just two yards from her stood Maya, her eyes still bottomless pools of blood and fire. At the bottom of the stairs was sprawled a strange, misshapen man in ratty old clothes. She recalled Maya mentioning he was the witch's son. He was on his back, motionless. So far none of them had noticed her.

"You've ruined everything," the witch said, sparks leaping up where she hammered the bottom of her walking stick against the ground. "I don't know why, or even how, but I've worked too hard to see all my efforts amount to nothing. You will pay for what you've done."

The witch raised her stick as she finished speaking and slammed it back down. The stone beneath it cracked and a shockwave blasted toward Maya. Maya slid backward a few feet as the wall of air hit her, but then her arms lashed outward, tearing the shockwave apart.

"Is that what you call power?" Maya asked as she wiped blood from beneath her nose. "In my day you would've been eaten alive by a newborn vyrnbest."

The witch grimaced and tightened her grip on her weapons. "Your day? And when was that? I see the face of a young woman, but beyond that lies something far older, and not human. So tell me, creature, what are you?"

Taylor didn't have to be psychic to know how that question was going to go over.

Maya sneered and moved her right arm in a sweeping gesture. The witch's staff ripped from her hands and flew against a wall where it shattered into toothpicks. The old woman screamed in rage. Taylor took that as her opportunity to go into stealth mode. There was a little girl who still needed saving.

Estera looked at the shattered remains of her staff, the ancient piece of wood passed down through her family for centuries. It had served her well for so many years, its enchantments preserving it against time and wear, but in one fell swoop the being calling itself Maya destroyed it. She would have wept if rage wasn't already boiling the blood in her veins.

"You'll pay for that, beast!" she said, her teeth clinched so tightly her jaw ached. "Now tell me what you are! What is your name!" Her knife shook in her hand as she held it forward.

The black woman sneered and took a step closer. "You underestimate me at your peril. I know the value of names, much as I suspect you do as well. I think I'll…"

A strange look crossed the dark face of the being opposite Estera, a look of confusion that changed into anger. The black shadow aura surrounding the woman flared, but then it suddenly disappeared. She appeared to be fully human again.

"Its name is Demael!" Maya said, her voice lighter than before, more feminine. "It wants—"

"Silence!" the darker voice said as the massive black aura returned in a rush. "Betray me and you betray yourself."

Ah, there it is, Estera said to herself. *I've tamed demons before, and with its name I will tame this one too.*

Working quickly, Estera reached into one of her many pockets and pulled out her wand, then waved it through the air. As the tip moved, it left a glowing red mark floating in the air–a circle with lines and symbols arrayed around the center. When she was done she said, "Demael, creature of blood and fire, with this glyph I bind thee!"

The possessed woman looked at her in confusion, but when the glyph flew toward her and wrapped itself around her, confusion turned to rage.

"You attack me with your paltry magicks?" the not-woman asked as she struggled to break free. "Fool! I brought ruin and pain to this world eons before your ancestors crawled from the slime and looked up in fear at the sun!"

Estera forced her face to remain still, but beneath it she was rocked to her core.

Could it be? Is it possible? Is this...a Primal? No, that's impossible.

Before her Demael twisted back and forth, its aura trapped as much as the body it inhabited was. Estera didn't worry. The binding glyph was strong enough to hold any evil being–there were rumors that once upon a time even Lucifer had been bound by it–she'd even put the creature's name in the glyph in Enochian, but when shadowy tentacles slipped free and grasped the glowing red circle surrounding it, a trickle of fear fell down her spine.

"You are bound, Evil One!" she said. "Attempt to breach the spell and it will destroy–"

She didn't get a chance to finish as the Primal flexed its aura in a titanic surge of power. With a massive heave, the dark tentacles broke the glyph into a million sparkling pieces. The released magical energy exploded in a surge that knocked her backward against her altar. She grabbed the black stone to help pull herself up, and when her hands swept the top of it she discovered it was empty.

The child! She's gone! My future!

She quickly searched around the altar but found nothing. When she looked to the stairs, however, she found her missing sacrifice in the arms of a young woman. Estera had never seen the girl before, but she had the stink of the Primal all over her.

"Stop! Bring back my prize, you stupid girl!"

The thief turned near the base of the stairs, her eyes wide like a raccoon caught in the trash. She then looked at the Primal, but shook her head. "She's a little girl, you bitch, not a trophy. But, if you want a prize that bad, here's a Kewpie doll!"

Moving quickly, the thief grabbed the doll from the girl's chest and hurled it at a far corner. Estera watched it tumble through the air with dread, seeing not just the doll, but her blood, sweat, and pain. If the doll was destroyed, she'd have to make another, and she didn't know if she could stand to pull yet another rib from her chest.

"No!" Estera pointed her wand at the flying doll and channelled her will through it to stop the doll's flight and bring it to her. She nearly fell down in relief when the doll did just that. It was saved. But, just as it was within her reach, it suddenly changed course and ended up in Demael's hands.

The Primal looked at the doll, then looked up at Estera. A lopsided grin split its face. "A soul trap. Very nice. I didn't think you'd be capable of magic this black. I'm impressed. Unfortunately you'll no longer be needing it." Demael hefted the doll one last time, then threw it to the ground where it shattered in an explosion of smoke and black light.

Estera's vision turned red, and everything within her screamed for revenge. Quickly she scrawled another binding glyph in the air, this time using *Lingua Tenebrae*–the Dark Tongue–a language with power beyond any other save *Enochian*, the language of God and the angels–to name the Primal and enhance the binding. Once Demael was bound again, she turned to the thief and lunged at her, her iron knife cutting the air before her.

I'm going to drain this little bitch dry, and then I'll use her soul to power a destruction spell not even a Primal can survive. Maybe I'll eat its soul too. What a glorious meal that would be!

The girl stumbled against the stairs and fell onto her backside. A dark smile turned Estera's lips upward as her knife buried itself in the thief's thigh. The scream that followed was music to her ears.

Taylor was overjoyed that she'd managed to get to the altar, grab the child, and sneak away without being caught.

She wouldn't have thought it possible, but here she was, the girl and her strange doll in her arms, with only a set of stairs between them and safety.

Holy shit! I'm a ninja up in here! This is—

"Stop" the witch bellowed behind her. "Bring back my prize, you stupid girl!"

Taylor knew in an instant that her luck had run out. She turned slowly, hoping she was wrong, but she wasn't. The witch glared at her like she'd stolen something, which she had. Taylor looked to Maya in the hope that her friend had regained control of herself, but her eyes were still as red and merciless as before. If anyone was going to save the day, it would have to be Taylor. Summoning her courage she said, "She's a little girl, you old hag, not a trophy. But, if you want a prize that bad, here's a Kewpie doll!"

With only seconds to act, she grabbed the doll and threw it as hard as she could at the wall on the opposite side of the basement.

The witch watched it fly with dread in her eyes. "No!" she shouted as she pointed some kind of stick at the doll.

Is that a goddam magic wand? Taylor asked herself with a laugh despite the terror racing through her veins.

To Taylor's horrified amazement the doll stopped its motion and floated instead toward the witch's gnarled hands. Taylor racked her mind for some way to stop the witch from getting what she wanted, but before she could think of anything the doll changed directions again, now toward Maya's hands.

"A soul trap," the possessed Maya said as she caught the doll, a hateful smile on her face that Maya would never be capable of. "Very nice. I didn't think a human would be capable of magic this black. I'm impressed. Unfortunately you'll no longer be needing it." As soon as the last word left her mouth, Maya slammed the doll to the ground, and it broke not with the bright cracking of porcelain, but with the crunch of bone. Taylor's stomach flip-flopped inside her.

As if a switch was flipped, the witch let loose a scream that tore through Taylor's ears like drill bits and traced that strange sign in the air, which once against surrounded Maya, trapping her in place. The witch then ran toward Taylor with murder gleaming in her beady eyes and a knife in her hands. The attack was so sudden, and the witch moved so quickly, that Taylor didn't have time to do anything but scuttle backwards and trip onto her ass. Before she knew what was happening, the witch was on her, and then a terrible pain exploded in her left thigh. Taylor couldn't help but scream.

"I'm going to bleed you dry," the witch said through clenched teeth, "and then I'll eat your soul like it's lunch. Welcome to oblivion."

The witch yanked the knife from Taylor's leg and held it up for another plunging stab, the iron blade coated in bright red blood, but Taylor managed to pull together enough brain power to shove herself back a couple steps and then kick the witch away. The witch stumbled and fell against the obsidian column next to her altar. Taylor tried to rise and carry the girl up the stairs, but huge hands suddenly grabbed her by her arms and pulled her back down.

"Who are you?" a slurred voice said as hot breath baked her ear. "What've you done to Momma?"

Momma?

"Nothing!" she replied. "I'm just trying to save a little girl!"

The rough hands shifted her around until the child was in view. "You... You're going to save Zoe? She's still alive?"

Taylor, thinking she detected a note of relief from the gnarled man holding her, took a leap of faith. "Yes. She's unconscious, but she's still alive. I just want to get her home to her parents. Are you going to stop me?"

The twisted man didn't immediately answer, which gave her even more hope. But, just as the hands grasping her loosened, the witch cackled and threw some sort of glittering dust in the air between them. Dark red bolts of electricity leapt from the witch's wand and crashed into her. The pain was overwhelming, and she loosed a scream unlike any before as she felt her soul being dragged from her. Feeling all her good intentions turning to ash, she strained to look at Maya, whose face drifted into her hazy view. She knew she had to try something. "Stop her, Maya! Please! She's killing me! Save me! You're my sister!"

For a moment Taylor thought she saw Maya's eyes change back to their normal, beautiful blue, but when she looked again after another bolt of energy lashed her face, all she found were merciless red orbs staring back at her.

"I'm not your sister, and your life means nothing," the Dark God said as she again struggled to be free. "You'll find no kindness in me."

Taylor's hope died as the pain overwhelmed her and her world turned into one long, tortured scream.

Maya raged inside her mind like a prisoner waiting to be led to the electric chair. Her friend was being murdered, the child she'd wanted so badly to save was still in danger, and she was locked away in her own body unable to do anything about any of it.

Let me out! she shouted from the depths of her skull.

The Dark God Demael's laughter rolled like thunder. *You poor creature. None of this matters. The only thing worth our efforts is gathering more power. My strength is returning, but the witch has magicks that were unknown in my time. Let her waste what power she has left dealing with the child you call sister, and then when I break free of this binding, I will end her life and take her power for my own.*

If she had fists, Maya would have clenched them tightly and shaken them in frustration over her helplessness. She didn't want to watch Taylor die, but the ancient being in control of her body wouldn't let her look away as the witch pummelled the young woman with arcing red bolts of energy.

"I'm gonna enjoy eating your soul, little girl," the witch

said, her face lit in crimson rage. "Dealing with the Primal has taken a lot of my power, so I could use the boost of energy. And who knows, I might just make a doll out of you and consume your life force. It won't give me the added years the child would have, but something is better than nothing, right?"

Maya was horrified by the witch's intentions, but within them was a tiny spark of hope.

If you won't fight for her, then I will, she told Demael as she closed her ethereal eyes and concentrated on adding her strength to the Dark God's. She knew Demael had no interest in saving Taylor, but he did have an interest in getting free of the binding glyph, so together they flexed and pushed and pulled at the glowing symbol surrounding them. Symbols within the glyph flashed, and it constricted even tighter. Quickly it became painful. Maya feared that their combined energy being squeezed into her small body would cause them to overload and burn up, but instead the Dark God used the focused power, squeezed it even tighter inside them until it trembled like a star about to go nova. When it reached critical mass, the unleashed energy hit the glyph like a freight train, shattering it in a blinding flash of light. They fell to the floor, her body too weak to stand.

We are free once more, Demael said, his ghostly voice weak, *but at a cost greater than I'd anticipated. You must let your friend die while we recover our strength. If she attacks us now I don't have the power to fend her off, and both of us will die.*

That was precisely what Maya wanted to hear.

"Hey, bitch," she said now that the Dark God didn't have the power to suppress her anymore, "you want to taste some real power?"

As if a light switch was flipped, the red lightning streaming from the witch's hands stopped and she turned.

"I dare you to try that shit with me," Maya said, curling her lips into a snide grin. *Come on! Come get me!*

The witch looked her up and down, and then she

returned the smile. "Breaking out of that binding had to be tough. I wouldn't have even thought it possible. You must be exhausted. Good. This will be quick and easy then."

What are you doing, you stupid girl? Demael raged. *She will destroy us both!*

The witch turned from Taylor as though she were completely irrelevant and stalked toward Maya's prone body. As soon as she was in reach, the witch extended her hands and grabbed Maya's head. The pain was immediate and intense as the witch reached beyond the physical world and began draining what power remained of the Dark God. Demael howled and tried to avoid the witch's probing like a dog running from a beast much bigger than it, but the witch wasn't shaken off. She had the Primal in her grasp, and was enjoying every drop of power she consumed. She was practically drunk with it.

"Oh, yes," the witch said, her voice thick with dark pleasure. "Yes, give me more, Ancient One. I've never tasted power like this. I want it all."

I was hoping you'd say that, Maya thought as she said, "Then here, have it!"

Before the witch or Demael could understand what was happening, Maya called forth a small reserve of energy she'd held onto and used it to push against the Dark God. Had she tried to free herself earlier, he would have stopped her before she even started, but now he didn't have the strength, though she could feel it was quickly returning to him. She had only seconds, so she pushed with everything she had.

I rebuke you, Demael! she shouted in her skull. *Leave my body now!*

You cannot do this! he told her. *You gave yourself to me of your own free will! You are mine now!*

I did let you in, Maya admitted, *but this is MY body, and you're not wanted anymore, so get the fuck out!*

Demael held onto her with all he had, but it wasn't enough, and with one final surge of power she expelled him from her body and into the witch. Now Maya could only hope she hadn't miscalculated.

"Yes!" the witch cried as she staggered backward and reached up to hold her head in her hands. "The power! It's so...so strange, but I will make it mine!"

The witch's brown eyes turned red as the Dark God ascended within her, and a wicked grin split her weathered face. "It seems I was wrong, child. Here is finally a vessel worthy of all that I am. You chose poorly, and now it will be your undoing."

The witch's hands rose, but then her eyes returned to brown and she snarled. "That's enough of that. You won't control me the way you did that mewling girl. You will serve me, Primal, and not the other way around!"

The witch looked satisfied with herself until her eyes turned bloody again. "You have considerable magicks, human, but my power increases even as we speak. You will know your place!"

Again the eyes turned brown. "Your power increases, and it's mine!"

The witch rejoiced, but then doubled over and fell to her knees. When she looked up, her irises were brown but the whites were red, as though both were in possession of the body at the same time. She trembled on her knees, and her hands shook as she again grabbed her head.

"No! It's too much too fast!" Her voice fluctuated strangely, as if two mouths spoke at once. "I can't contain all this power! Stop!"

But Maya knew the Dark God wouldn't stop. It was too consumed with the desire to take over the world and return it to what it once had been, too hungry to be the god of old once more. It wouldn't allow failure or feebleness to stop it, or even entertain the idea of it. Of all the things she'd learned while Demael was within her, that seemed his one weakness.

"Do not resist me!" Demael said, now back in control.

"My power will—"

The witch's shaking increased until she was nearly a blur of motion.

"—will not be—"

Maya gasped as the witch convulsed, her entire body rocking back and forth with unnatural speed. It was like watching a movie in fast-forward.

"—not be denied!"

Taking a deep breath, Maya readied herself for the witch to blow up or break apart, or even simply disappear in a puff of smoke, but slowly the witch's shaking came under control. Dread coiled in Maya's stomach like a snake. Seconds later, the old woman seemed perfectly normal.

"So, was that your plan?" the witch asked in her eerie double voice. "If so, you are even stupider than I thou—"

Blood erupted like a geyser as an axe suddenly buried itself in the witch's skull, splitting her face down to her nose. Her brown and black eyes rolled up, her arms sagged, and she fell over without another word said or breath drawn. Behind her stood Taylor, the young woman's chest heaving from exertion and her wounded leg quivering. Tears shimmered in her eyes.

"Did I do it?" she asked, her voice shaking as she slumped to the ground. "Are they dead?"

Chapter Twenty-Six

Shock hit Maya's system, and it took her a moment to understand what exactly had happened. When she felt like she was back in command of her faculties, she extended her sight into the aether. A sigh of relief slid past her lips when she saw that the witch's body was completely devoid of life and magic. No traces remained of her or the Dark God.

"Yes," she replied. "They're dead. Well, the witch is dead anyway. I think Demael is back under the mountain now that his anchor to the outside world is gone. Or he could be dead too. I don't know for sure. I'm not going to go back to Stillwater to check either. He's out of my head, and that's enough for me."

Taylor, looking paler than usual, hobbled back to her feet and stumbled toward Maya on trembling legs, then sat down beside her as if she could no longer hold herself up. "Holy shit. That was... Holy shit. I thought I was dead for sure. Thanks for distracting them."

"You're welcome," Maya replied as she leaned over and bumped shoulders. "Wasn't my intention though. I was actually hoping Demael's power would be too much and it would burn them both out. Nearly worked, too. When they recovered I figured we were done for."

Taylor chuckled, but there wasn't much humor in it. "And then came the axe. Ding dong, the witch is dead. No more children will die because of her."

"Speaking of which." Maya leaned forward to look at where she'd last seen the unconscious child. The little girl was still there at the bottom of the steps, but now she was also in the arms of Boden, the witch's son. Fat tears dribbled down his misshapen face. Yet one more casualty of the evil that had plagued the town.

"Momma's gone," he said as he rocked back and forth. "Momma's gone and I don't know what I'm gonna do."

Even though he was the witch's son, Maya could see that her evil hadn't been passed down to him, and whatever involvement he'd had in the kidnappings was more about love and devotion than any desire to see children hurt. He wasn't innocent, but he wasn't a monster either.

"I'm sorry," she said. "We didn't have a choice."

The lump of a man tried to wipe his tears off the girl's face. "Momma was a bad person. I know that. I still loved her. But I understand why you did what you did. Momma was nothing if not hard-headed." He banged his large knuckles against his skull.

"Will you be okay?" Maya wasn't sure why she asked, but the man's thick gray aura made him seem incredibly lonely.

"I dunno. Guess I'll have to be, huh?"

He wasn't as simple-minded as Maya thought. "I'll do what I can to help. The sheriff has some sins he needs to atone for, and so do those gypsies. With your mother no longer a threat, you might find them more willing to help than you'd think."

Boden sniffed and nodded, but he didn't seem overly convinced.

"What about the girl?" Taylor asked as she pulled a thick black leather belt from her waist and secured it above her leg wound like a tourniquet. She cursed as she cinched it tight. "We need to get her home. Her parents are probably losing their shit right now." The flow of blood from her stab wound slowed to a trickle, and then stopped all together.

"I'll take her," Boden offered.

Maya looked around the basement. It was a mess. "What about all this stuff? I imagine some of it is pretty dangerous."

Nodding, Boden stood up and pressed the little girl to his chest. "Do whatever you want with it. I never understood how Momma did what she did, and I never want to. Take all of it if you want. Means nothing to nobody now."

Surprised at the idea, Maya gave the shelves a long look. They were filled with things both strange and familiar. Books took up most of the space, but jars and pots and God only knew what else sat amongst them. "I don't know. No offense, but your mother was into some very dark magic. I don't know if I need that in my life."

"Then leave it," he replied. "Momma wasn't always bad, though. Years ago she was kind, her magic coming from the earth. After her head started to hurt and the doctors said she didn't have long to live is when she turned to that nasty magic. She thought it would save her, but I think it was what really killed her. It changed her into someone I barely knew."

Maya now had food for thought, and her perusal of the shelves was more intense. "So there could be some white magic books, huh? Okay, I'll take a look. Thank you."

"You saved Zoe," he said, turning the unconscious girl toward them. "If anyone can take Momma's magic and use it for good, I think it's you. Whatever you don't take I'll either burn, or bury, or both. I might just fill this whole damn basement in with dirt and be done with it. But right now I need to get Zoe home. Thanks for…never mind. Just please be gone when I get back. Today has been a very bad day."

"You ain't lying," Taylor replied, a bit of color starting to return to her pallid face. "And thanks. I hope things work out for you."

"So do I," Maya added. "I'm sorry things happened the way they did. You're a good person. Don't ever let that go."

Boden gave her a half smile, turned, and walked up the stairs, the unconscious child light as a feather in his misshapen arms. A minute later the house was silent.

"Help me look through all this?" Maya asked.

Taylor looked at her for a moment, then shook her head and laughed. "Not just no, but hell no. I am officially done with all this shit. If you want to stay in this crazy circus, fine, but I'm out. Out, out, out. Give me a boring job any day of the week. Hell, I'd even rather go back to school. Anything to avoid monsters and witches and ancient primordial gods. Am I being clear enough on that?"

"I'd say so," Maya replied, laughing as well. "Sadly, I can't quit. It's who I am, literally. I tried pushing all this away when I was a kid, and it didn't end well, so I accepted who I am and what I need to do. It isn't easy, but it's right."

"If you say so," Taylor looked skeptical. "Anyway, if you don't mind, I'm going to leave the room with the dead body in it. I'll be outside when you're ready to go. Just don't take forever. I happen to have a stab wound, in case you forgot, and if my leg rots off because you took too long picking through rat tails and eyes of newts, I'll kick your ass with my good leg."

Maya reached over and stroked Taylor's shoulder, then gave her a nod. "I'm a little creeped out too, so trust me, I won't be long."

Taylor grimaced, patted Maya's hand, and limped her way upstairs.

"Okay, girl," Maya said aloud as she stood up and approached one of the shelves. "This might be the chance to up our game to the next level. We've been lucky so far, but this one could have been the end of the road. I don't want to be powerless next time. Besides, being a psychic *and* a witch *has* to have its benefits, right?"

With that Maya looked at the top shelf and began searching for anything that could help her do more than just investigate supernatural threats.

Now she could also fight back.

THE END

About the Author

Justin R. Macumber is the author of the bestselling horror novel Still Water and several other titles. A proud member of the Horror Writers Association, when he is not hard at work on his next novel he is a cohost and reviewer for the popular Hollywood Outider podcast. He and his lovely wife live in the Dallas/Fort Worth Metroplex with a crazy pack of dogs and cats that run them ragged. You can find him online at justinmacumber.com.

www.ingramcontent.com/pod-product-compliance
Lightning Source LLC
Chambersburg PA
CBHW031727170626
46808CB00005B/1923